AN ENGLISH DILEMMA

OLIVIA ALEX

Matador
9 Priory Business Park,
Wistow Road, Kibworth Beauchamp,
Leicestershire. LE8 0RX
Tel: 0116 279 2299
Email: books@troubador.co.uk
Web: www.troubador.co.uk/matador
Twitter: @matadorbooks

ISBN 978 1788037 136

British Library Cataloguing in Publication Data.
A catalogue record for this book is available from the British Library.

Printed and bound by TJ International Ltd, Padstow, Cornwall
Typeset in 11pt Minion Pro by Troubador Publishing Ltd, Leicester, UK

Matador is an imprint of Troubador Publishing Ltd

AN ENGLISH DILEMMA

For my family – a source of inspiration and joy

ACKNOWLEDGEMENTS

This book would not have been possible without the help of friends. In particular I would like to thank CB and AH for their detailed comments on earlier drafts; JPB, PB and FG for their help and encouragement; RM and JF for their insightful and entertaining discussions over coffee; RGC who fielded a raft of questions and remained patient throughout, and finally to my many interesting and interested students who make lecturing worthwhile.

All the characters in this novel are fictional; the places are either purely fictional or used in a fictional way. No undergraduates were harmed in the making of this book.

Olivia Alex

DRAMATIS PERSONAE

Avon and Somerset Police
Detective Sergeant Caldicott
Detective Constable Stone

Academic Staff
Dr Jennifer Jordan – Senior Lecturer in English, Head of English
Professor Simeon Hardwicke – Professor of English, Dean of Humanities
Professor Gwendolyn Jones – Professor of English, Deputy Head of English
Dr Malcolm Lowry – Principal Lecturer in English Postmodernist Symbolism
Dr John Dryden – Lecturer in English
Dr Joyce James – Teaching Fellow in English
Mr Percy Smith – Lecturer in English
Ms Shelley Poppleton – Teaching Fellow in English
Rev Dr Clifford Martin – Lecturer in Theology and English
Professor Howard Carter – Professor and Director of Archaeological Studies
Dr Aisha Baigum – Teaching Fellow in Archaeology
Professor Michael Hastings – Head of History

Dr Penny Worth – Senior Lecturer in History

Dr Medusa Touchwood – Principal Lecturer, Head of Theatre Studies

Professor Silvanus Straw – Deputy Vice Chancellor, Principal Lecturer in Theatre Studies

Dr Amelia Halcroft – Lecturer in Law

Dr Ted Murray – Principal Lecturer in Law, Acting Head of Law

Miss Christine Vincent – Pro-Vice Chancellor, Reader in Law

Professor Andrews – Head of Business Studies

Professor Selina Bottomley – Professor of Business Studies

Dr Pat O'Flynn – Lecturer in Business Studies

Other Staff

Professor Graham Everson – Vice Chancellor

Tom – English Department Administrator

Holly – English Department Secretary

Robert Wiley – Marketing Assistant

Sandra Harris – Entertainments Manager

Students

Hajinder Patel

Bernice Pye

Tonya Fitzgerald

Franz Kafka

Ife Mantuwa

Donald McClellan

Rosie Anderson

Maya Dewley

Imran Khan
Reginald White
Ashley Roberts
Faye Goddard
Tammy Smith – PhD student in Archaeology
Nigel Downs – PhD student in Archaeology
Grant Roberts – PhD student in Law
Sophie Bellinger – PhD student in English

Other Notable Characters

Marcus – DS Caldicott's son
Liz – Marcus' Aunt
Stella – DS Caldicott's mother
Cedric – the cockerel

CHAPTER 1
TUESDAY, 12 APRIL 2016:
The University of Sedgemoor

It was 8.45 am on a fine Tuesday morning in April. An elderly and somewhat bashed up Renault Cleo lurched out of nowhere into the car park, strains of Nirvana's "Smells Like Teen Spirit" vibrating the windows. The man sitting in the black saloon car predicted that a greasy-haired student would materialise from the vehicle.

His mobile phone rang.

'Detective Sergeant Caldicott speaking…'

Contrary to his prophecy, an attractive and tidily-dressed brunette emerged from the Renault. He momentarily lost concentration… 'Sorry sir, I didn't quite catch that. The post-mortem *has* identified a match? I see… so there is now evidence to suggest that the two deaths are linked… Yes sir, I am in the university car park now. I've arranged to see the drama department first and then I will head over to the law school… Yes, I understand that the English department needs investigating, but I would like to gather knowledge from the other departments first…Yes sir, I will do my best to complete the investigation by the end of the week…Yes sir, I will keep you informed.'

The Head of English traipsed into her office and slumped into the chair positioned behind her mahogany desk. She sighed heavily at the sight of the pile of correspondence in her in tray, and the paper-knife that lay dormant by it. She had been in her new post for precisely five weeks and one day, yet it seemed like an eternity. She had never read so many unnecessary emails and never attended so many unnecessary meetings. To date she had unpacked only three out of her ten boxes of books; these books were now on the shelves behind her. The remainder of the boxes sat in a row along the wall from her desk to her door. Two large mock-Victorian armchairs rested in her window recess, behind the red velvet drapes; both of these were "occupied", one with her winter coat and the other with a pot plant badly in need of water. Against the wall, adjoining the window recess to the left-hand side of the desk rested a free-standing bookcase and a large recycling bin. The middle of her room was occupied by a solid pine chair. The chair was so ferociously bare in relation to the rest of the furnishings that it gave the appearance that merely to sit on it was punishment in itself. She took another look at her in tray, and then rested her head on the desk as though to go to sleep.

It was now three minutes passed nine and she was two hours behind with her work already. She mused on what a bloody awful role she had been saddled with. After all, most so-called promotions are fought for furiously in order to secure pay enhancements and/or power or at the very least, prestige. This headship had nothing to say for itself, just an ever increasing workload of the dreariest kind imaginable and it all had to be done by yesterday.

Why did she agree to do it? Well, she reflected, the truth was that she hadn't actually agreed to it, she failed to say "no" quickly enough to prevent being saddled with the title. No – that was not a fair reflection either; she was being too hard on herself. The reality was that Simeon Hardwicke had never given her the option to say no. That was the trouble with tall people, she thought; if you were over six-foot tall and built like a Viking warrior you could afford to be pushy.

'So that settles it then Jenny!' Hardwicke strutted around Jenny's office, his long flaxen hair flapping from side to side. You'll take over as head of department next Monday, and that will release me to become dean of humanities. After all, we have to have a certain semblance of separation of powers. But you needn't worry yourself too much; I'll be making all your major decisions for you, of course. Nevertheless, you can have the pleasure of signing the paperwork – Dr Jennifer Jordan, Head of English. That will look good for you, won't it?'

Jenny had been in the middle of marking student assignments when Hardwicke had waltzed in with this announcement. She remained positioned at her desk with a pen in her hand. 'Shouldn't you advertise the post?' Jenny asked in the vague hope that Hardwicke would realise his responsibilities.

'No time for that... I need to take up my new position immediately, in case Professor Everson has a change of heart and appoints one of his cronies from goodness knows where.'

For a number of years, Hardwicke had been demanding to be elevated to the position of dean of humanities, but up to now any sensible vice chancellor had refused his request, offering the post (when vacant) to an outside candidate. Finally, the arrival of a new VC, one Professor Graham Everson, gave Hardwicke the long hoped for break, and he was awarded the chance to take the crown. Hardwicke was quick to ensure that the opportunity was not lost.

'But what about Gwendolyn?' Jenny looked at Hardwicke. 'She's been your deputy for the past three years.'

'Ha!' Hardwicke's perambulations temporarily halted. 'She doesn't want it. Too damned lazy in my opinion. I sounded her out about it yesterday, just in case. Let's face it, that woman can do real mischief when she feels threatened. Besides, she promises to be retiring in nine months' time. Huh, I'll believe that when I see it. If we advertised for an external candidate, we would have to wait until December for their arrival. And I doubt if anyone decent would be applying anyway. On paper they may look excellent, but from my experience if candidates have good references then either they are rubbish and their current employers are pleased to get shot of them, or they are good at pulling the wool over their employers' eyes. We don't want either of that type here.' At this point Hardwicke acquired a wolf-like expression on his face. 'There is, of course, the third type, the ones that have shagged their way to the top. That might be all right if they are happy to throw it my way.'

Jenny chose to ignore this last statement and returned

to her marking; Hardwicke was notorious for his over activity.

'Well then, you should offer it to Dr Lowry,' she said with her eyes fixed on the paper.

'Malcolm? That washed-up idiot?' Hardwicke spat out in disgust. 'Apart from the fact that he drinks like a fish, he's gay. The VC won't like that.'

Jenny looked up in surprise. 'I've seen him blurry eyed – that's an occupational hazard, but what makes you think he's gay? I thought he liked women.'

'He gave me some frigging flowers last year, and told me I had a nice arse. I call that gay.'

Jenny laughed. 'Well, don't be too flattered, for your information he did the same to Joyce James. And anyway, even if he is gay or bi, that shouldn't be a bar to him becoming head of department.'

Hardwicke walked over to the window. 'For once I agree with you, but I am afraid that the university governors will not. More to the point, Malcolm may well have twenty important academic articles and three monographs to his name, but his dress sense is appalling. His jackets never match his trousers. I can't have anyone like that running the English department when I am dean of the faculty, you know.'

Jenny stood up and moved in front of her desk. 'But that's ridiculous, how can you base appointments on what a person wears? Besides, it would be good for the school. Malcolm is the world's leading expert on postmodernist symbolism, he is totally devoted to his research and he has recently won funding from the Bahamian Literature Project.'

'Huh – a free flight to the West Indies… that is going to do us a lot of good! We need serious cash and fast. Our student population is ever dwindling in both quantity and quality, thanks to the removal of the caps on student numbers for Russell Group universities. The ones we get nowadays can barely scrape a lower second, never mind a first class degree. Useless, the whole pack of first years.'

'You were happy enough to admit them.'

'Well,' he said, combing his hair with his fingers, 'I would hardly say "happy", desperate is a more accurate description. You know full well that I needed to show Professor Everson that English could still recruit; otherwise he might have closed down the department then and there.' He moved into the centre of the room looking directly at Jenny. 'It is now your responsibility to keep the punters coming in, but I warn you, Everson is obsessed with raising our percentage of "good degrees" to 92 per cent overall.'

Jenny looked shocked. 'Did you say 92 per cent? But that's impossible! Are you joking?' She slumped onto her desk in despair.

'I only wish I was. When Everson first told me his requirements, I asked him if he had got his figures around the wrong way, you know – 29 per cent. The look he gave me – I shudder when I think of it now.' He did so.

'"I have ambitions for my students," was all that Everson could say. I told him that the English department would do its best, but he may have to settle for a maximum of 65 per cent good degrees this year.'

Jenny sat bolt upright. 'Let me get this clear. By "good degrees" he means those with an average of 60 per cent or above which are in the upper second class category or the first class category?'

'Yes, it's all to do with league-table statistics. I'm afraid we are down in the bottom quarter and the VC wants us right at the top. It helps with recruitment, so I am told.'

'But that is going to be impossible. At the last count, only five out of our thirty finalists were anywhere near to obtaining an average of 60 per cent. On top of that, we have to count in those who have been rusticated for a year and allowed a final resit opportunity. We are looking at less than 20 per cent of good degrees this year. Did you make this clear to him?'

'You know, Dr Jordan, you are not as bright as I thought you were.' Hardwicke sneered his wolf sneer. 'I merely agreed with everything he said, promised him better students, and specified that we could at least triple our quota of first class honours and upper second class degrees in the English department. Obviously I couldn't say the same for History or Drama – they really will be scratching the proverbial bottom of the clearing barrel.'

Jenny gasped. 'You are expecting me to deliver your promises to Professor Everson?'

Hardwicke started pacing the room again. 'No, I'm not expecting you to deliver anything, but success or failure lies with you. You see now why I could not endure Malcolm as my head of department; he would be far too inflexible. Let's be frank here, you are going to have to work flat out to teach these bonzos anything.' He placed his hand on his chin, stroking his stubble. 'Your best bet is to show the students the exam paper before the day of the exam, and let them take notes.'

Jenny was horrified at this suggestion, as that assessment was supposed to be an unseen examination.

'I don't know why you are looking so shocked,' Hardwicke continued, 'I know for a fact that other unis do that, not that they could admit to it publicly. But believe me, I have a way of getting the information out of our colleagues elsewhere.'

Jenny didn't doubt that for a second. She was pretty certain that Hardwicke had slept with a member of every university's English department in England and Wales. Whether these were concurrent or consecutive events, she couldn't say.

'One more thing Jenny, your only hope of succeeding is to introduce step marking. In fact, let me help you with that one. I will demand it when I am officially dean. I'll do the same for all the humanities departments; after all, I am responsible for them all now.'

For not the first time in her life did Jenny feel the strong desire to commit murder. The whole conversation smacked of a complete lack of respect for education in general, and of her in particular. Why? Because she was a woman? Because she valued research? She was certainly a more rounded academic than her newly elected dean. This was typical of Simeon Hardwicke, aka Professor Hardwicke – and what a travesty that was. He no more deserved a chair than half of the students in the department. What had he ever achieved on the scholastic front? To date, five book reviews and a "Kiss Me Quick" guide to the Romantic poets – and some of that was incorrect. Hardwicke should run an option on Ray Cooney or, better still, Alan Ayckbourn; the whole situation was a farce.

Jenny could not help herself as she quipped, 'I presume that in order to solve this particular dilemma, I should now be leading the way on innovation in teaching and learning?'

'Of course, part of the job.'

'And the development of new modules?'

'Absolutely.'

'Well, good. I have long thought that we should run a final-year option on the Harry Potter series. After all, we might stand a chance that the students will actually read the books.'

'Yes, excellent idea, they will enjoy that. And they can watch the DVDs to firm up their revision. I don't think that we can squeeze them into the audience for the new play though; I hear that it is sold out. Although, on second thoughts, I might be able to chat up a box office assistant if I get a chance… See you are thinking like a true leader already!

Oh, by the way, I wouldn't waste too much time on the University Network of Teachers Committee; the only thing it has ever achieved was guffaws of laughter when it first announced itself. In those days the word "committee" was first… Yes, I can see by your face that you have worked out why it became an overnight sensation. Long before your time of course. Its embarrassment only stopped when the faculty of law had the stupid notion to rebrand itself after one of its benefactors, Christian King. "FCK Law" I ask you! If ever there was proof that the lawyers are intellectually inferior creatures to the rest of us, then that was it.'

Jenny was good friends with many of the law staff,

but she wasn't going to jump to their defence. It was pointless with Hardwicke. Jenny thought that the source of Hardwicke's venom with lawyers lay in his childhood desire to be called to the Bar, which had subsequently been thwarted by his poor A level results. She knew for a fact that his first degree came from a polytechnic, as they were called in those days. Not that she had any problem with that, but he clearly did.

'Ah, just another point, on Gwen's retirement, we will have a post going – do you want a teaching fellow or another lecturer?'

Jenny looked at Hardwicke in a quizzical manner. 'I thought that we needed to economise,' she said.

'Oh, don't worry about that.' Hardwicke swatted away her concern as one does a fly at the table. 'I will give the nod to the VC that we are expanding.'

'Well, if we can recruit lots of new students I think a teaching fellow will be useful to share the load.'

'Yes, but you can't expect an Oxbridge scholar to apply here for anything less than a lectureship.'

Jenny heaved a deep sigh. Hardwicke was obsessed with Oxbridge candidates. 'It would be good for the students to see that we are not prejudiced in our thinking. Shouldn't we consider appointing one of our own PhD students? It might encourage our best students to stay here if they think that there are job prospects at the end of their studies.'

Hardwicke scratched his chin thoughtfully. 'Yes, point taken. Not a bad idea… Teaching fellow it is then! That's quite good enough for one of ours. And we can save some money too. Sophie Bellinger could do it… Nice girl,' he added drooling like an old dog. 'She's just about to submit her thesis. Don't worry, I've got the examiners all carved up, so she is bound to pass it without any amendments, plus she has written three book reviews already this year. I'll get her to change the titles on these before she submits them, so that they look like *real* academic articles. I can instruct the VC as to what a gem we have here. Huh, he won't have a clue. Doesn't know the difference between his arse and his Archer.'

'And what about fairness and transparency in the hiring process?' Jenny persisted.

'Bugger that! I want something good to look at first thing on a Monday morning, not a dried up old prune.' Hardwicke was quick to note Jenny's look of annoyance. He added, 'Gwen, I mean, not you.'

Jenny was, in fact, irritated at the idea of a post being "carved up" rather than any reference to herself, but she was about to be angered for this reason as well. Hardwicke was a man who was in love with his own ideas. He continued,

'You could look quite nice if you made an effort – you know; wear a lower top and a shorter skirt. Oh, you might want to dye your hair – a blonde has more fun than a brunette... well, they do if they are with me...' Hardwicke's advice was relentless. 'And while you are at it, get into the gym and lose a bit of weight... You're quite short you know. What are you, five foot? At your height every pound counts.'

As Jenny was closer to five-foot four, this last remark irked her more than the rest. 'After all you're only thirty-seven not seventy-three, stop acting like it and get some action.'

And with that he left the room as abruptly as he had arrived, the ancient and somewhat threadbare paisley carpet barely being able to keep together under the stress of his pounding footsteps. *One day... just one day...* she thought, and unclenching her fist she had realised that in her anger her nails had dug into the palms of her hands leaving a bloody trail on her fingertips...

All of this had replayed in her mind as she lay there with her head on her hands. Hardly soothing, but it had evoked a dream-like trance on Jenny. God she was tired! She came to with a start at the sound of a knock on her office door. Tom her administrator had brought in a longed-for cup of tea. He studied her through his gold-rimmed spectacles for a few seconds in silence. It was now ten minutes past nine. The morning was flying by and nothing had been achieved.

'You all right, ducks?' he asked in his northern accent. It was halfway between a command and a question. 'I was only thinking as to how you've been saddled with this pig-in-a-poke of a job.'

'Yes, fine... and well yes... at least I know you can be relied upon to remind me what I am supposed to be doing.'

'Good, because I have one of your errant flock outside – Hajinder Patel. I've brought you his folder. He was supposed to see you yesterday for extra assistance but he forgot! Be gentle on him; he isn't the shiniest pebble on the beach.'

'So I've noticed. Okay, give me a minute then send him in.'

'Oh, by the way, he is an international student on a

Tier 4 visa. He only has eighteen months left to achieve a degree or his visa will be revoked.'

The student in question was a somewhat short youth of mixed Indochinese parentage. He was covered in acne and was clearly not a morning person. Jenny's keen sense of smell identified the potential cause of this student's poor academic achievement to date.

'Sit down. I've been reading last term's reports from your tutors. They don't paint a very pretty picture. Can you explain why you have got yourself into the position you have?' Patel bowed his head to the floor. No response.

Jenny tried again. 'I do feel that perhaps we are at fault in this institution by allowing you to stay here to sit the exams again, so I feel it would be in your best interest to return home, indefinitely.'

That did the trick. 'No, I mustn't go home. I will be a disgrace to my family.'

'Do you think that by staying here you are honouring them? Do you think you can avoid telling them the truth forever?'

'You don't understand; my father has a reputation to maintain. He wanted me to study law, but my grades were not good enough. I came here to get a degree and then do the additional law exams at home. If I am sent back now they will execute me.'

Jenny had the feeling that he wasn't exaggerating; at least, as far as this student was concerned it was a truly held belief.

'Look, I sympathise with your situation, but your visa time is running out. You really have to get your act together. The exams are coming up in less than a month.

You must pass every exam this time if you are to continue on to your final year.'

'Am I going to get a first class degree?'

'No, even if you pass each one, the best you can now achieve is a lower second class overall, and I would suggest that a third class degree is the more likely result.'

'But I've got to get a first!'

'I'm sorry but that is now out of the question with the grades that you have achieved to date.'

'Not if you allow me to take my resits for an honours mark.'

'On what grounds?'

'Medical grounds.'

'Any specific medical grounds?'

'Does it matter? The students know that you are as desperate for us to get good degrees as we are. Lots of them have got Hardwicke to give them a resit for the honours marks.'

So that was it, she thought, *just another of the slippery tricks that Hardwicke had in order to promote himself.* God, that man was a fiend.

'I'll tell you what,' she said at last, 'you go down to student welfare. You tell them that you have been overindulging in mind-bending drugs and require their support.' Patel finally appeared to understand something. 'They will put you on a clean-up programme, and in that case I can allow you to re-sit the exams that you previously failed without capping your marks at 40 per cent. However, this is your final chance. If you do not pass all your exams this time, note ALL your exams, I will have to terminate you.'

'Terminate me?'

'Sorry, I meant to say terminate your studies.'

'Thank you Miss, thank you so much. I won't let you down.'

Jenny was unsure if she had done the right thing or not. It was a huge dilemma. If Patel's studies were stopped now, he would be sent home and his shocking results to date would not count in the end of year statistics. If he passed, he was only going to scrape a third... and that would be another black notch against the department. Why did the university want more firsts and 2:1s overnight? Hadn't the management heard of grade inflation? What was the point of awarding first class degrees that would not be comparable to first class awards meted out at other institutions? But then only the other day there was a report about one of their competitors who awarded 67 per cent more first class degrees than they had in the previous ten years. Well, let the uni sink itself... what did she care?

But she did care; that was the problem. She cared for her students and wanted the best for them. But no matter how hard she worked, no matter how hard her staff worked, some of these students would barely scrape a pass. Did that mean they should not be allowed to take a degree at all? Surely it was wrong to dismiss all degrees as worthless if they were sitting at the bottom of a scale. For some of Jenny's students, a third class degree was a real and fantastic achievement. Jenny had taught lone parents on benefits, a woman who had brain surgery during her studies and a young man with autism. Where was the fairness in preventing these students studying just because they were not, on paper, likely to get a first?

Actually, all of these did. Jenny thought that the whole system was corrupt.

'And whoever decided to make the percentage of higher degrees a criterion in the university league tables needs to be shot,' she shouted.

Everyone thought it, but no one could say it to the Management.

"You are not ambitious enough for your students," was the reply that they would receive.

Jenny was left looking at a potential figure of 20 per cent of students reaching a 2:1 this year. Hardwick had told her that her minimum target was 65 per cent, over treble of what the school had anticipated. It would take a miracle to pull that off.

CHAPTER 2
TUESDAY, 12 APRIL: 9.40 AM:
Introducing Cedric

The English department was one of several departments making up the faculty of humanities. This faculty along with the faculties of law and business, education, medical sciences and engineering, completed the menu of the University of Sedgemoor, which had initially started life as Bridgwater Polytechnic in the 1960s.

Originally, Somerset's county town of Taunton was destined to be the central location for the polytechnic, however, when completing all the financial plans, the governing body decided that Bridgwater was a better bet in the short term, as land in and around the town was considerably cheaper to buy. The downside of this was settling in to a town that boasted a less than salubrious reputation locally. As a result, the polytechnic had struggled with student recruitment for all of its life.

The rebirth of all polytechnics as universities in 1992 gave the governing body the chance to rebrand, and at the suggestion of one of the lay members the decision was made to use the area name, as opposed to the name of the town. The University of Sedgemoor commenced life. The inspired name had borne fruit, particularly when a bright young thing identified that the initials "UoS" could easily be reduced to "US", and developed a range of advertising merchandise with the catchy slogans, "Become one of US" or "You are one of US" depending on the stage of admission. A more cynical colleague in the marketing department suggested that graduates should be awarded a mug with "You WERE one of US" embossed on it, but as that smacked of disenfranchisement, instead "You will ALWAYS BE one of US" was the final of the three slogans promoted.

It was part of the founding plan that all of the faculties were to be established within a three-mile radius of the Bridgwater train station, in an attempt to encourage more students to enter the institution's portals. However, as luck would have it, a large farm with numerous buildings and outhouses fell underneath the auctioneer's hammer at the relevant time. Since that property had the postal address of Nether Stowey, a governor with a literary interest decided that this would be the ideal place to build an English department, the name of the village being synonymous with one Samuel Taylor Coleridge of *Kubla Khan* and *The Ancient Mariner* fame. For this reason, the English department, along with its sisters in the faculty of humanities, became annexed from the rest of the university and some eight miles from student nightlife.

Some small effort was made to assist the hapless faculty of humanities to integrate, and when another expanse of farmland came up for auction, situated between Nether Stowey and Lawyer's Hill, it was thought to be a sign that the faculty of law (as it then was) should be ousted from Bridgwater (the buildings that this school had been occupying in the town, miraculously quadrupling in value and consequently sold) and shunted into no-man's-land. A shuttle bus service ran from the law buildings (known affectionately by the student body as "Shanty Town" due to their somewhat hastily built and flimsy construction) to the Nether Stowey site, then into Bridgwater. A massive drop in recruitment for law students indicated that this was without a doubt the most ludicrous plan that the governors had hatched to date and the faculty of law was quickly relocated for the second time in three years, to the humanities site, costing the university virtually all of the excess capital that it had raised by selling off the law buildings in Bridgwater.

The irritated law students still found themselves ostracised from Bridgwater, but at least they could socialise with the humanities students. This situation would have run smoothly enough for many years to come, except for another twist of the knife to the faculty structure. For some reason, business was added to the law faculty, but whilst law students remained in splendid (as opposed to squalid) isolation in Nether Stowey, business students were offered a former Hilton Hotel situated a mere stone's throw from Bridgwater station. If the law students were aggrieved with this, that was nothing compared to the sentiments frequently expressed by law staff. Perhaps this sense of neglect was a reason for the habitual bickering that Jenny knew occurred in the law school. On a sunny day, when windows were opened, it was frequently the case that arguments emanating from the law school wafted across the grass into the English department's offices.

After Jenny had spoken to Patel, she called to Tom, to ask him to step into the office.

'What's up, Jenny?' Tom asked.

'Tom, how many of our other students believe they are Sherlock Holmes?'

'You mean taking a "7 per cent solution"? How many shooting up? That's hard to say. I think that there a certain category of students who are on something, but mainly alcohol. Why do you want to know?'

'I wondered if there was correlation between those using opiates, or whatever, and their overall classifications. If there is, I might be able to prevent them sitting the exams on health grounds.'

'Good idea, but I don't think it is as simple as that. Certainly there are some at the bottom who are taking drugs, but I know of a couple who are at the upper second classification. Likewise, some of our students are not, to my knowledge, taking anything and only predicted a third.'

'Yes, that is inevitable. Well, worth a thought. Thanks Tom.'

It was now nine forty and only thirty minutes remained before she was due to take the lecture on *Hamlet* to the third year students.

> *O, that this too too solid flesh would melt*
> *Thaw and resolve itself into a dew!*
> *Or that the Everlasting had not fix'd*
> *His canon 'gainst self-slaughter!*

Was it solid or sullied? There was some debate on this issue, but whichever version was preferred, it mirrored her feelings. Her tea was cold and her in tray just as full as it was at ten to nine. Would it matter if she walked out of the door and out of the university for the rest of the day? Her eyes became blurry.

O God! God!
How weary, stale, flat and unprofitable,
Seem to me all the uses of this world!
Fie on't! ah fie! 'tis an unweeded garden,
That grows to seed; things rank and gross in nature
Possess it merely.

There certainly were a number of rank and gross aspects about this place! It would take a millennium to pull out all the weeds.

She finished her tea, and was just about to leave her desk, when she made the fatal error of opening the top envelope of her Everest-sized pile of correspondence.

It said: "Dr Jordan,

You bitch, whore, slut, your days are numbered."

'Well really, as if I haven't got enough problems without crap like this!' she said to herself. She was so angry by now and busy tearing the letter into shreds that she didn't pay full attention to a desk drawer on her right which had crept slightly open. She collided with it.

'Bugger – that's another bruise to add to my collection.' She reached down to close the drawer so that she might pass by in safety. The drawer was one of several still crammed full of Hardwicke's memorabilia.

'Oh, chuck it out my dear, I've got everything I need,'

he had said glibly. As if she was the cleaner. Might as well be, sorting out all the shit he had left behind.

She was about to empty the whole contents of the drawer into the recycling bag when her attention was drawn to a bundle of old newspaper cuttings. The story ringed was that of one of their English students who had died of some type of gastroenteritis in his room on campus the year previously. Jenny had semi-forgotten the incident but the paper cuttings brought it back into her mind.

It was the joke of the department that Henry Fielding was studying English here; the real comedy being that he was an excruciatingly poor student to tutor, or to put it in language that he himself might understand, he was as thick as two short planks. There was not one person who believed that he had achieved three grade Bs at A level as required to study at the university. There were rumours to the effect that Hardwicke had received a backhander from Henry's parents to allow him to join the English department, particularly as Hardwicke bought a new Mercedes at the time of Henry's arrival. Malcolm Lowry was all over the boy. It was easy to understand why. Henry was beautiful to behold, a living embodiment of a Greek god.

Poor Henry, he didn't even make it to the second year. Even if he had the innate intelligence, and that was questionable, his studies (as, she suspected, had Patel's) were marred by an overindulgence in drugs. Henry had become addicted to heroin during his first term here. That was the start of a not-so-slow decline. Everyone assumed that his stomach condition was brought on by an overindulgence of drugs, but the coroner gave an open verdict. Jenny presumed that suicide was another option. She remembered that Lowry was extremely upset at the time.

For some reason, unknown to herself, she decided to read the story again when she returned from her lecture, so she put all the newspaper cuttings back in the drawer rather than the bin. She picked up her bag, ensuring that her flash drive was securely tucked in one of the outer pockets, and walked out of her room, past Tom's desk, and down the corridor to the exit.

*

The architect who designed the humanities buildings had been inspired by a mixture of neoclassical architecture, blended with the works of the Pre-Raphaelite artists and the Romantic poets. He had gone to town with the English building, both on the inside, where each office was the recreation of a Victorian study, and on the outside, where overly decorative towers could be espied. The result created the look of a nineteenth-century stately home – only the butler was missing. She reached the majestic entrance, which acted as a barrier between the world of literature and the real world, and wished that the grandeur of their surroundings would inspire her students to study, rather than indulge in narcotics.

For the first time in months, the sun had dried out a large stretch of meadow situated between the faculty building and the main lecture theatre. The meadow was a natural short cut for her to take. The longer authorised route involved trampling along a gravel path, which, thanks to the lack of resources, at best wrecked one's shoes, and at worst broke your ankle. Gwendolyn had experienced both simultaneously six months ago. Much to Jenny's dismay, she was asked to cover Gwen's lectures on *Beowulf* for the following two weeks.

Depending on the time of year, the meadow was a host to many varieties of flowers. Hyacinths and crocuses gave way to daffodils, which in turn succeeded their majesty to the summer poppies. This was an in-between time when the daffodils had just finished their display and the poppies had not made their presence felt.

Thanks to the Somerset climate, for most of the year it was impossible to defy the signs marked "Keep off the Grass", for fear that the pedestrian would find herself knee deep in mud. However, an unusually bright spell for April had made non-compliance possible. So rare was this occurrence, that Jenny took full advantage of the chance for disobedience, smiling while she did so. Her sense of joy at this small act of rebellion was marred only by the realisation that she was not the only person to disregard the sign.

At first Jenny paid little attention to the slim, brown-haired man in a suit, but was soon forced to recognise that he was trying to catch her attention. She prayed that he wasn't about to make a complaint.

'Excuse me', the intruder said in a polite and not unwelcome tone, 'can you direct me to the faculty of law?'

Jenny felt an overwhelming surge of pleasure that the stranger was not the agitated parent or sponsor of one of her failing students. Her relief manifested itself into one of her rare (these days) warm smiles. She looked up at her accoster. He was smiling down at her with twinkling grey-green eyes. She was reminded of someone she knew, but couldn't place.

'Of course; you've taken a wrong turn at the aviary.' The man's grimace reflected her own feeling about the birdcage. 'Yes, I know. It makes the place look like a holiday camp. Someone thought it would be soothing for the students.'

'But they've put a cockerel in it…'

The man's disdain somehow amused Jenny more than she had been entertained for months and when the cockerel alerted the general public to his presence, as he did on a regular basis, Jenny burst into giggles. She didn't know how to answer the stranger's last remark of contempt, so she just shrugged her shoulders.

'You need to go back to the cockerel, he's called Cedric by the way, and turn right; then you go over the brick bridge and turn left. You should see the signs by then.'

She escorted the stranger to the other side of the grass… or was he escorting her?

'Thank you. Why Cedric?'

'It was a mistake. He was originally to be called Cecil, after Cecil Day-Lewis.'

'Daniel's father?'

'Yes, that's right; he was a gift from the local agricultural college, so the university wanted to put up a sign thanking them.'

'Huh, yes most heartily at six in the morning, I would say.'

'Yes, well, a signwriter was hired to produce the sign

which specified the university's thanks, etc. and when the sign returned, the name inscribed was "Cedric". So Cedric it was.'

By this stage they had completed their trespassing and were now safely on the tarmac path.

She noted that although the man was still smiling at her, he was also studying her intently. It unnerved her. She said quite firmly, 'This is where our paths diverge; I am taking a lecture in Wordsworth Hall.' She pointed to a white building, in the neoclassical style.

The stranger seemed reluctant to let her go on her way, and as though looking for an excuse to keep her, he asked, 'Did he live there?'

'Wordsworth? No, the hall wasn't built until 1985.' She couldn't help teasing the man. 'The name is on account of the host of golden daffodils that can be seen here.'

'Somehow I don't believe you, or has Cedric eaten them all?'

'I hope not, daffodils are poisonous aren't they?'

'I will have to ask one of our forensic experts about that.' The man bit his lip as though he had revealed more than he meant to.

Jenny decided to ignore that last comment.

'I'm not sure if you know anything about the university's establishment here, but the inspiration behind it are the works of the Romantic poets, hence the design of the buildings.'

Jenny waved her arm towards the lecture theatre and the English building. The comment produced another grimace from the man, as he perused the red brickwork topped with oriental domes.

'Did the Victorians have domes like that on their buildings?' he asked.

'I doubt it,' Jenny replied, 'but I think that they are supposed to conjure up the image of *Kubla Khan*.'

'Yes, well, no accounting for architectural taste I suppose. Thank you for putting me on the right track. I must not make you late for your lecture.'

As the man appeared to be in no hurry to move, Jenny scurried away to the lecture hall. However, intrigued by him, she made the fatal error of turning back to see if he had set on his path. Her quick glance informed her of what she had sensed – the man was still where she had left him. Furthermore, his face sported an intense expression that she hadn't seen when she was talking to him just now. There was something about this expression that she didn't like.

CHAPTER 3
TUESDAY, 12 APRIL: 12.15 PM:
Formally Introducing Caldicott

It was twelve fifteen by the time Jenny returned to the English building. Lost though she was in her own Kubla Khanesque state, she was not so oblivious to notice that Tom was still lurking in his office. This struck her as odd as Tom was a creature of habit and invariably he took his lunch-break at noon. He sidled up to her, and spoke in a low voice.

'Thought I had better warn you; you've a visitor. Quite a good-looking one, I might say, if you don't mind a Rabbie Burns impersonator wearing polyester suits.'

She looked up into Tom's mischievous brown eyes. 'Oh Tom, you're incorrigible.'

'In fact, altogether acceptable and commendable, perhaps even Byronesque.' He stopped to polish his glasses, as though waiting for her explanation. Jenny thought that she was about to get a telling off for some reason, but had absolutely no idea why. 'I have to say though, I do *not* approve of his profession.'

Jenny's heart sank. 'Oh dear, tell me the worst; is he here to carry out our audit?'

'That would be bad, but this might be considered worse. He is from the Unmentionables.'

Jenny was lost. Tom, she knew, had a language of his own devising, with every quirky phrase uttered pinpointing accuracy, in the way that champion darts players consistently score "one hundred and eighty" in their turn. But for this, she needed assistance. Tom looked at her in a disappointed manner.

'Here is his card.'

He handed over a small card introducing Detective Sergeant Caldicott from Avon and Somerset Constabulary (CID) Minehead and Porlock.

Jenny's face fell as she read the card. 'Uhh, a Man from Porlock – might have known that my dreams would be interrupted indefinitely. What does he want?'

'He said merely to introduce himself to you and ask a couple of routine questions.'

'That sounds ominous. Have you offered him tea?'

'Yes – he said that he preferred coffee, but would wait until you returned.'

'Very noble of him.'

'I've put him in your office. I didn't think you would mind.'

Jenny looked at Tom's inscrutable expression. This was not the Tom that she knew. Normally Tom would tell an unwanted visitor, in no uncertain terms, to make an appointment with her, police or no police; he wouldn't leave the enemy in her room. Something had affected his thinking. Perhaps he had developed a crush on DS Caldicott. No, there must be another explanation. Tom was now in a relationship with a junior doctor, and pronounced himself to be head over heels in love.

'Tom, would you be an angel, I know that you should

have gone for your lunch by now but would you mind making us a drink? And then do take a break yourself. I have a feeling that *my* lunch hour has been usurped, but I don't want you to sacrifice yours.'

'Yes Dr Jordan, anything to assist Cupid.' At which point he sauntered off to the staff kitchen.

Jenny didn't know which surprised her the most. Tom calling her Dr Jordan (he had never done that before), or the reference to Cupid. But that at least explained Tom's attitude. Tom must have mistakenly thought that DS Caldicott was a potential suitor. As if she would fall for a policeman… although Tom did give the impression that this was quite a good-looking policeman… She took a deep breath and opened her office door.

She didn't see him immediately as he was standing in the window recess looking out at the patch of grass that she had crossed earlier.

'Dr Jordan, sorry to intrude on you in your lunch-break…' Jenny started. She recognised the voice before she had a chance to look at the speaker. It was the "Birdcage Man" whom she had met earlier that morning.

'Coleridge,' Jenny said this with bitter disappointment, at the realisation that the attractive stranger was, in fact, here to cause her anxiety after all.

The policeman looked at her in surprise. 'No, my name's Caldicott.'

'I'm sorry, we have our wires crossed Mr Caldicott. My secretary described you as a Robert Burns lookalike, and I can vaguely see why but apart from the fact that you are thinner and taller than the original, I think that you look more like Coleridge.'

'And you are disappointed that I do?'

'No, not at all.' Jenny felt herself blushing and in an attempt to be light-hearted she added, 'Have you come to arrest Cedric?'

Caldicott snorted. 'Not yet, but if he keeps disturbing my enquiries, I might be forced to strangle him.'

At that point, Tom knocked on the door to announce the arrival of drinks. He set it carefully on the chair perched in the middle of the room and indicated that he had brought out the "special biscuits" for her visitor.

'I'll take my break now, Dr Jordan. Holly has just returned so there will be someone around to ensure you are not disturbed.' And with that he gave her a wink and closed the door. Tom's manner did not go unnoticed by DS Caldicott, but whatever thoughts he had on the subject he chose to keep to himself. Jenny was very glad about that as she felt herself blushing again, this time at Tom's audacity. She made a supreme effort to concentrate and appear professional. 'That's your coffee, Mr Caldicott,' Jenny said pointing to a pink flowery mug. 'Do help yourself to a biscuit, and please sit down.'

Jenny, realising that DS Caldicott had nowhere to sit, pulled out a chair from the window recess and dragged it forwards to be at right angles to her desk. Her coat, which had been resting on it, was rolled up into a ball and flung on the floor. Her apparent disregard for her own property made the man grin. She reached for her tea. 'In what way can I assist you?'

'Thank you.' Caldicott took his coffee, grimacing at the mug's design, and a biscuit which he promptly demolished. He sat down. 'I've taken over the caseload from DI Vaughan who has moved to the Met. She left a couple of loose ends to tie up, both involving the deaths of persons connected with the university.'

'Forgive me for asking Mr Caldicott, shouldn't the Bridgwater Constabulary deal with this area?'

'Yes, but Bridgwater is notoriously busy, and we are sometimes asked to step in. I have just come from the faculty of law – thank you for assisting me by the way, your directions were perfect. I spoke with Dr Ted Murray, who I believe is the current acting head of law, in the wake of the recent death of Professor Carstairs.'

'Yes. He died from gastroenteritis I believe.' Jenny looked down at the carpet that she was walking on, as though willing it to swallow her up.

Caldicott noticed that Jenny had been about to take a biscuit but changed her mind. *Hello*, thought Caldicott, *here's something that I haven't been prepped for. Was Dr Jordan in a relationship with Carstairs? If not, why is the woman looking so damned uncomfortable – was she in anyway responsible for Carstairs' death? This will need investigating carefully.* And to Jenny he said, 'We received the post-mortem results this morning. That is the main reason that I am at the university. There is enough evidence to suggest that the professor's death was caused by poisoning.'

'Oh.' Jenny, who had still been standing until that point, sat heavily in her chair. 'In what way does this relate to the English department?'

'Certain trace chemicals found in the professor's bloodstream also showed up in the post-mortem results of one of your former students.'

'Henry Fielding?'

'Precisely. Why did you think of him so quickly?'

Jenny did not appreciate this turn of questioning. Did he consider her to be a suspect? She would have liked to have spun him a story, but she was not very good at playing games. She would have to be truthful.

'I was thinking of Henry only this morning. Another one of my students came to see me… it was clear from his body posture and eye contact that he was going the same way as Henry.'

'I see. Is drug-taking a huge problem on this campus?'

'I think perhaps, yes, but it is hard to tell if it is worse here than at any other university. We are a relatively small community; this sort of thing is easier to spot. The new vice chancellor is trying his best to eradicate any peddling that goes on here, but I do not know how successful his attempts will be. Where I worked previously, the more the VC tried to stop it happening, the more it seemed to take place. Again that was a small, compact university, so it was easier to identify. I went to a large university myself, there was probably a substantial amount of drug-taking going on at the time, but I never paid much attention to it, I certainly was not interested in trying it.'

'No don't, it's a fool's game; except this is worse. There is enough evidence to suggest that dangerous chemicals may have been added to the normal mix; whether to deliberately cause harm, we cannot say at the moment.' Caldicott helped himself to another biscuit. He had not eaten for six hours and was suddenly aware that he was hungry. His actions did not go unnoticed by Jenny.

'But Tony… I mean Professor Carstairs, didn't

indulge in drugs, unless he had started very recently, so I am confused as to why the two deaths might coincide.'

'Thank you; that confirms what Dr Murray told me. It is, of course, possible that there is a contaminated batch of what appears to be a harmless tablet, a vitamin or mineral tablet for example, although the two incidents are twelve months apart, so that is probably unlikely. Can you talk me through Fielding's history? Your student's I mean, not the author's.'

'Well, I will try. To be honest, I was not in the best of places at the time for personal reasons, so I don't remember very much about Henry. Also, I have only recently taken over as head of department. Professor Hardwicke is perhaps in a better position to comment.'

'Yes, it was Hardwicke that told me that he had some newspaper articles that might be of use...'

'They are in the bottom drawer of my desk... Have a look by all means...'

'Thanks, I have already taken the liberty of looking through them.'

Jenny was taken aback. It was on the tip of her tongue to ask if the man had a search warrant but she stopped herself in time. Perhaps he didn't need one if he had been given consent by Hardwicke; it was, after all Hardwicke's property. It would do no good to deliberately antagonise the policeman. She would take it out on Hardwicke later.

Caldicott continued. 'By the way, you have a pretty vicious paper-knife there. Can I suggest that you remove it? I have a strong suspicion that "use at work" would not be a defence for that one.'

Jenny felt as if she had received an electric shock –

what else had he examined in her absence? She thought that she would like to get this over with as soon as possible.

'What would you like to know?' she asked him.

'When did Fielding start taking opium derivatives? Who did he hang around with? Did his circle of friends change after he started on the heavy stuff?'

'I suspect that he came to us already hooked on cannabis. In fact, I remember smelling it on him during his first week here. The heroin addiction started after he had been here for about two months; at least that was when he started to look washed-up and spotty. Sorry I can't really tell you any more than that; I didn't pay much attention to him as he was only assigned to me for lectures not seminars. I think he might have dropped out of lectures before the end of the first term. Can I ask why you want to know this? Are you trying to find the supplier?'

'Yes indeed. We don't want a repeat of this. Just one more question, if I may Dr Jordan. Can you tell me the last time that you saw Professor Carstairs?'

Jenny swallowed hard before answering. When she did finally address the question she looked at her desk rather than at her interrogator. 'I am not sure. I don't think that I have seen him since the end of last term.'

Caldicott, sensing that Dr Jordan was on the verge of clamming up completely, enquired gently, 'May I ask where this was?'

'It would have been at one of our Friday meetings in Bridgwater,' Jenny replied, and added as though in a trance-like state, 'everyone has to attend them.'

Caldicott reassessed the situation and decided that he would not pursue this line of enquiry for the moment.

'Well Dr Jordan, it has been a pleasure to meet you, formally. If you do think of anything else then please contact me. My mobile number is on the card, or you can email me.' He stood up to leave. As Jenny felt somewhat vulnerable sitting down, she also stood up. He added, 'By the way, what is your area of teaching expertise?'

She smiled at him, 'Is this relevant to your enquiries?'

He smiled back, 'No, just idle curiosity.'

'Well, most of my time is spent teaching Shakespeare, but my main area of research is Classical Greek literature.'

'Ahh, that explains why you sometimes lecture in the drama department. Quite a few Gorgons to deal with there I would say.'

Caldicott had brought to both their minds the horrendous spectre of Dr Touchwood. Her adopted first name was Medusa, and if anyone ever lived up to her name it was she. She had penetrating violet eyes, no doubt created by the use of coloured contact lenses, and dyed black hair with purple and green extensions plaited in. But it was her manner that was her most repugnant aspect. She was so full of false bonhomie. "Oh darling, that was absolutely marvellous," she would snivel at her least talented actor. "You simply must be considered for the RSC, you are a natural, isn't she a natural everyone? I said isn't she just too marvellous? We love you here; they will love you wherever you go."

'I understand that you are not lecturing Greek literature for the English department this year; you must think that is a pity not to use your valuable research?'

Jenny started to feel that the "Coleridge impersonator" had researched every aspect of her life. Why did he ask her about her research area when he already knew it? What else did he know about her? Good-looking or not, she could do without an inquisition. She started to manoeuvre him towards the door.

'It is a third year option, but the students are put off by aspects of the language, that and the fact that, unlike in some of the options, not many get a first class mark overall in the subject.'

'And you are not tempted to assist them?'

'I do not believe in grade inflation. I gather that I am in the minority on that account, particularly as our vice chancellor is incredibly keen to see our percentages of good degrees – first class and upper second class degrees – improve dramatically this year.'

'Isn't that a noble idea? I would have thought that all academics hope their students leave with a good degree.'

'Well, yes and no. If the students really did improve to the extent where they truly had earned their classification, of course that would be wonderful, but the trouble with stipulating quotas for this is that a number of less fastidious operators have chosen to adopt various unscrupulous techniques, which on the surface appear to be bona fide.'

'Such as?'

'Step marking. This is a mechanism used by several universities. In reality the step marking adopted is akin to a step taken by Neil Armstrong.' Caldicott looked blankly at her. 'You know,' she added, '"One small step for man, one giant leap for the overall grade". Let me give you an example.'

By this stage, Jenny became so wrapped up in her own problems that she had completely forgotten that she was being interviewed by a member of the CID. She ushered Caldicott back down to his chair and gave him the plate of biscuits whilst she took the floor. Caldicott would normally have found this behaviour irritating but for some reason he found Dr Jordan amusing. He certainly found her attractive, and was in no hurry to leave her company. He sat down in anticipation.

'In step marking you are asked to award marks on the "8" the "2" or the "5", at least that is our system. So you would award 52 per cent, 65 per cent, 48 per cent, etc. That seems reasonable enough and stops us agonising on whether a paper is worth 55 per cent or 54 per cent. Are you with me?'

'Yes, so far so good.'

'However, in theory, if we are looking at a piece of work worth 60 per cent we have two choices: go down to 58 per cent or up to 62 per cent. It always goes up… Again, that is not so bad, but here's the rub. If we want to give it 59 per cent the nearest mark is 58 per cent, agreed?'

Caldicott, having just bitten into his third biscuit, nodded his head in agreement, and started to smile. He was being instructed in the art of marking – something that was an unknown phenomenon to him. But mostly it was because he was enjoying the experience of being lectured to by Dr Jordan. Not many civilians are happy to tell a policeman to pay attention.

'Okay, so logically if we think that a question is worth 59 per cent, it should go down to 58 per cent, right? Wrong! We are told that it must still go up. You can see then that if this happens for each answer on a paper the overall grade is increased accordingly. End result? A candidate that probably deserves a 2:2 overall ends up with a 2:1. That is not so disconcerting in the grand scheme of things, but of course, it occurs for every classification so a candidate worth a high 2:1 finds themselves awarded a first class mark, much to their delight.

Now you might be thinking, "What is so wrong with this?"'… In fact, that was precisely what Caldicott was thinking, but as he had just started eating his fourth biscuit he was unable to say so. 'I can see you are…' Jenny looked kindly at him, as though he was a student in need of assistance. 'The problem is that the candidate that is truly awarded 78 per cent as of right, is then put on the same footing as a candidate who really should have been awarded 68 per cent… It's unfair in my opinion.'

'I see. And is there no way out of this predicament of the disenfranchised true first?'

Jenny sat on the edge of her desk, with her hands folded in her lap. She started to look past Caldicott, her bright hazel eyes staring out of her window, lost in her own world of academia. Caldicott was nonplussed by Dr Jordan's behaviour. He wasn't sure whether he preferred being commanded to sit down, or totally ignored. Here was a woman who would keep him on his toes. He was naturally attracted to brunettes, but this one had something different about her. It dawned on him that it was her openness that he liked; she said exactly what she thought, and made no attempt to deceive him. He found that refreshing.

She continued still staring out of the window. 'Certain countries work on a Grade Point Average, but we haven't endorsed that over here. Perhaps we should, then someone on a GPA of 80 per cent could be separated from those with 70 per cent as an average.' She stopped and looked at him. 'Have I said something wrong?'

'No, not at all. But don't you have external examiners to ensure that all the marking is at the right standard?'

'It's interesting that you say that. Usually the externals do not argue too much with what we do, primarily for the reason that they are operating the same systems in their own institutions. However, some externals are brave enough to speak out. In all fairness to the English staff, we are pretty reliable in our marking. But we haven't undertaken step marking before, and some of the staff are unhappy about it. The drama department used it last year, and my goodness didn't they get it in the neck from their externals at the examination board? But I mustn't be unprofessional and tell you why.'

At this point Jenny's eyes returned to the window, whilst her mind travelled back to a very ferocious scene at the board meeting ten months ago. Accusations had been flying left, right and centre, all to do with exam scripts being marked exceptionally generously in exchange for sex. She couldn't help but grin at the thought of it. Caldicott was quick to note the look of mischief on Jenny's face; he could tell that she was replaying the scene in her mind. Judging by her expression, he wished that he had attended the board himself.

'Pity,' he said.

Jenny looked at him and giggled. 'Yes, usually the meetings are as dull as ditchwater, but this was one for the memoirs. Let us put it this way, the allegations of services rendered to staff by the students eclipsed *Fifty Shades of*

Grey, and made the activities in that book appear perfectly normal.'

'Aren't they?' It was Caldicott's turn to be provocative, but he was easily outwitted.

'I suppose they are for you; after all, you deal with handcuffs all the time, don't you?'

Caldicott had to stop and think, 'Well, not normally like that.' They both laughed at that point. He wanted to carry on with this conversation. He had to remind himself that he was dealing with a potential suspect.

He continued on safe territory, 'Don't you have to comply with standards set by the Quality Assurance Agency?'

'Yes, a bureaucratic system if ever there was one, probably modelled on principles gleaned from *1984*. If the paperwork looks good, then the rest will follow. I won't say any more on that. No, it will backfire in the end; a first class degree from Sedgemoor will mean nothing to employers when they work out that some students are not up to that level. It will just discriminate against our best students. It is a pity as we do have some who are truly excellent scholars, who may not be able to fulfil their employment potential. This is just going to be an excuse for Oxbridge snobbery. Employers will only look at where the degree is from, not the candidate. It's wrong and I cannot buy into this inflated marking system, even if it means closing the department.'

'And is that likely?'

'Yes, very much so, unless I can turn it around and magic up a 65 per cent minimum classification figure of firsts and 2:1s. I'm told that the VC is aiming for 92 per cent.'

'And what are you predicted to get at the moment?'

'No more than 30 per cent, and realistically nearer to twenty.'

'That is a big jump, and how do you plan to increase your rates?'

'We only have thirty students in the final year, so one extra student obtaining a 2:1 would have quite a significant impact on the overall percentage. I have been holding re-enforcement sessions for the students over the Easter break, but of course, it is the ones who don't need to attend that turn up. The only other possibility is to find a mechanism to prevent the really poor students from sitting their final exams this year. That, I am afraid to say, is a more realistic plan.

'And are there no other ways to achieve this target?'

'No, other than that, I haven't got a clue how we can do this the honest way. Perhaps I should bump some of my hopeless students off!' Jenny laughed, and then went quiet realising that she should not be making this sort of joke with Caldicott. He gave her a curious stare. It unnerved her. 'Sorry,' she said, 'that was in poor taste.' She then added, 'I am talking about my work and preventing you from doing yours.'

Caldicott, staring at her intently said, 'I'm not in a hurry.' He smiled gently, 'Do you enjoy being head of department?'

'That's a strange question. Let's put it this way, I didn't ask to be head, the job got forced upon me.'

Caldicott started to recite Shakespeare, '*Be not afraid of greatness; some are born great, some achieve greatness, and others have greatness thrust upon them.*'

'Thanks, I didn't consider myself to be Malvolio.'

Caldicott grinned. 'Neither do I; more of a Maria.'

Jenny chose to ignore this interruption. 'And anyway, I would hardly call this greatness. *Uneasy lies the head that wears the crown* is a more apt phrase.

'Ahh, *Henry IV Part 2*, Act III, Scene 1, I believe.'

'Very good,' she said looking at him closely, 'better than our students could do.' To herself adding, *and probably most of our staff.*

'The person who should be head is Malcolm Lowry.'

'Didn't he write *Under the Volcano*?'

'*A* Malcolm Lowry did, but he's been dead for ages. Our Malcolm Lowry is an expert in symbolism in romantic poetry, but he is a bit of a loose cannon so he frequently gets overlooked for promotions. You know, he isn't compliant enough, doesn't buy into the corporate strategy plan.'

'Do you?'

'Not if it means inflating marks, but don't tell the dean of humanities that I said that. I'm on the verge of killing him already,' she said with some anger.

'Let's hope not.'

Jenny quickly hurried on. 'Well, just a figure of speech, you understand. He has saddled me with paperwork by the ton. As you can see,' she said pointing to her in tray. 'I am not very good at getting through it, mainly because I squander the majority of my time in meetings. In fact, I am due to attend a marketing meeting at 2 pm. All of the heads of department are flying over to the Bahamas in two weeks' time in the frantic act of recruiting students. Although, strictly in confidence, I think that most of the staff see it purely as an opportunity to party. Still, I ought to read through the marketing strategy…'

She pointed to a large file on her desk.

Caldicott appeared to take the hint. He stood up, and put the now empty plate of biscuits back on the chair. 'Then I will not detain you any further.' Jenny walked him back to her door, and held it open for him. Caldicott held out his hand to her, which she shook. He held onto her hand for a fraction longer than Jenny thought was needed in the circumstances. He looked down at her thoughtfully. 'Please do contact me if you have any information, about Henry Fielding or,' he added, with a warm smile on his face, 'if you need assistance in preventing the murder of your dean. Thank your secretary for the biscuits on my behalf…' Jenny momentarily lost concentration on his speech. She was irritated that a man who ate several biscuits stayed as thin as a rake… 'Don't worry about showing me out. I think I know the way. Goodbye for now.' And with that he was gone.

For the next twenty minutes Jenny engrossed herself in the marketing report, but the dreariness of its content, coupled with the intrigue of her lunchtime visitation prevented Jenny from reading to the end. She made the executive decision to put the file down, and open up the drawer of newspaper cuttings on Fielding. She emptied all the cuttings onto her desk, and was about to sort them into a pile, when she noted that the vicious drawer, her earlier assailant, still would not shut even though it was now empty. This annoyed her. She did not want another accident so she got off her chair to look at the back of the drawer. She pulled the drawer out, there was nothing on the bottom, but when she looked at the space that the drawer occupied in the desk, she saw a scrunched up piece of brown paper lodged between the end of the runner and the back of the desk. So this was what prevented the drawer returning to its rightful place? Jenny was determined to get one thing sorted out that day, so she leant forward until her fingertips reached the obstruction. A little more effort and Jenny's hands enclosed the ball of paper and drew it out of its hiding place.

Had today been like any other day, Jenny would have assumed that this was just a piece of Hardwicke's detritus fit only for eradication, and so her initial thoughts were to fling it in the bin. However, this was no ordinary day. The strange turn of events of that morning, Caldicott's enquiry into Fielding's death and the curious phenomenon of having come across the newspapers just earlier that day, put all her senses on high alert. Jenny unravelled the paper tangle to reveal a manila envelope, some eleven by twenty-two centimetres in size. On initial inspection, no address could be identified on the envelope, but she could feel through the paper that the envelope contained a secret and she suddenly felt a desire to be inquisitive and inspect the contents. With a deep breath she gingerly opened the stuck down flap in the hope of finding – what? Needless to say that when she pulled out the envelope's contents, she was very disappointed to discover only a dirty old tissue. Her utter contempt for the "treasure" fast-tracked its designation to the bin, but just as she was about to throw it in, she noticed some light pencil writing on the front of the envelope. That it was addressed to Professor Hardwicke came as no surprise, it was the rest of the pencil marks that amused Jenny. It read, "To Hardwicke. Please find enclosed some Naked Ladies for you. It is much hoped that you will enjoy each and every one of them."

Hardwicke liked his naked ladies all right; in fact, one might say that his only true passion was for seducing young women, or indeed any woman. Even so, the envelope still surprised her. She supposed that it must have contained pornographic images. Hardwicke would naturally have taken care to remove them from the office before leaving it. She suddenly didn't like the idea of the tissue, and quickly put it in the bin, before running off to wash her hands.

Her contempt for Hardwicke grew by the hour; whilst she was honest enough to admit that he was attractive, if one went for the Boris Johnson look, he never appealed to her. She supposed that he must be approaching fifty now, and in her opinion, it was high time he grew up. The only thing that appeared to remotely interest him was sex. That in itself wasn't an issue, what she detested was the manner that he set about getting laid. He did this by constantly passing himself off as an expert of random subject matter. At one point he held himself out to be an aficionado of antique gold; this was when he had been trying to get the knickers off the previous secretary. The poor woman stayed for all of two weeks before handing in her notice with no job to go to. Then he held himself out to be an expert of horticulture. This was the time he was banging one of the lecturers in the agricultural college. *A cock for a cock*, Jenny thought. It was after this that Cedric arrived.

Jenny added somewhat bitterly to herself that by displaying his supposed knowledge of music, art, theatre or flowers he would score a hit with his potential conquest. She had long listened to his mantra that it was easier to get a leg over if he expressed his feminine side.

"And about as feminine as a flame thrower," Tom had once remarked. "He just wants a no-strings-attached fuck, animal, mineral or vegetable – he isn't fussy!"

Jenny wondered if Tom had been one of Hardwicke's casual victims, but she would never dream of asking him. She had never considered Hardwicke to be gay, his remark about Lowry had confirmed that he was not over keen on being propositioned by men, but with Hardwicke it was likely to be about control, not sex, anyway. Yes, she could see him going with a man, if it fed his power lust. But Tom was one of her best friends at the university, and his friendship was far too important to spoil with idle curiosity, so she never asked.

"Tom," she would say, "It's hard to know who is the worst at choosing men, you or me."

"They're all bastards," was the ready reply.

I wonder if DS Caldicott is a bastard she thought. *Bound to be if he is in the police force.*

The clock tower chiming the half-hour brought Jenny back to reality. She would have to set off for her meeting in five minutes. For the second time that day, she put the clippings back into the drawer. This time, at least, the drawer closed fully.

'At least you won't be causing me any further injury,' she said to the envelope which she took pleasure in re-rolling into a ball and chucking in the direction of the bin.

It missed spectacularly and hid for shelter under the free-standing bookshelf.

She picked up her marketing folder and left the safety of *Kubla Khan* once more. The meeting was being held in Bridgwater, so she headed to the car park, which was situated behind the English building. Although only eight miles away, the slow and windy roads ensured that at least twenty minutes were needed to get there by two, so Jenny didn't waste time looking at any of the other cars parked there. She clambered into her Renault Cleo and sped off. If she had been more alert she would have noticed DS Caldicott sitting in his black Volkswagen, watching her intently.

CHAPTER 4
TUESDAY, 12 APRIL:
Late Afternoon

It was after five when Jenny returned to her office. Tom had ceased working for the day, but had left her a note pinned to her door.

"Dear Dr Jordan, (it read)

Rabbie Burns returned not long after I came back from lunch. He said that he had dropped something in your office, and would you mind if he looked for it? I could hardly say no, could I? I don't think he found it because he looked extremely displeased when he left.

Tom."

This is very odd thought Jenny. *I know for a fact that he didn't leave anything in my room, I would have spotted it.*

She said that before she looked at her desk, and at another pile of papers that had arrived for her when she was out. 'Oh well, maybe I wouldn't have noticed anything after all.'

She was about to sit down for a final attempt to read the newspaper clippings when her leg collided with the drawer again.

'No, this is too much! I know that I closed that f-ing drawer, I am absolutely convinced of that,' she said to no one there, and on receiving a sharp kick from its mistress, the drawer obeyed and aligned itself properly in the desk.

Jenny drew the only possible conclusion from this. DS Caldicott had opened the drawer. The man had the audacity to come back when he knew that she wouldn't be there. Why didn't he ask her if he could take the papers when he was here at lunchtime? He would have been welcome to them.

Jenny felt slightly depressed at the thought that she had bored him so much with work talk that he couldn't wait to leave her company. She would have much rather stayed chatting to him than read that stupid nonsensical marketing report, but he seemed eager to use it as an excuse to leave. Perhaps that was the technique he used with all his potential suspects, although why he thought that she was a suspect goodness only knew.

The final chore of the day was to go over to the theatre studies block and return a batch of third year essays to Medusa Touchwood. This was to be the sole task that Jenny had performed on time since she had been landed with the role of Head of English. She knew that the theatre studies department frequently worked late, especially if they were performing, but Jenny secretly hoped that Medusa wouldn't be there. That woman was too much at any time.

"Oh darling, we love you, cherish you, worship your wise words of wisdom. Why don't you become one of us? Leave the English stiffs and join us in theatre studies."

In some ways Jenny would have liked that, but they were "oh so drama". They had to perform to the letter of the spirit of the times. Women were not allowed to take part in any Shakespeare production (which meant that as the majority of the students were girls, Shakespeare was rarely performed) but for some reason this did not apply to Greek tragedies. The concession here was that the performance took place using the correct Greek attire. This, in the main, meant wearing nothing more than a flimsy cloth. To compound the audience's embarrassment, staff had to dress accordingly. She had seen Medusa's generous bosoms more times than she cared to count, but that was not all. Due to the shortage of male students, the male professoriate, Straw, Woodman and Leon, were often called upon to take part in these productions. Jenny had seen their tackle more often than she had had hot meals at the university. Had they been in their twenties, this might have been all right, but as the youngest of the trio was forty-nine and the oldest nearly seventy, it was not a joy to behold.

Professor Silvanus Straw was particularly repulsive. Although named after a god, he fell short of the mark by a mile. He made Hardwicke look like Zeus in comparison. Straw was a short, pugnacious little man, sporting silver hair, which, for reasons not apparent to anyone else, was held in place by a hairnet – and he smelt like a cabbage.

Needless to say, the euphoria of a successful first night performance frequently led to an impromptu party. Nothing wrong with that, but these after-show parties frequently turned into an enactment of a Greek orgy.

Jenny had developed an armoury of excuses not to stay to one of these spectacles – not that she was averse to casual sex, but as so often in these arrangements, there was no one vaguely appealing available. Jenny felt it unprofessional to have sexual relations with any of the students, no matter how attractive they were; as for the staff, nice enough in their own (clothed) way but undressed… gross; the whole lot of them! Hardwicke had tried it on with her once, but she deflected his advances and made her escape. The ultimate nightmare occurred when Professor Straw propositioned her. She went home and promptly threw up. Some things were worse than being celibate, she decided.

She had now reached the staircase which led to Medusa's study. Medusa occupied most of the top floor of what would have been the attic in a Georgian farmhouse. The other theatre studies staff had offices on the first or ground floors. The stairs were somewhat old and rickety, as to be expected in a grade two listed building, and a number of students had successfully sued the university on the basis of the ill-repair of the steps after they had taken a tumble down them. A handrail was finally on order, but had yet to arrive.

As the farmhouse had limited space, most of the rehearsals took place in a converted barn across the pathway. This was also the venue for public performances, and for those "oh too sensational" parties.

When Jenny entered the building, she found it to be empty, and presumed that everyone was in full rehearsal in the barn. Had Medusa been present, her voice would echo throughout the building shaking its very foundations and rattling all the glass.

Just as well that she is not here thought Jenny, *that woman is one horror too many for today.*

However, when she reached Medusa's office she was

surprised to see that light glowed through the door frame. She knocked on the door, but there was no reply.

Perfect thought Jenny. *I will just leave the scripts on her desk if the door is unlocked.* It was.

On opening the door Jenny had the feeling that she was not alone. 'Probably the ghost,' she said to herself. It was rumoured that an old farmer made frequent appearances in the theatre studies department. No one could identify the spirit and there were those, including Medusa, who flatly denied any such thing. Jenny reflected on the fact that the ghost only seemed to appear when the frantic orgies took place. *He probably likes to watch* she thought.

Having put her parcel of scripts on the table, Jenny made her way back to the winding staircase. She had reached the first floor landing and was halfway down the second flight of stairs, when she was hit on the head by a flying missile. The contact in itself was not severe, but the surprise at being hit made her lose her balance. In her tired state and semi-dark surroundings, she lost her footing on the uneven step and ended up tumbling down the rest of the stairs.

*

When Jenny opened her eyes she discovered a number of strange faces staring at her. 'Hello love, you come back to us?' A paramedic spoke in a very cheery voice.

'What am I doing here?' was all Jenny could say.

'You've fallen down the stairs. You took a nasty tumble. Don't you remember?'

'Not at all, I just…' Jenny tried to speak, but found it too much effort.

'We'll take her in,' another voice said.

Jenny was transferred into an ambulance and shipped to the local hospital, where various tests were performed on her. At one point she fell into a deep sleep. Vague macabre dreams followed in rapid succession; images of tigers and cockerels intertwined with the fertility rites of Bacchus, and the most unpleasant spectacle of an overexcited Professor Hardwicke. The nightmare might have continued indefinitely had her slumber not been rudely disturbed by a softly spoken voice that she instinctively recognised as DS Caldicott's.

Whilst feeling that she had been rescued in one respect from her visions of Hell, this sensation rapidly dissolved into a sense of persecution. She had seen the man twice in that day already, admittedly the first time was a pleasant mild flirtation, but the second time… She started to feel victimised. Primarily though, she was embarrassed to be caught bandaged like a mummy. This was hardly the picture of professionalism that she had tried to promote earlier. It never crossed her mind to wonder why she was concerned about that.

Drat that man, she thought, *he's been in my face all day!*

It would have surprised Jenny had she known that her sentiments were mirrored by Caldicott's own. *Bloody woman* he thought. *Poking around where she isn't needed, and now look what has happened.* His professional training had, however, modified these thoughts for public edification.

'Good evening Dr Jordan… No, don't try to get up. I don't expect that you feel up to any questions tonight, but just in case we need to take swift action, can you tell me if anyone else was present when you fell down the stairs?'

'I don't think so. I'm sorry, I don't remember anything very much. Something hit my head, not heavy, but it surprised me and I fell. But I don't recall anyone being around, except George.'

'George?'

'That is the name we give to the resident spirit who makes an appearance from time to time in the theatre studies office.'

Caldicott gave her a look to suggest that her injury must be a serious one. As though reading his mind, Jenny said, 'Yes, I know it sounds mad but a number of people have claimed to have witnessed supernatural activity in Medusa's office.' And to herself she thought *and lots of other activity as well.*

As though echoing her thoughts Caldicott said, 'Yes, I should think that office has a lot to tell if only four walls could speak.' That made Jenny laugh. She felt better, instantly.

At this point the doctor came over to tell Jenny that all the test results were clear and that she had been discharged. He added that an ambulance would take her home as she was unaccompanied. 'Mind you,' he said cheerily, 'I'm only allowing it because you work at Sedgemoor, and "You are one of US".' She smiled wanly at him; the logo meant nothing to her in her present condition.

Caldicott continued, 'I will leave you now and visit you at your house tomorrow.'

'I'll be at work.'

'I don't think that it's wise for you to go there tomorrow.'

Jenny wondered if he was warning her off. 'I have to go in.'

'Are you lecturing?'

'No, but I am booked in for a student meeting at eleven thirty. I really need to speak to the student in question. She is on my hit list.' Then seeing Caldicott's stern expression she continued, 'The student needs remedial support to improve her studies. I don't think that I am the right person to talk to her though. You would have far more success than me.'

'In what way?'

'She responds to good-looking men,' was the reply.

That comment surprised Caldicott. Women had told him that he was attractive, but it was always when they wanted to take him to bed. Dr Jordan, in her semi-conscious and bandaged state, had said it purely as an observation, a statement of fact. It confused him.

'How long will your meeting take?' he asked.

'Hopefully no more than thirty minutes. I don't remember having anything else to do.'

'Not even your paperwork? You must have amnesia,' Caldicott retorted.

Jenny glared at Caldicott, but to her annoyance that amused him. 'Sorry, that was an unprofessional comment. However, in all seriousness looking at you at the moment, I would say that you have a perfectly valid reason for not going into work.'

Jenny shook her head, an action she regretted instantly

as it caused her a great deal of pain and made her wince. This spasm did not go undetected by Caldicott.

'I can see that you are determined to go in, but may I suggest that you don't arrive much before the time of your meeting? Let me assist you by leaving a message now on your office answering machine, telling your administrator that you will not be in until mid-morning.'

'Thank you. That is very kind of you. Do you have the number?'

'I'll find it. If you think that you will be available after twelve, then I will try to come to your office between twelve and twelve thirty to see if you are able to remember more details of this evening.'

Jenny would have loved to say "no, don't disturb me", but she knew that Caldicott would insist; after all, he had a job to do. Very weary from all that had happened that day she nodded her head and gave a brief smile. She fainted. When she came around, Caldicott had gone. She surprised herself by wishing that he hadn't.

*

For his part, Caldicott was very disturbed to see Dr Jordan pass out. It reminded him of a time that he had hoped to shut out for good. Part of him wanted to stay and ensure that she was all right, but another part just wanted to run away. He chose the latter course, and cursed himself for being a coward. He thought that Dr Jordan would rate him poorly for disappearing so quickly. Why did he care what a suspect thought of him?

CHAPTER 5
WEDNESDAY, 13 APRIL

It was eleven fifty when Bernice Pye eventually rolled up at Jenny's door. Jenny had given up on her and was in the staff kitchen putting a frozen pizza in the oven for her lunch, when Bernice finally arrived. Bernice was a kind-hearted girl, but spent all the day preening herself and finding tops low enough to emphasise her near perfect breasts. All the staff wondered if these, her two biggest assets, were real.

If only she spent as much time on her books. Her casual attitude, her lackadaisical approach to studies put a heavy burden on Jenny's heart. There was no hope that this one would achieve anything more than a lower second class degree overall, and in reality probably a third. This was doubly painful as Bernice was the chair of the English department's student society, and as such, Jenny had to negotiate with her on arranging events for students. Also, for some reason best known to Professor Hardwicke, Bernice was involved in assisting the department's marketing trips abroad.

'Oh the Bahamas is just GREAT,' she simpered. 'I've been there on holiday several times, gives you a wonderful suntan. Lots of good-looking rich men out there and the heat makes you feel... you know,' she tittered, 'hot.'

Jenny didn't like the direction in which this conversation was heading. She said, 'I don't think that I will have time to sit on the beach, unfortunately. I have seen the itinerary and I'm afraid that I will be very much stuck inside various buildings.'

'Oh, what a shame!' said Bernice. 'Does that mean that I have to come to a bunch of stuffy meetings, too?'

Jenny was lost. 'I'm not sure that I understand…'she began.

'Oh, don't you know? I've been invited to attend!' Bernice announced. 'Professor Hardwicke asked me especially, particularly as I know all the best places to go.'

Jenny was taken aback; students had never attended marketing trips before. She thought that there couldn't be anything worse, particularly with this student. Perhaps she might get the men's attention initially, but as soon as she opened her mouth all the university's credibility would fly away.

Absolutely typical of that letch Hardwicke, she thought. She was certain that he'd already had his fingers in this Pye. Jenny thought that she should forbid Bernice from going, but what was the point? She knew Hardwicke would overrule her objection, *and besides*, Jenny thought to herself, *it protects me from unwanted attention. If everyone is chasing Bernice I can be left alone in peace.*

To Bernice she merely said, 'Oh, it would be useful to have someone who knows the place well.'

It was rapidly approaching ten minutes past twelve and nothing had been achieved in this meeting. Jenny had called it primarily to keep Bernice on track with her studies, but had lost the willpower to carry through this mission after five minutes. She tried one last time. 'Bernice, we must discuss your work record to date.'

'Oh, must we? Can we talk about it another time? I'm really happy with my predicted grades. Simeon, says that he is sure that he will give me top marks.'

'Yes, I am sure that he will,' Jenny said to Bernice, and to herself she thought, *he will probably rig that somehow...*

Jenny had long suspected Hardwicke of breaching the anonymity marking protocol by exposing the student's name from under the supposedly sealed corner of the examination booklet. She had to confess that she had done it herself – not to award higher marks to favourites but to find out which idiot had completely failed to garner one shred of knowledge from her module.

While all this was going through Jenny's sore head, Bernice was chuntering on in her own world.

'I'm getting a lift to Bridgwater Station in a minute as I've got a train to catch. Oh, by the way, I received this.' Bernice handed a piece of paper over to Jenny. It looked like the poison pen letter that she had received. This one read, "Plastic Boob Girl. You will be next."

'Do you have any idea what this is about?'

'Nah, I think some of the girls are jealous of these.' At this point Bernice started juggling her breasts. Jenny found it difficult not to look at them. 'Hopefully it is nothing,' Jenny said.

'Can I go now?' Bernice asked, and without waiting for an answer, she left, taking the letter with her.

Jenny suspected that Bernice had a sugar daddy in London, as every week she seemed to have acquired new clothes. If only she had obtained the answers to her assignments as well! There is only so much you could do with a bimbo, and Jenny had a sneaking feeling that the best thing to be done with Bernice was to end her programme. She was in completely the wrong department. Theatre studies would have been the one...

That's a great idea, thought Jenny, *if I can get her transferred to theatre studies that will be one less third class degree for the English department to balance out.*

Jenny cheered up immediately and for the first time that day, she felt in a positive mood. It was at this time that Caldicott announced himself. Something had happened which had clearly put him in good humour. *Probably the sight of Bernice*, thought Jenny.

'Hello,' he smiled as a guilty schoolboy might when caught stealing sweets.

'Did you have the pleasure of bumping into Bernice?' Jenny asked. This outright assault caught Caldicott off guard, and he answered in a less than professional manner.

'Couldn't fail to, the corridor wasn't big enough for us all... Sorry, shouldn't have said that, blame it on fatigue and hunger. I haven't had lunch yet. How are you feeling today?'

'I'm alive, though not particularly kicking. I think that I am in need of sustenance too.'

'Then as we both need food, and at the risk of being even more unprofessional, let me drive you into town and find a place to eat. We can talk on the way.'

'Oh, I don't think that I am up to going very far. Do you eat pizza? I put one in the staff oven twenty minutes ago, I've only just remembered. If it hasn't burnt to a cinder you are welcome to share it with me, it is supposed to feed two.'

'Perfect,' was the reply, although when Jenny brought in the somewhat charcoaled pizza, both agreed that it was inedible, and set to order a delivery. This took some time to negotiate. Caldicott was extremely put out that Jenny refused to share a large meat supreme pizza, despite her insistence that she was a vegetarian. He seemed to put it down to her temporary amnesia that she had forgotten that humans were omnivores. When the order was finally placed the questioning began in earnest.

'My first question: Do you remember anything about your fall last night?'

'No, nothing at the moment, although the duty doctor said that I may recover more details at a later stage.'

'Fine, we will leave it at that. Second question: Do you know of any reason why someone would like to see you out of the way?'

'Absolutely not. Why would anyone want to do that?' Jenny bit her lip. 'Apart from Hardwicke, who I believe to be capable of anything, the only other person that I thought that I was on bad terms with was Professor Carstairs.'

'Can I ask why?'

'I would rather not answer, and normally I wouldn't, but as you are investigating his death... Tony and I were in a relationship on and off for three years. It all went particularly sour at the end. He was Dr Carstairs when I first met him, and was a lot of fun to be with, but his career was always more important that his relationship with me. Most of the time we were together he would just complain about his lack of progress at the school of law. In all fairness to him he should have been promoted years ago, his research profile was second to none. Similar to poor old Malcolm here… This is nothing new. Talk to any of us, and the majority feels the same. You know, people who can't produce scholarly articles get promoted above us, which would be all right if they were trained for management, and were skilled at it. Inevitably, they are neither trained nor naturally skilled. One of the lawyers refers to this as PMSP – Performance Management Safety Promotion, the idea being that you promote those who haven't a clue about their jobs to keep the idiots away from the front line and keep the customers safe from harm. It's not a new phenomenon, I expect it happens in your job as well.'

Caldicott raised his eyebrows. It was pretty obvious from this expression that he had experience of this in his work. Jenny noted this and moved on.

'What is interesting, and it happens a lot in the school of law I gather, is that as soon as anyone gets a sniff of power, they become poacher turned gamekeeper. They forget all their earlier promises to their colleagues about fairness and transparency and turn, quite frankly, into monsters. The previous dean of law is a case in hand. A real bitch if ever there was one. When she was given her title, she allegedly went down the corridor saying "I'm dean, I'm dean," until one of the bright sparks asked "Which Dean, James Dean or Dean Martin?"

'You get the picture… and I gather from talking to friends in other institutions that the same thing happens there. The difficulty is that lecturing is seen as a doss job, and in some respects it can be. If you are only here for the money, and not interested in research, then you can come in for a couple of hours to do your teaching and go home. No one will challenge you – nor should they. True academics are all, by their nature, freethinking radicals. We all work better when we are free from rigid control. We have to be in our chosen, protected environment to flourish. I can't think through anything of a detailed academic nature here, I get too many interruptions, so I write at home in the evenings. It's even worse now that I am the head of department. However, some lecturers abuse the system. It has not been unknown for people to cancel their tutorials to go off for a game of chess.'

Caldicott looked at Jenny with a mixture of amusement and shock on his face. Jenny started to laugh at his expression.

'No really!' she continued. 'This is a particular problem of the faculty of business so I am told. One of the business lecturers was found on the golf course by the previous VC. The funny thing was that they were supposed to be in a meeting together and both had phoned in sick. Obviously there could not be any repercussions for the lecturer as the VC couldn't sack him without sacking himself as well!' By this time Caldicott had a broad grin on his face, but Jenny suddenly felt a pang of guilt that she was straying off the point. 'Sorry, I could talk about this for hours, but it doesn't really help your enquiries.'

'On the contrary, it is extremely insightful and therefore potentially useful.'

'Well anyway… my relationship with Tony – the embitterment that festered in him became bigger than "us". Our relationship was clearly running its course, these things happen, but neither of us had got round to finishing it completely. And then I thought that I was pregnant. I made the mistake of blurting this out to Tony when we were in a restaurant. You should have seen him. He went ballistic and we had a most unpleasant row in public, all about his bloody career being ruined. After that I told him that I didn't want to see him again.'

'I see, and when was this?'

'Around the time of Henry Fielding's death. If I had been less focussed on myself, I might have been able to help Fielding in some way.'

'There is not one person that I know of, who has not let personal issues affect their working environment, but I have no doubt that Fielding was beyond your help.' A swift change had come over Caldicott whilst saying this. Jenny noted it but chose to ignore it.

'Third question: How did you know that daffodils were poisonous?'

This surprised Jenny more than the previous question.

'I thought everyone knew. I remember when I was a child my father took me to church. The vicar thought that it would be a good idea to eat daffodils as part of his sermon. Haven't a clue why. He was taken ill very quickly and had to have a few days in bed. Why are you asking me this?'

'Because the two deaths showed similarities with daffodil poisoning.'

'But you don't usually die from eating daffodils, do you? I thought it only happened if you ate a lot of the bulbs. There was a story I read about Dutch farmers feeding their cattle daffodil bulbs during the Second World War to stop them starving. Unfortunately, the cattle died of poisoning instead. I haven't heard of any human deaths… I didn't know it was possible.'

'Someone seemed to think it was. They sent us a letter informing us of daffodil poisoning.'

'This makes no sense; Tony died in the hospital.'

'The hospital which trains your university medical students… the hospital that you were in last night… It might be easier than you think. Did either Fielding or Carstairs get involved with a medical student or even a doctor to your knowledge?'

'I really have no idea about Fielding, but I am pretty certain that Tony didn't. He had a hatred towards anything medical, including the personnel. He was actually quite unusual in this respect in that he didn't waste his time chasing any of the students. I don't mean that he didn't get offers; female students are notorious for making advances towards the staff. Partly the power attracts them, but I suspect these days that the students are hoping that it will guarantee them a first class degree.'

It was at this point that the pizzas arrived. Tom, back from his noon departure, was swift to act as maître d' and summon up some plates and cutlery from the stores.

'Jenny, you must eat something,' he said as though telling off the policeman from preventing her from having her lunch, and waltzed off again to answer the phone.

'I don't think your administrator likes me,' Caldicott said to Jenny.

'*Au contraire*, if he didn't like you, he would have left your pizza in the box,' Jenny replied.

They had just started to eat when the subject of the conversation quickly rushed in. 'Oh my God! There has

been a car crash near Dunster. One of our students…
smashed up… DS Caldicott… eurgggh.' He rushed off to
be sick.

'Tom? Tom! Sorry, I will see if the caller is still on the
phone.'

'No, this appears to be my business, though why the
devil they didn't phone my mobile, I don't understand.'

'You may not have a signal. The service is notoriously
bad around here.'

Caldicott looked at his phone. 'Yes, you're right.'

Caldicott spoke to his colleague and then returned to
Jenny.

'I think you had better sit down. They have found a
student's ID card in the wreckage; that, I gather, is all that
is recognisable. Dwaine Saunders.' He added gently, 'I
know that you are not supposed to have favourites but
was he one of yours?'

Jenny spoke quietly, 'To be honest no, he was another
target for remedial support, but he was a nice enough lad
in his way. I presume we are speaking past tense here?'

'Without a doubt. We will, of course, contact the next
of kin. Do you have that information?'

Jenny sighed. 'When Tom is back he will find out the
numbers for you… oh, but he was one of our Bahamian
students, so you may have to wait a few days for the family
to arrive.'

'I don't want to ask you this, but would you be
prepared to identify him if we needed you to? Only as a
last resort, of course. We will try the family first, naturally,
although it might be a matter of dental records.'

'Oh God… well, I can help you there. His dental

surgery here was Crown Dental Practice. I remember because he made a joke last week about having to have a crown replaced at Crown DP.'

The office phone rang again. Jenny answered it. She called to Caldicott, 'It's Constable Daly for you.'

When Caldicott returned to Jenny's office, he looked at her intently as though trying to fathom out how much she could withstand. Jenny sensing the meaning of this appraisal anticipated him. 'Tell me the worst,' she said.

Caldicott hesitated. 'Saunders was not on his own. A female has been pulled out alive, if not exactly in one piece. I will let you know when we have any further details. In the interim please keep this to yourself, I cannot cope with hordes of journalism students turning up and interfering with my enquiries. Huh, so much for a quiet location.'

He left without collecting his pizza. Jenny looked down at hers. The tomato base seemed to spread out, reminiscent of blood flowing from a crushed body. She cast the pizza to one side, her appetite well and truly ruined, and rested her head on her hands.

CHAPTER 6
WEDNESDAY, 13 APRIL:
Late Afternoon

Jenny achieved nothing that afternoon. Not only was she still feeling sick from her own injuries but she was absolutely shaken by the tragic news of the car crash. Caldicott had phoned up from the hospital to inform her that the female student was none other than Bernice Pye, and could she give him details of the next of kin. Jenny had supplied that information, and asked if there was any other way that she could be of assistance. He asked her if she could retrieve the students' files and meet him at the Carew Arms in Crowcombe at 18.00 hours, but only if she was feeling well enough herself. She agreed to do that. She asked Tom to bring her everything they had on Bernice and Dwaine to hand over to DS Caldicott later that day. Tom made some comment about a good excuse to go on a date, but Jenny was lost in thought and his remark went in one ear and out the other.

Dwaine's mother had also phoned up the English department. She was in tears. Jenny could do little to comfort her, except tell her what a great student Dwaine was, that he was doing brilliantly and so forth. 'All lies of course,' she said to Tom after she had put down the phone. He nodded in an understanding way. Dwaine's mother did not need to know the raw truth.

The only saving grace in all this, she thought *is that it is going to increase my percentage of firsts and 2:1s.*

She immediately felt remorseful that she could have such selfish thoughts at a time that she should be mourning one, if not two of her students. She resolved to be more charitable and find out if there was anything that she could do.

"Say a prayer for Dwaine," was all his mother had said.

Fatigue swept over Jenny like a tidal wave. She put her head on her hands and fell asleep. When she came to, she decided to call it a day.

*

Jenny lived in a mid-eighteenth-century cottage in Bishops Lydeard, some ten miles from the university. Described by the estate agent as a "beautifully quaint one-bedroom end-terrace property," Jenny found it too small to enjoy living there, but at the time of moving to the area, it was all that she could afford. Although not far in terms of mileage, the route home involved driving over the twisty and at times, ruthlessly dangerous single-track roads across the Quantock Hills, usually taking the best part of forty minutes to get home. The longer (in mileage terms) but more straightforward route was to drive over the Quantocks and through the village of Crowcombe. From there, she took the A358 which was an easy drive back to her house.

It was twenty minutes past five when Jenny reached Crowcombe. This meant that she barely had enough time to get home and back before six, so she parked in the Carew Arms car park. She didn't want to wait in the pub for forty minutes on her own, and as it had started raining she couldn't sit outside. Instead, Jenny meandered down the street to the church, hoping that it was open.

On normal occasions the idea of going into the church would have horrified her, but such was her state of mind that she didn't seem to feel her usual reluctance. Besides, hadn't she promised to say a prayer on behalf of Dwaine? The red brick construction looked warm and friendly; not forbidding as many a church can look. Additionally, she was somewhat curious to go into a church called the "Holy Ghost". She wondered whether she might meet him. The rain was getting heavier and the skies darker by the second. A thunderstorm was on its way. Jenny was relieved that the door handle turned for her.

The Holy Ghost at Crowcombe is steeped in history, so a leaflet informed her. It specified that the earliest part of the present church was the fourteenth-century tower and north wall. It added that the most dramatic event in the church's history occurred in 1724, when the spire was struck by lightning and came crashing down into the church. The rumble of distant thunder gave an atmospheric backdrop to this story.

To her surprise, Jenny felt a sense of peace in the building and walking around the church she identified a number of features that she was instructed to look for – the east window by Clayton & Bell, the fourteenth-century font and the medieval bench-ends. Jenny identified various images carved into the bench-ends including the pagan images of the green man, but her favourite was the carving of Crowcombe men fighting a two-headed dragon. This summed up precisely how she felt about working at Sedgemoor. Jenny wandered back down the sixteenth-century south aisle and wondered what it would have been like to have lived in Somerset then. She was determined to ask her colleagues in the history department.

By this time, the church had become shrouded in darkness and an ominous flash of lightning lit up the pulpit, swiftly followed by the rumble of not so distant thunder. The rude awakening of the storm brought her back from Tudor England into reality. With it came the realisation that she was no longer alone in the building. For some reason she was petrified. Her heart began to pound and a sharp pain crossed her forehead. Jenny gasped. She would have slumped to the ground had the unknown entity not caught her by her arm.

'Sit down,' it said quite violently. Jenny turned around. Her worst fears were recognised. It was that bloody policeman. 'Christ,' she said with some anger.

'No, I am definitely not he. What are you doing here? I told you to meet me in the pub. You should be resting!'

Jenny was stuck for a second as to how to reply. She wanted to say "It's none of your fucking business what I am doing here," just to give the man a set down, but instead she blurted out, 'I've come to say a prayer for Dwaine.'

Ironically, this seemingly mild response dealt a much larger blow to Caldicott than an outburst would have done. He immediately let go of her arm. She sat down on one of the benches.

'Sorry,' he said, 'I shouldn't have interrupted you.' He turned to go.

'No, don't go,' Jenny cried out. Caldicott looked surprised but obeyed and sat down with her.

'You shocked me...' Jenny began, but for some reason couldn't find any words to add. They sat in silence together for a number of seconds, until Jenny finally found her voice. 'What's the latest news on Bernice?'

Caldicott sighed. 'When I left she was in a stable condition, but she has been put in a medically assisted coma. She is expected to recover, but will be scarred for life.'

'Oh, poor girl. I mean, she is an appalling student, but as a person... and Dwaine, not the brightest star in the sky, but nice enough. What on earth were they doing in Dunster? She told me she was going to London.'

'We will have to wait a while to question her...' He stood to go, 'I will leave you in peace and wait outside for you.'

*

Jenny could not find the right approach to prayer. It was something that she had long abandoned doing. Looking for inspiration from her guidebook, she found a Celtic prayer printed there, entitled "Peace". There wasn't one person she knew who didn't need to find peace.

*

When she finally went outside she noticed that the rain had stopped, and the sun was trying to break through the clouds. The policeman was standing by one of the graves. This, unlike most of the other graves, bore fresh flowers. Jenny was suddenly awakened to the fact that Coleridge, or whatever he was called, needed to find peace too. She stayed still, not wanting to disturb him. She was certain that there had been no flowers on the grave before she went into the church – had he put them there? Was that why he was so angry at seeing her? Perhaps, as much as he had interrupted her quiet contemplation, she had interrupted his. She resolved to be more compliant with his enquiries, should he pursue his questioning. When he finally turned around, he smiled at her. 'Let's have a drink,' he said. 'I think we both need one after today.'

CHAPTER 7
WEDNESDAY, 13 APRIL:
Early Evening

Once they had reached the Carew Arms, Caldicott ordered drinks. It was now a quarter past six and the pub was well and truly open. As the rain had saturated the benches, any chance of sitting outside was thwarted, so finding a table was not an easy task.

'Have you been here before?' Caldicott asked when they were finally seated.

'Yes, once. I came with a friend and her six-year-old son. He lost his first tooth in the garden, quite literally. We were rummaging around in the clover for the best part of an hour trying to find the wretched thing. We gave up in the end. I've never seen a child cry so much. He thought that the tooth fairy wouldn't pay up, if he didn't put his tooth under his pillow.'

As Jenny had said all this with a straight face, Caldicott adopted an equally serious expression. 'Did she?'

'Pay up? Yes, I believe she did in the end.'

Jenny had been looking directly at Caldicott but turned away and laughed at the ridiculous nature of the conversation. When she turned back to look at him, she could tell that he hadn't taken his eyes off her. She found that very unnerving. It was though he was trying to read her mind.

He continued: 'They serve food, but not until seven unfortunately, but I thought that as we didn't get to eat earlier you might like something now, or rather I certainly do.'

'Are you still on duty?' Jenny asked. 'I mean, isn't there a chance that you will be called out again?'

'God I hope not, I would like to stay still for a bit. I seem to have done nothing but chase around the countryside these last two weeks. They said that this was a quiet post; it is anything but. You, of course, know the area, but I hadn't fully appreciated that a ten-mile journey over the Quantocks takes as long to drive as thirty miles on a motorway.'

'Yes, it can be frustrating at times, but then I lived in London at one point in my life and it used to take forty minutes to go one mile on the North Circular at rush hour.'

'Been there and done that. But to answer your question, my shift ends at seven, so yes, I am currently on duty, but at seven, I am free. In the interim, I would like to ask you some questions (Jenny grimaced again), and if I am still here at seven, I hope that you will be my guest.'

'Said the spider to the fly. Very well.'

'I would hardly call you a fly, and I don't much appreciate being called a spider. I can't stand the things. Right, well. I need to ask you this first before I forget. Do you remember anything extra about last night, that you haven't told me to date?'

'You mean about my accident?'

'I'm not so sure that it was an accident; that is why I want to know.'

Jenny looked horrified. 'I wasn't tripped.'

'I understand that, but you said that something had hit you. I don't mean that someone necessarily wanted to do you harm but they might have meant to scare you off, or play a prank on you. You mentioned this blessed ghost, what was he called?'

'George.'

'Yes, could George have been more of a physical presence?'

'I suppose it is possible. You mean one of the students pretending to be George to frighten anyone entering the building?'

'Perhaps.'

'I don't know, I really... I did feel like I was being watched. I felt the same in the church earlier, and that was you. So I suppose it could have been a *someone* rather than a *something*. Why are you so convinced that there was someone there?'

Caldicott studied her intensely for a few moments before making up his mind. 'All right, I will tell you, because you will learn this for yourself anyway. At some point during the evening, someone else had gone into Dr Touchwood's study. They may even have been in there when you went in. Can you describe the office exactly? I presume that the office was unlocked. Were the lights on?'

'Not the main lights, but the table lamp was on. Yes, the office was unlocked; I would not have been able to enter it otherwise. Some of us have master keys to the offices; Professor Hardwicke holds a generic key for the offices in the English department, so does Professor Jones. I have a feeling that a number of the theatre studies staff have master keys, certainly Medusa does. They are supposed to be just the master keys for the specific building, but I think that the locks duplicate in some way. You would have to check...'

Caldicott made a note of this. 'Go on,' he said.

'To be honest, I was relieved that Medusa wasn't there. That woman is... well, I'd better not say.'

'Say it; after all, I have met her already. I would like your opinion on her.'

'Well, she is an example of the worst kind of feminist around: Women who give chauvinistic men an excuse for their bad behaviour; the type that use their sex to get men to do what they want, and then claim that they, themselves, have been used.'

'That's a very astute observation, and you've known her for...'

'Too long. She seduced my best literature student two years ago at one of their after-show parties, and just before his finals. Christopher Middleton was his name. He was the most gorgeous student. I was very jealous about this, as I had planned to have a go at him myself...' She said this in a way designed to provoke a reaction.

Caldicott pretended to be shocked, 'Dr Jordan, I am surprised at your unprofessionalism.'

'... after he graduated, of course. I don't know what happened precisely, but he ended up with a 2:2 rather than a first class degree.'

'You think that he was given something more than Medusa's body?'

'Possibly, but I have no proof. I will say this, if I was dean of humanities, I would have absolutely no hesitation in closing down the whole of the theatre studies department, if they didn't clean up their act.' Jenny thought of some of the spectacles she had seen and she shuddered.

'Do you think it possible that Dr Touchwood is in any physical danger?' Caldicott continued.

'No. Well, no more now than last year when one of the theatre studies students was raped on the campus. I understand that there was an arrest made at the time, but the case was dropped due to lack of evidence.'

'Yes, I've been reading up on that. That is why I went to see Medusa yesterday morning. The student transferred to another university, some distance away. My colleagues were furious that the CPS dropped it so quickly, especially when the investigators thought that they had a DNA profile match. It looked good to me, too, when I studied it yesterday.'

Jenny thought, *is it only yesterday that I met this man for the first time? I feel that I have known him for years.* She closed her eyes in order to think. She had some important information but she couldn't quite grasp it. And then in a flash she replayed her life from over a year ago, her relationship break-up, the rape and Henry Fielding's death.

'How silly of me, there was a suspicion that Henry Fielding was involved in the rape. I don't think it was ever suggested that he carried out the act, Henry wasn't like that, but by that stage he was well into every drug going, poor lad. The rumour went round that he had offered something to the victim, which had a stupefying effect and left them vulnerable to the attack later that night. My understanding is that Professor Marlowe was heavily involved also, but was never questioned. It wouldn't surprise me if he was, as he is in allegiance with the Devil. He is Australian and he has gone back home on a sabbatical for this term, so I'm afraid you won't be able to get hold of him that easily.'

'Ahh… I see. Thanks, that's very helpful, the notes that I have been handed said nothing about him.'

Jenny had suddenly thought of the role that Medusa might have played in the rape. Yes, she may well have lured in a young victim for someone else…That was just her style, a perfect Marquise de Merteuil in fact.

Jenny asked, 'Do you know for certain that someone went into Medusa's office? Are you sure she wasn't just attention seeking? She has a tendency to do that. As I had an accident, she would probably want to get one better, cry "rape" or "murder" or something. Sorry, that's a horrible accusation. I need to learn to keep my thoughts to myself.'

'No, don't do that, it's a relief to meet someone who is prepared to say what is in their mind to a policeman. It would make my life a lot easier if everyone did so.'

Jenny looked at Caldicott with a quizzical expression on her face. She was disconcerted to find that he was smiling, his grey-green eyes twinkling at her. This was not the first time that he held this expression when looking at her. She wasn't sure if she liked it or not. As far as Jenny was concerned, an embarrassing pause occurred at this point, which was saved only by the sound of her mobile phone ringing.

'Excuse me,' she said to Caldicott. 'Hello. Oh! Hi

Sacha, any problem…? Oh… I see… Well… I've been better… no… no, I'll survive… Sacha honey, can I call you back? I'm being interviewed at the moment… No, not for a job, unfortunately… Okay, speak to you soon.' She switched off her phone and put it in her bag and turned to Caldicott. He looked slightly put out.

'Sorry, my brother-in-law. Nothing urgent, my sister's asked him to check up on me. But you were going to tell me why you know someone was in Medusa's office.'

'Are you looking for another job?'

It was on the tip of Jenny's tongue to ask the man what business it was of his, but this was one thought that she was able to keep back. 'Well, it never hurts to look, does it? I've been told that there is a job going in Durham later this year, which I would be suited for.'

'That's a long way to go from here.'

'Yes, it is… though I probably wouldn't get it if I applied. These things tend to be a carve-up. You usually have to work in a place part-time before they think seriously about hiring you. Either that or sleep with the right people… But we are straying off topic… Medusa's room?'

Caldicott surprised himself by saying, 'You know, I would much rather talk about you than Medusa's room.' Then after a slight pause and by a considerable amount of self-control he added, 'When she returned to her office last night, she found that a slogan had been sprayed on her wall, the one opposite her desk, in what looked very much like blood. Did you see anything like this?'

'No, I don't think so. What did it say, or I suppose I am not allowed to ask?'

Caldicott smiled, '"Wicked Witch of the West, your time is fast approaching".'

Jenny laughed. 'How brilliant! Well, yes, she does look like the archetypal witch I suppose. What did Medusa say?'

Caldicott's smile vanished in a second and he gave Jenny a look of utter loathing, 'I've had a very trying week. Please don't make me remember that scene!'

Jenny found this all hilarious. 'Oh, you poor thing!' she said.

Caldicott reached for the menu.

'It's still not seven yet,' Jenny continued to tease.

'Oh yes it is as far as I am concerned; let's make our choices, so we can order on the dot.'

Jenny chose the butternut squash lasagne, and received another glare from the policeman, whilst he went for an 8 ounce sirloin steak and chips, what Jenny referred to as "boys' food".

Jenny became thoughtful. 'So are you saying that I might have been attacked because the graffiti artist thought that I could identify them? But how would throwing something at me stop that?'

'Well, think about it, it nearly worked. There are two scenarios; if your assailant, and I am pretty sure that you were hit on purpose, wanted to make your attack look like an accident, they would hope to initiate a fall down the stairs. On the other hand, if they really knew their anatomy, they would aim for your temple. A blow to a specific spot can kill you with sufficient force.'

'Whatever hit me certainly got the side of my head, but it wasn't a particularly hard hit, it felt as if I was hit with a rolled-up pair of socks, and I didn't get the impression that it was supposed to hit me at all. But it did, and I lost my concentration. That, on top of the already trying day I had had…' At this point she looked directly at Caldicott, '… Well, I just fell.'

'Think, Jenny, think! What else did you see?'

Jenny found it pleasing but also impertinent that he called her by her first name.

'Mr Caldicott,' she began pointedly.

'Kevin.'

'Mr Caldicott,' she started again staring at him quite hard this time, and then burst into giggles. 'No, you really can't be a Kevin!'

'Why not?'

'You look too sophisticated for that.'

'I will take that as a compliment. My mother may take that as an insult however, seeing as how she chose my name. I will ask for her forgiveness on your behalf.'

Jenny was still laughing at this. 'No, it's no use, I really can't think of anything. Besides, if I am right, the wall you are talking about is the one where she hangs up her cloak and it was there. I saw it out the corner of my eye.'

Caldicott's eyes widened. 'No, you didn't. Medusa told me that she had her cloak with her. What you saw… Jenny! No wonder you were a target. You may have scared off whoever it was from committing a serious crime. We may have to give you police protection.'

'That would be a waste of taxpayers' money.'

'I'm serious. We have a number of unsolved crimes on your campus and I do not want you to be another victim.'

'I really don't think that anyone is out to get me;

well, not in that way. Of course the pleasure of being in a middle management position is that you are squeezed by both sides. You can't satisfy your boss, but your workers feel betrayed by you.'

'Nevertheless, you need to take care. And don't be afraid to ask for help if you feel in danger.'

At this point, any further conversation was temporarily halted by the arrival of their meals. This was just as well as Jenny did not know how to respond to this last comment. As for his part, Caldicott was trying to put various pieces of information together. None of this made any sense at the moment. It was though he was trying to read three detective novels at once.

A few minutes of silence followed whilst Caldicott attacked his meal ferociously with his cutlery. Meanwhile, Jenny picked slowly at her food; she really was not in the mood to eat much. When she noted that Caldicott had slowed his eating down, Jenny took to questioning him. She was curious as to why a seemingly intelligent and relatively sensitive man should enter the police force.

'I took a first degree in forensic science, but to be frank, I wasn't good enough, or interested enough, to go on to do intensive lab work. By the time I had spent three years looking down a microscope I really didn't want to do that for the rest of my life. After I graduated I worked in the field for three years but then, something happened and eventually I chose to do this job.' He stopped to take another mouthful of his steak. 'Why do you ask?'

'I am always interested in finding out what motivates people to do the jobs that they do. I imagine your job must be very challenging; is it?'

'Yes indeed. I had to complete two years as a PC before I could transfer.' Caldicott swallowed the remainder of his drink. 'That was hard enough but becoming a detective at any rank requires a heck of a lot of work. It's not easy and it's not for everybody, but I was lucky to find it less demanding than most of the others who transferred at the same time as me. What keeps me going, us going, is the sense of satisfaction you get, if, after working flat out on a case, the jury finds our suspect guilty.'

'Yes, I can understand that.' Jenny sipped her drink thoughtfully. 'Why Somerset? I would have thought there would be less crime here, usually.'

'I was working in Slough and wanted a change. This job came up first. So far, I don't regret coming here, but I've only been here a month. Saying that, I now realise that I made the mistake of renting a property in Wiveliscombe. The Avon and Somerset policy is to relocate to within twenty miles of the posting and I wanted to be as far away as possible from Minehead, but I didn't realise quite how long it would take to get back to my flat from there.'

Jenny laughed, 'Just you wait until August; it will be a nightmare for you with all the caravans heading down to the coast.'

It can hardly be said that their conversation equalled the works of William Blake, but Jenny, despite her aching limbs and head, was enthralled. It was a long time since she had been out for dinner with an attractive and interesting man. Albeit that she was apprehensive of being Caldicott's prime suspect, Jenny was enjoying herself immensely. Then she remembered that she was there primarily to assist police enquiries, and felt guilty for enjoying herself. Caldicott was swift to notice Jenny's mood change, and believing her to be bored discussing his employment, made an effort to engage her about her own.

'So, what are the students like at Sedgemoor? I get the impression from all that you have said that they are not the same calibre as when we were studying.'

'They seem to be getting worse by the year. Take our second year students. We have been studying English dramatists this term, but honestly they don't know the difference between Sheridan and the Sheraton. I asked them in the lecture what they liked about Sheridan and one alert student told me he particularly like the Shine Spa in Dubai. What was even more disturbing was when another bright spark piped up with, "Doesn't Sheridan play football for England?" I had to explain that I thought he meant Teddy Sheringham who *used* to play but not anymore.'

Caldicott laughed at this. It was a pleasure for him to be meeting someone with intelligence for a change. Most of his interviews were held at a very basic level. 'No, I can't believe it's as bad as that,' he said.

'It's worse. I was particularly put out on Monday when one of the third years, *third* years mark you, asked me if they could pass the exams without reading *any* of the set texts. I had to point out that they were studying for a literature degree, which by definition required them to read books!'

'I'm glad you said that,' Caldicott started. 'You have reminded me.' He reached into his pocket and drew out a paperback book in a plastic bag. 'This book was found in Saunders' car, it has your name inside the front cover. Can you tell me anything about it?'

Jenny looked at the cover. It was *Christine* by Stephen King. 'Oh,' she said, 'I lent that to one of the students a while back, can't remember who. Is it significant?'

'Probably not. What is significant is the cause of the accident. I'm afraid what I am about to reveal will give you even more to worry about. A mechanical failure has been identified, but the long and short of it is that it could very easily be a deliberate act of sabotage, although as yet, we have no concrete proof of that.'

'Oh God...'

Caldicott said bitterly, 'I was supposed to be clearing up murders not adding to them. Was Saunders one of the group junkies?'

'Quite possibly, certainly his studies were poor, destined to be reducing my percentage success rates of firsts and 2:1s, but I didn't have him down as a habitual user.'

'And Ms Pye?'

'I'm pretty certain that she had a sugar daddy arrangement. I know for a fact that her parents do not have a significant amount of money. When she first came here, her fees did not clear in time and she couldn't start until the third week. Not only that but she wore clothes that made me look fashionable. Then after her first Christmas break, this was two years ago, all changed. Obviously, she is a naturally beautiful girl, but she arrived with her hair in a chic new style, make-up, nails manicured and togged out in fashion by Dior. She has to be kept one way or the other... Between you and me, and please don't let on to him that I have said this, but I am pretty certain that Professor Hardwicke has been working on her. Whether he is the main payer or just one of many I couldn't say. Come to think of it, I can't imagine Simeon paying anyone for sex. He would see it as failure that they didn't give it to him for free. But as for Bernice taking drugs? No, I really can't see that being the case.'

A sudden thought struck Jenny; she sat bolt upright. 'Wait a minute, she told me that she had received some type of poison pen letter yesterday. She took it with her; something like "You will be next". I didn't pay too much attention to it at the time, as I had received something similar on Tuesday…' Jenny then realised the implications of her words. 'Oh!'

Caldicott intervened, 'I told you that you were a target. Now will you believe me?'

'I should have forbidden Bernice from leaving; then she would have been safe.'

'I am going to tell you that I don't think that it would have made any difference, so you mustn't beat yourself up about it. Did anyone else know that Bernice was getting a lift with Saunders?'

'Sorry, I don't know. Would you like the names of students who were friends with them both?'

'Thank you, that will be very helpful.' By this time Caldicott had finished his meal.

'Tom is the person to ask. Tom knows everyone. I will ask him to supply you with a list tomorrow. I've got their files for you in my car, not that they will say much…'

'You've stopped eating.'

Jenny looked down at her food. 'Sorry, I've lost my appetite what with my stupid fall yesterday and all this dreadful news today. It's really annoying but I have some blind spots in my memory. I feel that I know something of use, but I cannot recover it. I probably just need a good night's sleep.'

For a moment, Caldicott had considered ordering a second course, but thought that he would be impolite if he ate on his own. Instead he asked, 'Would you like a coffee? I need one before I drive back.'

'Tea would be nice,' Jenny replied.

After they had finished their drinks, Caldicott walked Jenny to her car. She handed him the files.

'Thank you,' he said, adding, 'You know that you shouldn't be driving so soon after suffering from concussion, don't you?'

'Yes. However, I got a taxi to work this morning as my car was in the university car park but I would have felt better if I could have driven myself in. I'm sure the driver was practising for the Silverstone Grand Prix. I couldn't face another journey like that.' Jenny nearly turned green at the thought of it.

'I can give you a lift. I will be following you back for most of your journey, anyway.'

'No, but thank you.'

'Are you absolutely sure that you don't want a lift? I promise to drive slowly.'

Jenny laughed. 'That is very kind but in the morning I will be at my house and my car will be here. I will be fine.'

'Very well, but I am probably failing in my duty to allow you to do this. Will you send me a text when you get home just to put my mind at rest? Do you have my number?'

'Yes, I've got your card in my handbag.'

'Good, don't lose it, and if ever you need me, any time night or day, please contact me.'

'Okay.' Jenny thought that Caldicott was being far too officious and was not sorry to leave him.

She drove home quite slowly. The night had come in and a slight mist was settling on the ground. On reflection she wished that she had taken up Caldicott's invitation, her concentration was failing her and once she had turned off the main road, she suddenly felt alone and frightened. So much so that when she arrived at her house, she did a complete check of each room, holding an umbrella in her hand. Having ensured that no one else was in her house, Jenny relaxed once more. She undressed, put on her dressing gown and made herself a cup of tea, to help swallow her painkillers. Once in bed, she texted Caldicott telling him that she had arrived home. She put the phone down on her bedside table and laid her head on her pillow.

CHAPTER 8
WEDNESDAY, 13 APRIL:
Late Evening

Despite all the horrors of the previous two days, Jenny went to sleep immediately, albeit that she experienced particularly vivid dreams. In her trance she stood upon Westminster Bridge, looking down at the Thames embankment bearing a host of golden daffodils. Or were they daffodils? Undeniably they were flowers, beautiful ones at that, moving in unison as showgirls performing an introductory dance at the Moulin Rouge, and now they were not flowers, they were the showgirls themselves as Toulouse Lautrec painted them so many times during his life, half-dressed, their voluptuous bosoms on display for all to see. She could even identify one of the persons on the stage. It was Medusa, as she had seen her so many times before, bare-chested, dressed as a priestess from ancient Crete, standing there in the middle of all of the naked ladies enacting out the role of Clytemnestra. She was carrying what looked like a broken doll, no doubt her daughter Iphigenia, so rudely sacrificed by Agamemnon just to sail to Troy. And there was Agamemnon himself, the cause of all the misery. It wasn't his wife who had run off to Troy, he needn't have interfered, certainly not sacrificed his beautiful daughter.

But that is the trouble when men's egos become too great; they forget humanity in pursuit of ambition.

This Agamemnon was hiding behind a mask, like so many of her colleagues at work in reality. Clytemnestra threw down the broken doll, and picked up a stranger from the audience. They had rampant sex, and then all the performers started screwing anyone available. Agamemnon picked on a young person, but male or female it was impossible to say. Whoever it was did not want to be touched and started fighting the King; the mask slipped to reveal Silvanus Straw. A man stepped up on the stage to arrest him.

Jenny woke up in a cold sweat. She did not want Straw invading her body in any shape or form. Then quickly realising it was only a dream, she fell asleep almost immediately. This time she dreamt of *Kubla Khan*, and a rather nice man from Porlock, who she didn't mind being interrupted by...

*

If Jenny spent a relatively peaceful night, it was not so for Caldicott. As he lay in his bed thinking through the last two days of his life, he felt miserable. Had he acted in an unprofessional manner by dining with Jenny? He didn't feel that he had at the time. But on reflection, perhaps he had. He worked through the College of Policing Code of Ethics in his mind. It told him he must:

ensure that any relationship at work does not create an actual or apparent conflict of interest not engage in sexual conduct or other inappropriate behaviour when on duty

not establish or pursue an improper sexual or emotional relationship with a person... who may be vulnerable to an abuse of trust or power

They certainly hadn't engaged in a physical relationship, he thought ruefully, whether on or off duty, nor could she be classed as "vulnerable", and it was essential to get to the bottom of a number of oddities that the university deaths had brought up. However, on reflection, he thought that it might be perceived to be a "conflict of interest" from an outside perspective.

Looking through the case facts with a cold eye, there was enough evidence to arrest Dr Jordan. She was the only person to date identified as having been in the right place at the right time to perform the act of vandalism. Her subsequent fall down the stairs was real enough, but that didn't mean that she hadn't sprayed the graffiti on the wall before leaving Touchwood's office. Not that anyone should be prosecuted for that. The Touchwood woman was a horror. Nevertheless, there were only minutes between the office being left vacant by Touchwood, if the gorgon was to be believed (and that in itself was open to challenge) and the arrival of Dr Dryden, another member of the English department, who was helping with the theatre studies production. He had, at the request of Medusa, who appeared to have made him her slave, entered the building to collect the stage-prompt copy, so carelessly left in her office. Dryden said that having found Jenny sprawled on the floor he had rushed up to

Medusa's office to make the emergency phone call. There was a matter of some seven minutes at most. No one was seen running from the building. True there were plenty of hiding places, but the theatre studies department was rehearsing in the barn. This production involved the whole of the department – students and staff alike.

When questioned, not one person was unaccounted for, and the only person to enter the barn after the rehearsals had begun was Dr Touchwood and the only person to leave was Dr Dryden. It was Dryden that, in addition to finding Jenny, had detected the graffiti. Was he responsible for putting it there himself? Caldicott decided he must ask him further questions, and found that he was delighted to have an excuse to go back to the English department.

'Which other departments are on that site?' Caldicott asked himself. 'English, of course, then connected to English the history department, and archaeology.' Was that all? Not that many students in total, but enough to take up time. The law department was a stone's throw away, as well. He might need assistance to interrogate everyone on the Nether Stowey site. He would call on some of his team members for that. At the moment, though, it all came down to just two people –Dryden and Jenny.

But that wasn't his biggest concern. The truth was that far from him being in a position to arrest Jenny, Jenny had arrested him. Perhaps if their first meeting had taken place in her somewhat gloomy office, he would not have noticed the joy and the mischief buried inside this gypsy-like creature, but that had not been their first meeting.

He had accidently stumbled upon her on the forbidden grass. (For this he must thank Medusa, whose directions to the law school had been useless.) He had, at that time, no knowledge of who Jenny was, or of how much time he would spend in her company during the following forty-eight hours. In her office, she looked stressed and tired, and any age up to mid forties, but outside she had looked so young and carefree he thought briefly that she might be a student. As he watched her delighting herself by carrying out an act of pure rebellion, he identified a kindred spirit. Weren't they both repressed by their surroundings? Weren't they both repressed by their work? Clearly, Jenny had ambition and talent, but this was almost beaten to a pulp by the frenzied line-management whippings.

"More teaching, more research and more paperwork! And no pay incentives whatsoever, not even a word of thanks." That was what Jenny had uttered. "They want a higher percentage of "good" degrees, and more students. It's a huge dilemma. You can't have both; it has to be one or the other. Where can we get these students from? We can't conjure them up out of fresh air. Who would come here, if they can go to London? Yes, it is a beautiful area, but it is cut off. Let's be realistic, we don't even have a direct train line. Or if they do want to stay in the area, they would have to be silly to turn down Bristol or Exeter if they had the chance to go there. Whip! Whip! Whip! What gets me is that it is the ones who are lacking in talent that end up managing the place."

His job was not dissimilar in its demands. In his case it was more arrests and fewer crimes and more satisfied customers. And more paperwork!

If only he could win the lottery, he could tell the bosses to "Fuck off!" He suspected that Jenny was on the verge of doing the same. And it was a pity, he reflected, as he felt that both of them were doing an effective job for their respective communities.

But would he really leave even if he could afford to? Probably not, what would be the point? Since the death of his wife ten years ago he hadn't had anyone to share his life with, not on a permanent basis. He felt it very cruel that she died in her twenties, for her as much as him. But cancers, like serial killers, show no mercy to their victims.

He would have been happy working in a lab indefinitely, until Lucy had died. Afterwards... he needed to find some peace. He identified straight away that it would have helped his grieving process, if he could have pinpointed someone responsible for her death. Of course there was no one. The cancer, a pernicious brain tumour, had taken hold and that was that. It could never have been for one second an issue of medical negligence. He almost wished it was. He wanted someone to blame. In the absence of a suspect, he blamed himself for everything that had happened. In this he knew he was being irrational and unjust. It didn't help if he told himself that either.

In an effort to shake this bleakness, Caldicott sold their house and handed in his notice. He took his money and spent a year travelling around different countries in Europe and beyond. He had a number of sexual dalliances, but they meant nothing to him. It was only when he reached the Bahamas and met Meg, a widow in her mid forties that his pain started to lessen. They shared a mutual experience of loss, despite the twenty years' difference in their ages. She comforted him for four months, and he almost started to live again, but then to both of their surprise she fell pregnant. The irony of this was a setback to Caldicott. It was only when Lucy and he were trying to conceive, that the cancer was detected. He told Meg that he couldn't stay, that he wasn't ready. She understood. All she asked of him was to acknowledge their child, and visit from time to time. Marcus was born seven months later. By that time Caldicott was back in England.

Before saying goodbye, Meg had told him to change his career and do something which would help him to harness his need for justice. Identifying criminals from their DNA profiles had always given him a sense of satisfaction, but he needed a more physical role. Eventually, he decided to retrain as a detective.

Caldicott was excellent at his job. One of his key strengths was that he was extremely fair. He would not arrest anyone just to make up his quota, no matter how much pressure he was under to do so, nor how damning the evidence might be. He would make certain that he analysed every detail before he acted. Further, once his suspect was in court, his meticulous preparation of the case file ensured that counsel for the prosecution had everything it needed to secure a "guilty" verdict from the jury. But this case was different. This case was testing his heart as well as his head.

Wherever he had been during the last two days, Jenny had been there too. Moreover, he was certain that she knew something that would help him solve the case, or was it cases? Take her knowledge that daffodils are poisonous; it is supposedly common knowledge, but how many people really know it? It would have impressed him normally, but struck him as significant that plant alkaloids had been found in Henry Fielding's body – albeit not from daffodils. Then there was her visit to Medusa's office at the time when vandalism was occurring or about to occur. But the strangest of all coincidences was finding her in the church. The church with its lonely gravestones left unattended by relatives...

His wife had been cremated and her ashes spread over the Quantocks – that was her wishes. It was a place that she had loved as a child. He, though, wished he had a finite spot to think of her. Perhaps that was why he chose to come back to this area, to be near to where she was, spiritually if not physically. In order to compensate for a lack of a physical marker, whenever he passed the church in Crowcombe, he would always put flowers on an untended grave. He was certain that Jenny knew that he had done so today... did that matter? No, of course not, but he should explain one day, after this was all over... but was it right to get involved again? Perhaps it was time to move on; a person cannot grieve forever.

"You're young and handsome," Meg wrote to him, "you have given me the most precious gift in the world – a beautiful son, he looks like you. But you... you need to find yourself and someone to love you as you now are. There is someone out there for you."

Was there? Was there really? Even if there was, why did he think it might be Jenny? Urgh he must go to sleep. God, he hoped that Jenny would be all right. She was in more danger than she realised.

CHAPTER 9
THURSDAY, 14 APRIL:
Morning: Dryden In Action

When Caldicott arrived at the university the next day, he was disappointed to learn from Tom that Jenny was unavailable as she was snowed under with students' appointments that morning. The student she was currently with was on the verge of being expelled, so Tom didn't dare interrupt that meeting, he said. Tom estimated that she would be free around eleven thirty.

'In that case,' Caldicott asked, 'is Dr Dryden available?'

'I'll just look at his timetable,' Tom replied. 'Wait one moment... Yes, he should be. He will be teaching again in about twenty minutes, so now is a good time to catch him. Second door on the right. Oh, Mr Caldicott, Dr Jordan asked me to draw you up a list of Dwaine's friends. Here you are.'

Tom handed over a list of names to Caldicott.

'Thank you.'

Caldicott strolled down the corridor. He did not like the smell of cigars emanating from Dr Dryden's office. Wasn't smoking of all kinds strictly forbidden in the college? Well, that was nothing to do with him; he had other things to worry about. He knocked on the door.

'Who's here, beside foul weather?' came the cheery reply to his knock, although the caller was less jovial when he saw who it was.

'King Lear,' Caldicott announced. Dryden's office was twice the size of Jenny's. Six chairs arranged in a semicircle faced Dryden's desk. Dryden indicated the end chair to Caldicott.

'Oh, Inspector, have a seat.'

'Detective Sergeant. I haven't been promoted since Tuesday.'

'No, well you certainly won't be promoted if you stay around here. Some of us have been hanging on to the title of lecturer for the past twenty-odd years; still, at least I'm not a teaching fellow. What can I do for you?'

Dr Dryden was a man who wouldn't see fifty again, but was lucky enough to still sport a full head of greying hair. His round face matched his round stomach, and he failed to take anything seriously, except for his dinner. Caldicott could not work out why he might be in a relationship with Medusa. He thought he would start by seeking an answer to exactly that conundrum.

'Well, Nancy and I go back a long way'… he started. 'Ah ha!' he announced in full pirate impersonation. 'I can see by the puzzled look that you don't know that Medusa is not her real name. Heaven only knows why she chose that one of all the beautiful names available, it's not exactly a character of goodwill to all men. I think Nancy likes to shock, that's what it is all about.

'We were lovers many moons ago now, but that was before she started working with men half her age. She was very beautiful when she was in her twenties, but now she just looks like an old boot. I suppose that's a sexist remark, but that's that. You can't change an old fossil like me as she calls me. You see, we have a love-hate relationship. But she shouldn't sleep with the students, not ours anyway. Goodness only knows they do not need any distractions. We need to fight them tooth and nail to get a decent answer out of them on the exam. They seem to think it is their God-given right to be awarded a first class degree. Well, I've got news for them; they are not getting a first out of me unless I feel they really deserve it. They think that because they pay fees these days, they have bought the certificate. Trouble is, and let's be frank here; you can safely say that they pay what can only be described as an extortionate amount of money each year. Not that we aren't worth every penny you understand, but what are they going to do with a humanities degree? Except go into teaching of course, or the police. I gather some of our best have joined the Avon and Somerset Constabulary. But if they want a proper job'… Caldicott chose to ignore this remark, it was clear that Dryden was attempting to provoke a reaction… 'they must get a first today. I often think that I could give them the exam paper and the model answer a month before they were due to sit the paper and they would still muck it up. In fact, strictly between ourselves, I heard a malicious rumour that that was precisely what the business school was doing – ha! And they still only got 10 per cent of students to the upper second level. I told Dr Jordan that we should do this, as a joke you understand, but she didn't think it was funny. That's the trouble with women in management; they lose their sense of humour, or their looks. Bless her; Jenny seems to have lost both, and all in the space of a month. Shame, utter shame, lovely woman, very reliable and not a bitch like many of the staff in the university, male and female, but the poor woman is on a hiding to nothing with our current third years – dreadful the whole batch of them, except for one or two. But that's the root cause of the trouble. In my day it was only the one or two that could go to university at all, and we fought tooth and nail to get a degree. Nor did we complain if we didn't get a first, we were just too grateful to be there at all. I only got a Desmond, a lower second to you, but that was all I needed then. It hasn't held me back. It was good enough in my day and it should be good enough today, but it isn't. It's an absolute joke how some universities manage to get 70 per cent of their students a first or upper second. Today's first is yesterday's third. We all know that, but no one is allowed to say so, or we will be disciplined. Colleague of mine got sacked from the University of… I'd better not say where… last week, just because he had the audacity to fail ONE student. I ask you!

'But now… sorry, you got me on my favourite theme, we are all under pressure, particularly Jenny… Poor girl. It gave me a hell of a jolt finding her at the bottom of the stairs to Nancy's office.'

Dryden had finally stopped for breath; Caldicott was quick to take his chance. He pulled out his notebook and flipped through the pages.

'Yes, that is what I wanted to talk to you about. Now in my notes I wrote down that you went over to the building to fetch the prompt copy at eighteen thirty-seven?'

'Yes, there or there abouts.'

'And are you absolutely certain that you saw nobody except of course Jen… I mean Dr Jordan during this time?' (Caldicott's slip had not gone unnoticed by Dr Dryden.)

'Well, I'm pretty sure that I didn't. It is absolutely clear in my mind that I saw no one before finding Jenny at the bottom of the stairs. After that point… all I can say is that it is possible that someone was on the first floor, but if they were there, then they didn't make an impression on me. But then don't forget, I did have a nasty shock finding Jenny like that. For one moment I thought she was dead. Thankfully she wasn't, as I realised when she started making ghastly noises. To be honest that was worse! I thought that she was going to be sick. My only desire was to get her an ambulance. This bloody area, I didn't have a signal on my mobile or I could have phoned from there. I didn't want to leave Jenny like that. Someone might have taken advantage of the situation…' Dryden gave Caldicott a penetrating stare and then pointedly turned his gaze to a copy of Simeon Hardwicke's book that happened to be on his desk.

Dryden continued, 'On reflection, it is more than possible that someone might have crept down after I had gone up to the second floor.'

'And you are sure that there was no one in Dr Touchwood's office?'

'No. The only place to hide would be behind the door, or under the desk. As I went round to the phone I would have stumbled across anyone lying underneath it, and by habit, I closed the door when I came in. That was why I saw the writing. Had I left the door open, I wouldn't have seen that reproduction Cro-Magnon scribble.'

'Thank you, and you can't recall anything else about the building, about Dr Jordan, anything on the stairs, a missile…?'

'Actually, come to think of it, now I remember, it has only just struck me as you are asking me again, I recall Jenny's bag being in my way going up the stairs, I had to step over it, but when I came down, I am pretty sure that the bag was in a different position.'

'And the contents of the bag?'

'Well, yes that is why I am sure now that it had moved, because only the bag was there when I went up, and on the way back her keys were sprawling down the stairs.'

'Could Dr Jordan have moved it even if she was temporarily unconscious?'

'I think that is more for you to decide than me, don't you think?'

'Was the bag attached to her body when you first saw it?'

'I really couldn't say.'

Caldicott jotted down a couple of points, before putting his notepad away. 'Very well, thank you for your time. I don't think I have any other questions at the moment. Let me know if you think of something else.'

'Yes, of course, Inspector.'

Caldicott was pretty certain that this was a deliberate jibe from Dryden, but the man was smiling in a good-humoured way. 'Don't worry,' he said, 'you will be a DI before long, that I am certain of.'

Caldicott was less than certain about that, and of late was less certain that he even wanted it. 'By the way,' Dryden continued, 'what about the car accident involving our students? Do we have an update on the girl? I suppose it was a car accident?'

'Miss Pye is in a stable condition, I understand. As for the car, it appears that it may have been sabotaged.'

'Oh really? That is fascinating. Was it Saunders' supplier getting payback?'

'You knew about his drug taking? Dr Jordan wasn't so definite.'

'Ah well, that's not surprising. I think most of us thought he was clean, but then I had the experience of following him all the way to the lecture hall at the end of last term, giggling his head off. The boy could barely keep in a straight line. It was pretty clear he was on something. I made the mistake of walking too fast and catching up with him. The wind wafted the not so mellifluous odour of cannabis, of whatever kind it was. Made me start coughing. I had to get some water before I started lecturing. A great irritation. Lodged itself in my memory.'

'Thank you; that ties in with what I've learnt about his extracurricular activities. I am hoping to meet some of his friends, to get a better insight into his life. Do you know where I might find any of these students?' Caldicott handed over Tom's list to Dryden.

'Ah well, as luck would have it for you Inspector, his tutorial group is due to roll up here at ten thirty. I call them my Thursday morning horror group. The only literature they know anything about is *Frankenstein*. In my professional opinion, I do not believe they have even read that book, yet alone all of the books required on the syllabus, but they do a good job of attempting to bluff through the hour. I find it amusing to see how much rubbish they come out with. Why don't you interrogate them now? It will give you a real insight into what we are dealing with here. And if you know anything about Keats, you can ask them about that into the bargain.'

'Excellent. Are you sure that it won't set you back with your teaching?'

'No, I will be glad for the rest. It's tiring doing all the talking, you know.'

That last remark surprised Caldicott. He had hardly been able to get a word in edgeways for the past twenty minutes! Dr Dryden clearly had a mischievous sense of humour, but would that make him a practical joker?

'Ah, here they come now. Enter in you motley crew.' Caldicott drew out his notebook again.

Three students dawdled in, looking particularly hungover and depressed. Caldicott studied them carefully. There was a black girl, wearing jeans and a T-shirt, and a lanky Asian youth in severe need of a shave, and a petite blonde, wearing a skirt her mother would not approve of. It was obvious that the blonde had been crying. As for the other two, one of them smelt of cannabis. He couldn't identify which one at the time; he later worked it out that it was the black girl. This surprised him as he had originally put it down to the Asian youth.

Yes, drug taking is rife, thought Caldicott. No wonder Jenny was having a bad time trying to get them to improve their studies.

'Well, my lovelies, we have a rare treat for you today. We have with us a real policeman, one Detective Sergeant Caldicott. Let me introduce you to my talented students. Rosie Anderson, Ife Mantuwa and Imran Khan, sadly not *the* Imran Khan but I gather a very good cricketer for the university team.' This he said very loudly for all to hear, but in a low voice he said to Caldicott, 'That is the only thing he can do. Heaven knows how he got a place here.' He continued to the students, 'Detective Sergeant Caldicott would like to ask you a few questions about Dwaine.'

'Oh no! It's awful, awful,' wailed the blonde.

'Now Rosie, calm down. Sit down all of you. Ife, do sit down, you are blocking out the light. Where is McClellan?'

'I haven't seen Donald today, sir,' the Asian youth replied.

'Well, never mind Imran, you will have to answer on his behalf. Oh, just before DS Caldicott starts his interrogation, does anyone know anything about Franz Kafka?'

It was on the tip of Caldicott's tongue to say, "Yes, he was a Czech writer", but just in time he realised that Dryden was asking the whereabouts of another student.

As if reading Caldicott's mind, Dryden added, 'Kafka is one of our Eastern European students, whose name is on my list, but whose body has yet to undergo metamorphoses from ink into flesh this term.'

Caldicott smiled and Dryden chuckled to himself, mainly because his play on words was completely lost to the students, but he was pleased to find that someone in the room had knowledge of literature.

He continued, 'Lord, what fools these mortals be! Never mind… Over to you Mr Caldicott.'

'Thank you, well I…' Caldicott did not get any further, as his speech was interrupted by a late arrival.

'Ah McClellan, so good of you to join us for lunch,'

Dryden said somewhat sarcastically. Caldicott liked this man. Not only did he have a vicious sense of humour, but more importantly, he had rescued Jenny, or had he? Could Dryden be the culprit? Caldicott didn't want him to be. Meanwhile, the student was explaining his late arrival.

'Sorry, sir, I had car trouble.'

'Well, one can only hope that it was less trouble than our late friend Mr Saunders suffered.'

At this point Rosie started snivelling again. 'We are here to face a grilling from Mr Caldicott, on that very matter. Back to you Mr Caldicott.'

'Thank you. I gather than you all know Dwaine Saunders well.'

'Some knew him better than others,' said a sneering McClellan looking pointedly at Rosie. She started a fresh outburst of hysterics.

'See what you done now you bastard!' Ife had risen up to Rosie's defence. 'Yes, we all knew him well. He was our friend. Some of us took advantage of that, didn't they?' Ife was staring hard at McClellan by this stage. She continued. 'He was good to us, would always buy us drinks, give us lifts…'

'Supply some of you with drugs,' McClellan interrupted derisively.

'Shut up man!' Ife retorted.

'Perhaps you would like to ask direct questions to the students Mr Caldicott, before we have a barrack-room brawl in front of us,' Dryden suggested.

Caldicott was looking on at the students with some bemusement. He started to understand what a monumental task Jenny faced. 'Good idea,' he said, although he was rather annoyed that the students' argument had been interrupted. 'Did anyone know that Saunders was planning to give Bernice a lift yesterday?'

'Yes, well all of us knew because he told us so in the *Beowulf* lecture.' Ife pronounced *Beowulf* as if it were some ancient swear word, a look of utter contempt overcame her quite attractive features.

'Goodness,' Dr Dryden interrupted, 'don't pronounce it like that in front of Professor Jones, it will break her heart.'

'Sorry Mr Caldicott. You were about to say Rosie…?'

'I was about to say that it was probably only us who knew. Bernice said that she had been summoned to see her boyfriend at short notice. They were meeting in Minehead, but not to tell anyone. I think she wanted to use that as an excuse for bunking off her meeting with Dr Jordan.'

Dryden and Caldicott exchanged glances.

'Why would Miss Pye want to leave her meeting with Dr Jordan?' Caldicott asked.

Rosie continued, 'Because Dr Jordan was on her case about her results… and other things… and you don't want to get on the wrong side of Dr Jordan.'

'No you don't!' added McClellan. 'Though she be but little, she is fierce!'

'Very good McClellan,' Dryden interjected. 'Dr Jordan will be pleased that you have learnt something from her Shakespeare lectures, although if I were you I wouldn't quote that line to her face.'

An amused Caldicott pursued a different line of enquiry. 'Do you know which car belonged to Dwaine?'

Ife said, 'Yes, of course, it was the most expensive one in the car park… white Mercedes with tinted windows.'

Rosie corrected her. 'No, Professor Hardwicke has got that one. Dwaine did not have tinted windows.'

McClellan said, 'No, you're wrong; Hardwicke without, Dwaine with.'

Caldicott continued. 'Do you know of anyone who would like to see either Dwaine or Bernice out of the way?'

Imran spoke for the rest of them. 'Only Dr Jordan. She has made it clear that she wants to get rid of her failing students. She is always on to us to meet our targets.'

'Isn't that her job?'

Ife started, 'Yes, but as if it is going to matter to us. We are here to have a good time. We didn't choose to come to a concentration camp. All these boring lectures that we have to attend, I mean it's ridiculous. And if that wasn't bad enough we are supposed to prepare for tutorials.'

Rosie cut in, 'Well, Dr Dryden here is very nice to us, and Dr Jordan is okay, but some of the other staff are… well… dull. Especially Professor Jones. Sorry Dr Dryden but you know it's true; she could bore for England. We'd do better if they gave us time off to watch *Beowulf* on DVD, rather than listen to Professor Jones. I mean, at least we can see some nice arses.'

Ife agreed, 'Yeh! That Kieron Bew is well fit. Actually,' she turned directly to Caldicott, 'you look a bit like Kieron Bew.'

'No he doesn't,' Imran joined in, 'he looks more like the guy who plays the skinshifter.'

'Thanks for that!' Caldicott interjected.

'Oh, the guy who plays Koll is good-looking, when he is in human form,' Rosie said.

Dr Dryden roared with laughter at his students' apparent disregard for Caldicott's authority.

'It's not just that lectures are boring,' Imran continued, 'some of the staff don't know anything. We are paying nine thousand pounds a year for this, but Professor Hardwicke said that Wordsworth wrote the poem, "The Tiger", and Blake is supposed to be his area of research.'

'And that is the truth,' McClellan added. 'For once, we knew more than the staff!'

Dr Dryden looked shocked. 'My dears, you shouldn't say that about your lecturers.'

'Well, you won't snitch on us,' said Rosie.

'No, he can't,' added McClellan, and turning to Caldicott he added, 'it has gone down in the university folklore, that our beloved Dr Dryden had the audacity to throw Professor Hardwicke's book in the bin, in front of last year's class.'

'Yes, well enough of that,' added Dryden, but he was clearly amused by the students. Caldicott attempted to reassert control.

'If we could get back to Saunders, are you sure that there is no one who bore him a grudge and/or might have the skills to sabotage his car?'

This sobered up all of the students.

Imran spoke for the rest. 'Dwaine was very popular, but he owed somebody some money. We heard him telling Dr Lowry that. Dr Lowry was his personal tutor. He said in the class something like, "If only I was given more time, then I could sort it all out, but I'm being pressured to pay up and I can't do it and study".'

Caldicott asked them all, 'Did Dr Lowry give any response to this?'

Imran added, 'I think he told him to seek a loan from the university.'

Rosie continued, 'Yes, that's right, he did, but I don't suppose he had time to do so.'

Caldicott continued, 'And is there anyone here who would have the skills to tamper with a car?'

Rosie was pleased to be able to pay back McClellan. 'Yes, our Donald here is a motor enthusiast, tops up his student loan by freelancing for a garage.'

'Aye, I do, but I have never been near to Saunders' car. Don't work for those who can't pay. That's my motto.'

Caldicott rose to leave. 'Well, thank you for your time. I'll let you get on with your tutorial. Please contact me if you think of anything extra…'

Dr Dryden escorted him to the door. 'Got what you came for?'

'Not entirely as I had planned but extremely enlightening. I've certainly been given something to think about.'

'A pleasure to have some intelligent company in my tutorial for a change.' And shaking hands with Caldicott said, 'Good luck.'

And as he closed the door behind him, Caldicott became lost in thought. Someone had given him a significant clue this morning, perhaps more than one clue. He would have to think things through.

One thing he was now sure of; Dr Dryden had not been

responsible for Jenny's fall, but someone was. He would not stop his enquiries until he had identified the culprit. It may well be a harmless joker, but Caldicott suspected that a much more malevolent force was at hand. Caldicott ambled back to the office, but Tom shook his head when he saw him return.

'Sorry, an emergency has cropped up with a student. It will take a couple of hours to sort it out. Dr Jordan has left a note for you.'

Caldicott picked up the handwritten note. He struggled to read it.

"Dear Mr Caldicott, (it read)

I am in meetings all afternoon, but if this is urgent then please phone me at 13.00 hrs. Otherwise, I am free tomorrow after two fifteen.'

'Thank you. Please inform Dr Jordan that it is not urgent and I will be in contact soon.'

'Will do,' was the reply.

CHAPTER 10
FRIDAY, 15 APRIL:
The Friday Congregational

It was now Friday morning. Once upon a time, Friday was the day that all staff went to work in an extremely positive frame of mind, primarily because the weekend lay ahead of them. But with the arrival of the new vice chancellor, all this was changed. Friday now became the morning of mourning for the university's staff, and absences due to medical appointments, annual leave or mere sickness, quadrupled in two months. This was due to the introduction of the summoning for the weekly "congregation meeting".

Secretly, staff had begun to organise a strike over these meetings. This was until the union representatives were tipped off that in another university, union reps were first to receive their redundancy notices. It all went quiet after that.

The meetings achieved nothing but raising everyone's blood pressure and for those working on the Nether Stowey site, it meant axing in the region of three hours of the precious research time by having to go to the Bridgwater lecture theatre.

Jenny, although thinking these meetings, along with

every other university meeting, were a waste of time, quite enjoyed them in a macabre way. It gave her an opportunity to study some of the other staff who she would never normally meet. It did also reveal certain budgeting facts, which would not have been shared by Hardwicke.

She always made a point of sitting in the front row of the circle, mainly because it made her feel like one of the naughty monks in the thirteenth century, who used to amuse themselves by pouring melted candle wax on the tonsures of those in the row beneath. It also gave her a good view of the enemy, in particular, Christine Vincent, the ageing bleach-blonde from the law faculty.

Miss Vincent, who partly to do with her initials, and partly to do with her face, but mainly to do with her attitude had earned herself the nickname of Cruella de Vil. Every time that she had stood up on the rostrum to speak, Jenny was alerted to the fact that here was a woman who appeared to have no dignity whatsoever. During Jenny's relationship with the late Professor Carstairs, he had informed her that this was a person to steer well clear of at all costs. How Cruella had risen to the role of pro-vice chancellor was beyond everyone's imagination; that is to say, it *wasn't* beyond their imagination. Two things were for sure – it certainly wasn't on her academic achievements, or on her teaching feedback. This left only the third route available...

No one would really have minded any of this had she been pleasant, but the woman didn't even pretend to be nice. She would frequently belittle the young female staff. This was not the case with the male staff. Cruella liked to take the role of Queen Bee, constantly delighted to have numerous drones flying around her.

One of these, Dr Adams, decided that he could not cope with her sexual harassment any longer and left the university within a year of his arrival. The university was forced to pay him in the region of twenty thousand pounds damages for constructive dismissal. His place was taken by Dr Albertini, who luckily for him, was married to a beautiful singer with an exquisite voice. She acted as his bodyguard against the clutches of the man-eater. Poor Professor Marchant was not so lucky. Within one day of his arrival, Cruella had set a man trap for him. He had aged by thirty years overnight.

Cruella was utterly vicious to Jenny whenever they met. It took Jenny a number of months to work out why. Cruella hated any woman that stopped her sleeping with her desired target, and in Jenny's case this meant Carstairs. In fact, one of the reasons that Carstairs was in no hurry to end the relationship with Jenny was because it gave him protection from Cruella. *Not a very flattering reason for staying together*, Jenny thought.

This Friday, Jenny sat by Amelia Halcroft, one of the young law lecturers. Amelia was the living personification of Aphrodite; tall, naturally blonde and stunningly beautiful. In fact, she was all the things that Cruella wanted to be. Cruella hated her. This made Jenny like Amelia even more than she would have done otherwise. They often went to the pub together on a Friday night.

'Hi, I haven't seen you for ages, how are things going?' Amelia asked her.

'Hell,' said Jenny. 'It's this ridiculous quota of good degrees; we are never going to make it.'

Amelia replied, 'Yes, I entirely understand. We have

116

the same problem. But at least you don't have to work with some of the grims that I do, all vying to be in charge. It's almost a replica of the gas chamber effect. You know, who can clamber on top of the pile to get air.'

'Huh, steady on!' spluttered Professor Carter, the director of archaeological studies who was sitting the other side of Amelia. 'Not this early in the day.'

'Sorry Howard, I didn't see you there. I didn't mean it in an anti-Semitic way, just a parallel example.'

'Oh, no offence taken my dear. Now, had one of your colleagues said it... that might have been a different matter.' He looked pointedly in the direction of Christine Vincent, who for some unexplained reason was wearing her crocodile smiles for the audience.

'The VC cometh,' Vincent called out.

And duly the great man himself, Professor Graham Everson VC, arrived to a fanfare of recorded trumpets. The audience burst into cheers and frantic clapping.

'Really this is going too far!' said Carter. 'It's turning into a Billy Graham concert.'

Jenny said to Amelia, 'Do you think he will check to see who stops clapping first? You know, the first to discontinue clapping gets sacked...'

'Ssh,' said a newcomer who sat on Jenny's left. 'Can't you feel the force, the magnificence of the occasion?' It was her English colleague Dr Dryden.

'Oh belt up, John!' she said.

'Oh, it's not fair. I would have such a nice time in the faculty of humanities; instead I am a slave to the boring old law department,' said Amelia.

'Well, if we can recruit a lot of students, which is

highly unlikely,' Dryden said to Amelia, 'we will bring you in. Always keen to have a pretty face around.'

'John, be quiet. The VC is watching you.'

'Let him, I'm waiting for my turn to tell him what I think of him.'

The music stopped and everyone's conversation drew to a close.

'Well, thank you all for coming here on yet another magnificent Friday morning, and I am delighted to introduce you to yet another of our quick snippets about how I am improving this university. First we will hear from the estates' bursar, and then we will move on to some positive news celebrating the Queen's ninetieth birthday. But first I want you to stand up. Yes, all of you stand up!'

'Oh Christ,' said a voice from behind. It was Dr O'Flynn, a lecturer from the business department. He had recently joined the faculty of law and business from his previous job in Queen's Belfast, and was seriously regretting his move. Amelia stifled a giggle.

'I want you to raise your hands, yes raise them up, up, up in the air, all of you, yes all of you.'

'Are we supposed to be doing a Nazi salute?' asked Dr Penny Worth, a historian.

Jenny was on the verge of bursting into hysterics. The fascination for her was the bunch of sycophants who lined up in the front two rows, listening to Everson's every word.

The VC continued, 'I want you to raise your hands in love, love yourself, love this university, love each other… Feel the love… Feel the love…'

'There's been a damn sight too much feeling the love

in the theatre studies department recently,' sniggered Penny. That was it for Jenny. Tears welled up in her eyes as she tried to stifle her laughter.

'Now then, give the person next to you a big hug! That's it, a great big hug!'

'Do we have to?' Dryden asked.

'I'm insulted,' said Jenny, 'you wouldn't refuse Amelia.'

'No, but she is young and beautiful,' he said. Jenny punched him on the arm.

'Will that do as a hug?' she asked.

'Thank you, sit down,' the VC commanded.

The group of reprobates all sat down desperately trying to compose themselves, but there is always one who goes too far, isn't there? And it was always Dryden. He leaned back and asked O'Flynn, 'Hey Pat, how would Everson go down in Northern Ireland, you know with the paramilitary organisations?'

'Christ, he'd be shot by both sides!' came the response. This was too much for Amelia; she collapsed into infectious giggles, which soon spread to Jenny on one side and Professor Carter on the other.

'Over to you Frank,' the VC called as this very sad looking accountant took up his position on the podium.

'Hmm yes well, I've been asked to talk about accounts,' said the sad man. 'Here you can see the accounts of 2011-2015. We have only just managed to break even each year. In fact, it is fair to say that we are going to see a deficit this year. So it is essential that we economise as soon as possible or we will have to face redundancies.'

'That's right, just fill us with confidence,' said O'Flynn to those who could hear him.

Jenny nearly spat out her tea.

When the sad man left the stage, his place was taken by Sandra Harris, the entertainments manager.

Putting on her favourite Prince track "1999", she started to dance and act out the celebrations planned for the following month. It appeared that there was to be no expense spared. There were to be trips to London, trips to New York, half the staff were going to the Bahamas... It was going to be a great celebration!!

Whereas the group were in hysterics during the VC's act, the stone-cold truth about the colossal waste of money had a sobering effect on everyone.

'Is it just me thinking this,' asked Jenny of anyone around her, 'but wouldn't we be in a better position financially if we didn't have all these events planned?' Everyone was in agreement with this sentiment.

After this, Jenny switched off to any further presentations. Had she been attending a more important meeting, she would have made every effort to concentrate, but what was the point? The university had been led into the valley of death for years. Definitely time to get another job she decided.

Jenny spent the next ten minutes daydreaming about Caldicott. She had missed his visit the day before, as she had been knee deep in students. She wondered how his enquiries were going. *I wish they would hurry up and end!* she thought, but she knew that with Dwaine's death the process was going to be slow. 'I'm sure it must be something to do with drugs,' she whispered to no one in particular.

'Yes, I should say he is definitely on drugs,' someone close by had answered.

'Well, thank you for that,' the VC announced. 'We are now going to be handing you over to the department of business and Professor Selina Bottomley who is going to discuss business strategies.'

A tall, leggy blonde sashayed across the stage, her contours emphasised by her lycra outfit.

Dryden started to smack his lips at the sight of the woman, and there was an audible "cor" from numerous men in the room. Percy Smith, Jenny's youngest lecturer in the English department, was one of these.

'For Christ's sake, you're supposed to be lecturers not lechers,' Penny spat out. 'It's like working in a *Carry On* film with you lot.'

'I wonder what business she used to run.' Percy's remark was unfortunately timed as everyone in the hall had suddenly gone quiet, so his words were heard by all.

'The young man is an embarrassment to us,' Gwen, sitting three rows further down, mouthed at Jenny.

For all her good looks, Selina was fighting a losing battle with her presentation, primarily because it was vacuous. 'And so in order to enhance our quality pro forma, we thought it might be a good idea if we taught the students rather than letting them teach themselves... We are also trying to increase student motivation and morale, so we have bought two guinea pigs to act as study buddies for our weaker students.'

'God, now you see the rubbish we have to deal with in our faculty; that's where all our research funding goes,' Amelia said to Jenny.

'There are only so many ways to present emptiness in a positive light,' another voice told her.

Jenny drifted off again. It had been three days since her fall down the stairs and although her head was better, it still caused her pain from time to time. Today, perhaps it was the stifling atmosphere of the room, or the almost euphoric sense of servitude that some of the staff seemed to have for the VC, but she could smell degradation in the air. She just wanted to get out. She wondered how Kevin was… Kevin… of all names…

She came to with a start when Amelia tapped her arm. 'Wakey, wakey, time to go! You were supposed to be motivated by it, not inspired to go to sleep. Jenny… are you all right? You look ill.'

'Took a tumble on Tuesday and been overdoing it,' said Dryden.

'Oh really?' exclaimed Amelia.

'Well, I…' Jenny was about to explain, when Amelia's attention was drawn to an Adonis-like figure some fifteen metres away. He was waving to Amelia with one of the nicest smiles that Jenny had ever seen.

'Wow, who's that?' Jenny asked. 'He's gorgeous.'

'That's Grant, my PhD student,' said Amelia miserably.

'Why the sad face? You lucky cow.'

'Too long to explain now, Jenny… Are you free tonight? I could do with a girls' night in!'

Penny, who had just seen Grant, shouted out 'Phwoarr! Who's that guy who looks like a young Kevin Sorbo?'

Jenny jumped at the mention of the name Kevin. 'Come round to mine and we will get a takeaway,' she said to Amelia.

'Great. See you about seven.' Amelia chased after her PhD student. As Jenny watched, Echo and Narcissus came to her mind. She hoped not for Amelia's sake, she really was a nice girl.

*

Jenny had spent the early afternoon in secret anticipation that Caldicott would arrive but that was not to be. At half past three she received a message from Tom saying that Caldicott would not be able to come to the campus today, but hoped to have some news soon.

'Lovers' tiff?' Tom asked.

'What do you mean? It's purely professional,' replied Jenny.

'Hmm, yes that's what they all say,' he replied.

The disappointment of not seeing Caldicott made Jenny sit up and think. *This is ridiculous; I only met him on Tuesday. I know nothing about him. He may be married with children for all I know.* But somehow she didn't think that he was. Would it be too forward of her to ask him? *Others would, but I'm not sure that I have the nerve,* she thought sadly.

CHAPTER 11
FRIDAY, 15 APRIL:
Girls' Night In with Amelia

Amelia arrived on the dot at seven.

Jenny smiled, 'I wish my students were as punctual as you. Come in.'

'Oh Jen, you are looking worse than this morning,' was all that Amelia could say.

'Thanks, just make me feel better, why don't you?'

Amelia looked mortified. 'Sorry, I didn't mean to upset you... I've bought some beer... I thought we might need it. And some cigarettes, although I think you have stopped smoking haven't you?'

'Well, I have but after the week that I have had I might start again. Let's order this curry and then I'll fill you in, or would you rather go out?'

'Oh God, no! I'm in hiding – I will tell you about that as well.'

Having phoned up the local curry house and placed an order for a delivery, Jenny and Amelia poured out their beer and started to set the world to rights.

'Is it just me or is everything at work spiralling into disaster?' asked Amelia smoking her second cigarette.

Jenny agreed. 'It does seem like that and things are getting blacker by the second.'

'Is it true that your student's death was caused by sabotage rather than mechanic failure?'

'It's possible, at least that's what DS Caldicott thinks.'

Amelia's face lit up. 'I understand from Tom that your policeman is extremely attractive, and Tom thinks that you two would make an ideal couple.'

Jenny was flabbergasted. 'When on earth did he tell you all that?'

'Oh, yesterday.'

'Don't you just love Tom? Such a gossipmonger! But he's hardly *my* policeman…'

Amelia was not letting Jenny off the hook that easily. 'Is he good-looking?' she persisted.

'Yes he is. A bit on the tall side to look good with me though.'

'Well, what are a few inches between friends?'

Jenny burst into laughter. 'Amelia, you're turning into Roy "Chubby" Brown!'

Amelia blushed profusely. 'Sorry Jenny, I didn't mean it like that, I didn't mean to offend you.'

Jenny was bemused at Amelia's reaction, and asked her, 'Goodness child, you haven't offended me, where has your sense of humour gone?' But Amelia completely ignored this invitation to offload her concerns, and attempted to change the subject. 'John told me that you fell down a flight of stairs; is that right?'

'Well, I am not sure, but I must have fallen down a number of stairs, judging by my bruises.'

'But that isn't like you, how could you have got it so

wrong? I mean, how could you have lost your footing? Even when you've had a drink you've always managed to keep in a straight line.'

Jenny was thoughtful. 'I don't know Amelia. I think that I have been exceptionally overwrought lately. Then on top of that, hearing about Tony... did you know that it is possible that Tony was poisoned? No, I can see by your face that is news to you. I don't know what to think, or what to feel any more. And this bloody job... but enough about my problems, something is bothering you – now out with it.'

'It's Grant,' said Amelia eventually.

'Your hunk of a PhD student? I thought he might be involved somewhere along the line... I suppose you have fallen in love with him?'

'Oh Jenny, how could you guess?'

'Well, it doesn't take a genius to work it out. Besides, I defy anyone male or female not to fall in love with him. I mean, he's the sort who makes nuns open their legs in anticipation.'

'Jenny! You shock me! How can you say such a thing?'

'Because it's true... Tell me about him.'

'He's Canadian. He's working on a comparative piece on variations of manslaughter between UK and Canadian law. Oh my God, he is just the perfect student. Always polite, always cheerful, even when I tell him that I don't like his work – and that is a very rare event. He's recently applied for his upgrade from MPhil to PhD and he has only been here twelve months.'

'That's good isn't it?'

'Yes, for him. Not for me. I will get it in the neck for

losing six to twelve months' fees from an international student. We aren't doing any better financially than you these days.'

'But that doesn't bother you does it…?'

'Oh Jenny, I will be distraught if he leaves early. I haven't got the nerve to say anything to him now. I mean, it wouldn't be professional for me to seduce my student, would it?'

'Not at all, but you wouldn't be the first. A number of PhD students marry their supervisors so I'm told. Building up mutual trust and respect, etc. You could declare your love and then step down as his supervisor.'

Amelia went quiet as she considered what Jenny had suggested. 'I don't want to do that,' she said finally. 'Working with Grant is the only thing that keeps me going. I can't seem to drill a single case into my undergrads.'

Jenny sighed. 'Don't worry, it's the same here. I daren't discuss Dickens with the first years. I mean, not only do they snigger at the name, but they do not seem to have absorbed one piece of his literature.'

'What do you mean snigger?'

'Oh come on Amelia, you know the joke. "Do you like Dickens? Yes, but not on a first date!" I asked them in the seminar only last week to name his significant works. It went like this.

"*Oliver Twist.*"

Good, next…

"*David Copperfield.*"

Okay, a novel that doesn't have an eponymous character…?

"*Nicholas Nickleby.*"

A novel that **doesn't** have an eponymous character; in other words, a book that isn't named after one of the characters in it…

"*A Christmas Carol.*"

Yes… good.

"*A Tale of Two Cities.*"

And then they were stuck…

"*Wuthering Heights*?"

I had to say, "No, that was by Emily Bronte, but you are thinking along the right lines."

After thirty seconds' silence, a tentative voice called out, "Full House?"

Full House? I said, Full House? We are not playing Bingo here. I think you mean *Bleak House*, and ladies and gentlemen, let me tell you that this is a *Bleak House* if you can only name me five of Dickens' works. I had had *Great Expectations* of you all, but I can see that we have fallen on *Hard Times*. You have left me feeling like *The Wreck of the Golden Mary*, and I must set off on *The Long Voyage* to *The Old Curiosity Shop* to buy *The Pickwick Papers* and meet *Our Mutual Friend, Barnaby Rudge* with whom I am having *A Holiday Romance*. He has promised to tell me *The Mystery of Edwin Drood.*'

'Is that the lot?'

'No, I've missed off *Dombey and Son, Martin Chuzzlewit* and *Little Dorrit,* and there are some more short stories. Saying that, I defy anyone to get *The Public Life of Mr Tulrumble, Once Mayor of Mudfog.* Besides, I don't want to emphasise that story in class as it sounds too similar to Mr Tumble from CBeebies, and that is something I want to steer clear of at all costs.'

'What's wrong with Mr Tumble?'

'Nothing whatsoever, my nephew loved the programme, but I don't want to see him mentioned in an essay on Dickens written for their examinations!'

'Oh Jenny, you've cheered me up,' Amelia smiled but then quickly looked sad again, 'but that isn't all.'

'Don't tell me, Cruella has been having a go again.'

'Oh yes, and it's worse than you think. She keeps finding things wrong with my work, but only when Grant is around. Then she keeps asking him to my face to go round to her office so she can "sort out my mistakes" but I haven't made any.'

'Amelia, sass up! She just wants to fuck him. She hasn't got a chance when you are around. You are young, beautiful, intelligent and free. She might be free, but she is not any of the other things! She is as jealous as hell of you; I know that because Tony told me that when we were together. In fact, all the female staff are, and not just those in your own department. Medusa would hate it if you strayed over to humanities. But I have to say this for Medusa, faulty though she can be, fundamentally she is not normally a malicious person. She is like a cuddly lamb compared to your Cruella.'

'But what can I do?'

'You have three choices as far as I can see. One: Get another job and then tell Grant how you feel; Two: Tell him how you feel anyway and blow the consequences; Three: Stay in your current job and keep quiet until he has graduated. If he is the person you think he is, he will not want to jeopardise either your position or his own… but when he has completed his doctorate… grab him! In the meantime, try to keep him away from Cruella; I am sure that he likes it even less than you.'

At that point their curry arrived, and they sat down to eat and drink the rest of the night away. After several bottles of beer, Amelia was talking so loudly that Jenny didn't hear her phone ring at first. When she finally realised it was ringing, she decided to ignore it. Had she known that it was Caldicott, she would have answered it straight away.

*

Caldicott did not know Jenny's plans for the evening, but he was hoping to speak to her. He had found an excuse to do so and was pleased with himself. However, Jenny did not answer the phone; neither did she call him back. He supposed her to be out somewhere, and felt strangely perturbed. He would try again tomorrow.

CHAPTER 12
SATURDAY, 16 APRIL

It was a very hung-over Jenny who answered her phone the following morning.

'Hello...? Oh hello... Sorry, I have just stumbled out of bed... umm... oh, what now?... Well, uh, the place is a tip and I'm a bit embarrassed to let anyone around, but give me twenty minutes or so... have you got my address? Yes? Okay...'

Caldicott had the feeling that Jenny was not alone. She was absolutely entitled to do as she pleased. It was not his business, he told himself. Nevertheless, he didn't like it, and he particularly disliked the fact that it bothered him at all. He must adopt a more professional approach he said to himself.

Duly twenty minutes after he had phoned, he knocked on Jenny's door. She answered the door in a sheepish manner, still wearing her dressing gown, which roused his suspicions further. He stopped on the threshold. She was right – the place was untidy to say the least. Remains of the takeaway from the night before were strewn across the table, and what appeared to be an empty crate of beer was stacked against the outside wall. The smell of cigarettes still pervaded Jenny's cottage; he hadn't noticed her smoke

131

before. His biggest surprise, though, was the presence of two cars outside her cottage. He felt irrationally jealous.

Jenny did not pay attention to his reactions; she was too busy squirming at the state of her cottage. On top of this, she now realised that she had been so busy trying to clear up some of the debris of last night's takeaway that she had not got out of her dressing gown. At least thankfully all of the rubbish was off the floor now, and the sofa looked okay. But why did she forget to get dressed? That was stupid, she said to herself. Caldicott had given her ample warning. What happened to those twenty minutes?

She had wanted to see Caldicott, that was without a doubt, and she would have been delighted if the day before he had informed her of an impending visit, so his arrival could only be a good thing. However, at the same time, she was desperate to impress him. She was disappointed that his first, and no doubt his last, visit had occurred at the time when her living room looked in the worst imaginable state. The trouble with the cottage was that it was too small to entertain in any shape or form. The ground floor consisted purely of a lounge and kitchen-dining area all in one narrow room and so it was not possible to close a door on the dirty dishes festering in the sink. She used to pride herself on how immaculate her cottage was, but that all ended when she became head of department. Jenny's only other rooms were a bathroom and her bedroom on the floor above. Even if she had wanted to invite Caldicott upstairs, and part of her would very much like to take him upstairs, there was an even worse mess there and she simply could not have brought herself to do it. Not that he was here for that reason. He had informed her that he had some news.

'Sit down, somewhere. Sorry it's such a mess. Would you like coffee?' she asked him. 'I think I can find some clean cups somewhere.'

'Yes, that would be nice; white, one sugar. You've had a bit of a party here, haven't you? I didn't realise that you smoked.'

Jenny was nettled. It was bad enough that her habitat was untidy, without him being so observant, but she supposed that was his job. However, he shouldn't be so upfront in his rudeness; she would tackle him on it. But first she would get dressed; she would feel less vulnerable then.

'I don't smoke any more but I have friends that do… Excuse me a minute, I will just throw on some clothes while the kettle is boiling.'

Jenny climbed up her stairs, which were situated in the middle of the room along one side. Caldicott, having watched her walk up the stairs, and having observed that a dressing gown was all that Jenny was wearing, had a mad desire to follow her upstairs and rip it off her. This would not do, he thought. He sat himself down to try to keep himself out of mischief. What was the matter with him? This was a suspect.

The kettle boiled. He considered asking her if he should make the coffee, but somehow he thought that she would see it as an insult. Instead, he sat still and waited for her arrival. He hoped that she wasn't making too much of an effort to dress; he rather liked her as she was.

Jenny didn't keep him waiting for more than a couple of minutes. She decided that as she had ruined all her chances by now, it did not matter what she threw on, as long as she felt comfortable in it. He watched her intently as she came back down the stairs. He thought she was beautiful, but noted that she was very pale and hanging onto the banister for dear life. He was concerned. There was no doubt about it; Dr Jordan had taken one hell of a whack to her head earlier in the week. No more was said until she sat down with the coffee. In order to keep his lust in check, he reverted to a more formal approach.

'If you don't mind me saying so, Dr Jordan, you are not looking too well today.'

So it's back to Dr Jordan, is it? Jenny thought. *Oh dear this is a professional call, just when I thought I might be onto something good.* Out loud she said, 'Well, actually I do mind you saying so, but I am sure that you are right; after all, observation is your forte is it not?'

Caldicott mentally kicked himself. *Wrong approach, stupid man!* He thought. *I've been warned that these academics are just like glorified actors: insecure, egotistical and oversensitive, but I thought that this one was more level-headed.*

Jenny noticed his whole body tense and thought that she had been overly rude. She had a tendency to be short with people. Sometimes it was the only way you could shake off unwelcome attention. But she didn't want to warn this one off, quite the contrary. She decided that she would have to soften her approach if she wanted to give him the (correct) impression that she liked him.

'You're right; I'm not at my best. It is all my fault for trying to drink Amelia under the table last night; not a good idea after concussion earlier in the week.'

She saw him visibly relax at that point. *Why?* she asked

herself. *Was it because I mentioned a female name? Maybe he thought I had a man in my bed, and that was why he was being so formal.* The realisation that he might have been resentful of a supposed lover made her smile. It was as radiant as the one she had given when he first met her crossing the grass. He smiled back in response. It lifted her heart.

Had Jenny been a more manipulative woman, at this point she would have played upon the jealousy that she had espied in her suitor, but Jenny didn't participate in those sorts of games. She often wished that she could, because she was pretty certain that she would be more successful with men if she did. Men were stupid. They only seemed to want women who led them a merry dance… It was no good; she would have to be herself.

She continued, 'Amelia is one of the law staff. You may have met her when you went over to the law faculty. You would have noticed her. She is my ideal of female perfection; a tall, golden-haired, nymph-like creature.'

'She sounds intriguing. Perhaps I should go and interrogate her, although I have to say that I prefer Hermias to Helenas. I hope she didn't drive back under the influence.'

This was not the first time that Caldicott has introduced Shakespearean characters in his conversation. Was he trying to impress her, she wondered? The irony was that he seemed to know more about English literature than her students did. Would it be impertinent of her to ask him to sit the English exams? He might just help push up her overall percentage of "good" degrees. She smiled at the thought.

'No, she definitely took a taxi. Her car's outside. At least, I think she's left. I don't remember seeing her this morning. She's not sleeping behind the sofa is she?' Jenny looked behind her sofa, just in case.

'You must have drunk a lot if you don't know if she left or not.' He laughed.

'There was a lot to catch up on,' she said. To his annoyance, Caldicott felt himself blush. Jenny relieved his embarrassment, 'Mainly about my concussion!'

'No better?'

She shook her head. 'Ouch, shouldn't have done that… But you wanted to talk to me…?'

'Yes. Well, two things, neither of which are the best type of after hang-over conversation. Firstly, you will be pleased to hear that your student Bernice is now in a stable condition, but I gather that she has some pretty unpleasant operations to undergo next week. I don't expect that she will be in a position to sit any exams this term.'

Jenny sighed. 'Well, that might not be a bad thing for the English department. Sorry to sound heartless but she really is the most dreadful student. I had been thinking that she might like to stop her studies where she was, and transfer to the theatre studies department. It would be one fewer weak student for us to cope with. And I thought that theatre studies might have suited her better, particularly stripping off… hmm… though perhaps not if she is scarred.'

Caldicott did a double take at Jenny. 'Did I hear you right? Stripping?'

'Yes, let us say that the theatre studies department likes everyone, staff included, to bare all during their performances.'

Caldicott couldn't help but ask, 'And do you, if you are working with them?'

It was Jenny's turn to blush. 'Not if I can help it,' was all that Jenny could say.

The ambiguous answer delighted Caldicott for some reason, but he thought that he had better go back to his rehearsed script. 'We managed to retrieve the poison pen letter from her bag. I have brought it with me. Would you mind looking at it again to confirm that this is the same one you saw?'

'Of course.'

Caldicott handed Jenny the letter in a plastic bag. She looked closely at it. 'This is definitely the same letter, and I am pretty certain that it is the same writing as the one I received. Hmm... I've seen the writing somewhere else too, but I can't remember where. Can I scan this with my printer here? Then if I remember, I will contact you.'

'Yes, by all means.' He probably shouldn't let her do this, he thought, but what the hell.

Jenny continued, 'Is this similar to the writing in your "daffodil letter" and on Medusa's wall?'

'That's an astute thought,' Caldicott smiled. 'Yes, to the daffodil letter. As for the writing on the wall... probably, but the nature of the writing was different, so it is hard to say for certain. I know it's not yours, as I have seen your handwriting on the note you wrote me the other day. I can read this.'

'Bloody cheek!' said Jenny laughing, momentarily forgetting that she was being questioned.

'Onto the second matter, and this is perhaps more sensitive for you, we decided to re-evaluate Professor

Carstairs' post-mortem. It appeared that there was a possibility that some of the initial samples for testing had been contaminated with an alkaloid, so these samples were re-ordered. We also investigated his house and his kitchen in particular. It seems that Carstairs liked cooking, is that correct?'

'Oh yes, not that he ever cooked much when I was around.'

'Did he experiment with herbs, wild plants and so forth?'

'Sometimes. Did he pick the wrong type of mushroom?'

'I would rather not say any more at the moment as we are still redoing the tests, but I thought it might help you to know that in all probability your former partner met his death accidently.'

'Thank you. I am glad to know that. It has been worrying me all week the thought that Tony was deliberately killed. It's bad enough that he died the way he did.'

'Do you miss him?'

'Yes and no. He made me become the sort of person that I never wanted to be; a mean, nagging bitch. I detested myself for it. But it wasn't as though he were blameless. I used to stay at his a lot but I became absolutely sick of being the one who did the laundry, emptied the dishwasher, etc. If I put in a pizza for myself, he managed to eat it all before I had realised that it was cooked. But the biggest bone of contention was his obsession with marking everything I did. It drove me insane. He would say, "Jenny, I give that cake a 2:1 for effort. Oh dear, that cleaning only gets a third today. Put something else on, you are looking like a 2:2 at the moment." I'm afraid that I never got a first for anything I did. It's the main reason we never married.'

Caldicott laughed at this point. 'It's the little things that become the big things, I remember!'

'Are you married?' Jenny asked, delighted to find an excuse to do so.

'Umm, I was, but my wife died…'

'Oh, sorry I asked,' said Jenny, and she was. 'Dare I ask if you have any children?'

'I have a son from another relationship, but he lives with his mother.'

Jenny saw that she was getting too close for comfort with her questions, so she decided to get back to safer ground. 'But I am curious. Why were the original tests incorrect?'

'We are working on that at the moment, but I think that is something that the English department does not have to worry about.'

'I presume no news on Dwaine's car?'

'We are still investigating the matter. It all depends if anyone saw the car being tampered with. It might be that another car was the target.'

'I don't think I even know what car he had. I am not that interested in cars, I'm afraid. Have you checked this with the porter's lodge? They have a file on all cars that are owned by staff or students.'

'Yes, it was a white Mercedes. Normally this would be a rather expensive purchase, so there are not many of your colleagues or students who have one of those. In fact, there are only two others. One belongs to your dean and another belongs to a student in the medical school, who lives on this campus. Can you think of any reason why either of these would be a target for sabotage?'

Jenny adopted a somewhat frosty exterior. 'I think, Mr Caldicott, you know very well that there is no love lost between myself and my dean. I told you myself on our first official meeting that I could happily kill him, however, I haven't yet. Nor do I know how to sabotage his car, except perhaps to induce a leak in the brake-fluid system.'

Caldicott looked at Jenny keenly. 'You know, you really need to stop being so open with me. It is precisely an issue of brake fluid that we are looking at, although sometimes these errors occur naturally, especially if the driver hasn't been maintaining his car effectively. I gather Dwaine was short of money, so if he didn't have his car serviced, it might very well result in this.'

'Yes, he was terribly behind with his fees. We were not supposed to be teaching him, but the view of the English department is that it only diminishes our chances of getting the students up to a decent level of education. They can't graduate until they clear their debts, but stopping them attending lectures and seminars is counterproductive in an age when we want more firsts and 2:1s. Not that Dwaine would have got more than a lower second, even if he had attended every class going.'

She continued, 'In terms of Hardwicke being a potential victim? Well, I can think of a number of people who would happily say goodbye to the man. Hardwicke is a misogynist and most of the female staff would like him removed, but he also manages to offend the men as well. He is just an unpleasant person, and that's all I can say. He is rude, doesn't apologise if he should, makes inappropriate remarks and so forth. Also, if you remember, there was some trouble last year with the rape of the theatre studies student and I do seem to remember that Hardwicke was called in to interrogate staff. It didn't go down well, and a few staff swore revenge. I probably shouldn't be saying all this to you.'

'On the contrary, I always find your outlook refreshing. That is why I always ask you first.'

'I don't know any medical students so I can't assist you with the other one I'm afraid.'

'I didn't think you could.'

Here the conversation came to a natural end. Caldicott had to readjust his thinking before starting it up again.

'I'm going on annual leave on Wednesday for two weeks. It has been booked up before I started here and for personal reasons, I have to go; otherwise I would postpone my trip. DC Stone will be looking after the cases in the interim. I am hoping that he will clear everything up quickly. Either way, I will call on you when I return. Thank you for the coffee. I need to go and finish as much paperwork as I can, so that I do not get a whipping from my line manager on my return. I don't think that I will complete it all unless I work all night...' he smiled, '... but then I expect that you know all about that,' he said pointing to a pile of unmarked second year assignments.

He longed to say more but although this might be the place it certainly wasn't the time for either of them. Until the deaths at the university were cleared up, until he had found the graffiti artist, he did not feel free to speak his mind to Jenny. He sincerely hoped that on his return he would find it all sorted by his colleague. But he had worked with DC Stone for a month now, and in Stone, identified a man without any creative thinking. If a crime was in front of his nose, he probably wouldn't spot it. Caldicott was also concerned for Jenny's safety. As much as he hoped things were over, he sensed that they had only just begun. He wished he could postpone his trip.

'I am sure that DC Stone will assist you if you need help, so please call him.'

'Is that likely?' Jenny asked, surprised.

Caldicott looked apprehensive. 'Hopefully not. Anyway, you are flying out to the Bahamas next week are you not? So that is one week that you can't get into trouble at Sedgemoor.'

Jenny visibly relaxed. 'Yes, I'm looking forward to the sun although I really don't think that I will see any of it. Meetings you know.'

'Yes, I do. Well, thanks for the coffee. Have a pleasant weekend.'

And with that he was gone, leaving Jenny with a sinking feeling in her heart. She supposed that he couldn't say any more than he had said to her, even if he had wanted to, as he was still investigating the university. How she wished it was all over.

Jenny's mind turned to Carstairs. It was a pity that he never fully achieved his ambitions, but rarely did any of the staff here. The only people who were promoted to professor were the ones who should have been demoted to cleaner. It was the same at every university, she was told.

"Professor usually means, bull-shitter, arse-licker or related to someone who has a deep pocket." Dryden had once said. That was after Hardwicke had been given a chair. When asked which category Hardwicke fell into the reply was, "All three!" It had stuck in everyone's gullet that Hardwicke, a man with a superficial knowledge of literature, should be promoted. Jenny was glad that she wasn't overly ambitious. *Poor Malcolm Lowry*, she thought, *always overlooked.* He had seemed really miserable for the last year, ever since his promotion had been turned down in favour of Hardwicke. It really did stink.

*

To cheer herself up, and as a way of evading the pile of marking sitting in her cottage, Jenny decided to go shopping in Taunton, later that day. Whenever Jenny felt down, she would get a buzz from spending money on something that she had longed for. The trouble was when the money came to an end a horrible feeling of guilt kicked in, so the whole process was somewhat self-defeating. *Still, I do need to get some clothes and sunscreen for the Bahamas*, she thought, *and I don't want to leave everything until next weekend.*

Her shopping trip was extremely enjoyable. She parked in the town centre and spent over two hours looking at clothes and accessories. She didn't buy very much, but she purchased all the things that she genuinely needed. That really cheered her up. Her last stop for the day was to be the Starbucks which sat behind the Market House in the town centre.

She took one step into the cafe and then quickly left it. Sitting at a table with his back to the door was a man who looked very much like Caldicott. Sitting opposite him was a beautiful, albeit somewhat older, brunette. The brunette was holding the man's hand. Jenny didn't dare go in any further. If it really was Caldicott, and she was pretty certain that it was, then she didn't want him to see her.

So much for paperwork, Jenny thought. She now realised the meaning of the swift goodbye this morning. He was seeing this woman. Jenny felt a huge wave of misery hit her body. *This is ridiculous*, she said to herself. *What had he ever done but be slightly less than professional? Perhaps he takes all the women he meets out to coffee. He had dinner with me, but he has never tried to hold my hand, so why am I so upset?* Then she realised that she was upset because he hadn't tried to hold her hand! She walked back to her car with her shopping and drove home. Amelia's car was gone by that stage. She thought that was a pity; she would have liked to unburden herself on Amelia.

For the first time in over three weeks, Jenny finally summoned up the courage to tackle her pile of Shakespeare assignments that required marking. In the vicious mood that she was in, there were no firsts, and due to the lack of compassion for mankind only three reached an upper second class mark. 'Buggeration,' she said, 'I will have a look at these again tomorrow, and hopefully I will feel more charitable towards them.'

Tomorrow came and went, so did Monday. Jenny did not hear from Caldicott, nor did she try to make contact. She re-marked her essays, and found it in her heart to award one first and five more 2:1s. A total of 23 per cent higher grades, she had said to Dryden who was second marking them. 'Try your best to improve on that.'

'Not likely is it?' He smiled.

'No, not at all,' she agreed. 'But at least none are plagiarised, unlike some of the ones you gave to me,' she added sadly.

*

Caldicott had wanted to phone Jenny on Tuesday, before he went on leave, but he couldn't find an adequate excuse to do so. He was left in confusion by his feelings on Saturday. He desperately wanted her, but she was the prime suspect. No, he couldn't speak to her until everything was over, one way or the other.

CHAPTER 13
WEDNESDAY, 20 APRIL

For Jenny, the week had dragged on. It was now Wednesday morning. A planned faculty meeting was cancelled. Jenny was delighted as she would be able to catch up with her ever increasing backlog of work.

Having deposited the last of her essays with Dryden, she picked up yet more correspondence from Tom and sat down to open her emails. She had answered all of two out of seventy of these when Gwendolyn invaded her office.

'Dr Jordan, dear Dr Jordan,' she started.

Oh no, thought Jenny, *what is this going to be all about?*

'It's about Mr Smith; I really need to speak to you about him.'

'Why, what has Percy done now?'

'What hasn't he done? Well, firstly that immature comment at Friday's assembly.' Gwen pulled a face which equalled that of a fried haddock.

'Oh, I wouldn't worry about that,' Jenny said lightly, 'everyone thought it was funny. Besides, Professor Bottomley really did look like a prostitute.'

'Really, I thought better of you than that.'

'Gwendolyn, is that all?' Jenny was getting fed up with

Gwen. The woman was a tittle-tattle. Jenny had known that for ages. There was a secret code sent to the "in-crowd" (of which Jenny used to be one), when Gwen was stalking the corridor. Everyone would rush back to their desks and aim to look incredibly busy. It was well known that Gwen would report back to her line manager as to who was in and who should have been around and wasn't. When Gwen was safely stowed in her room, a signal would be sent around, and everyone would congregate in one office for a good chat. Most of the staff thought that Gwen's activities were funny, but they were confused as to why she wasted her time doing this. The answer was simple, but Jenny did not find it out until she took over as head. It was to cover up for the fact that Professor Jones knew sweet FA about English literature, as evidenced by the significant number of student complaints that Jenny had received.

Jenny was shocked to realise that the woman was even more of a fraud than Hardwicke. She had not believed that it was possible. She now understood why neither of them had complained about the other. The truth of the matter was that neither knew enough about their subject matter to work out that the other knew nothing about theirs. No wonder Gwen took five months to lecture on *Beowulf*; that was all she knew about. And Jenny had developed a sneaking feeling that she only knew as much as she did from watching the recent TV series, which, she was informed, didn't even accurately portray the book. *Is this why we have poor results?* Jenny asked herself.

Gwen was screeching on, 'No it is not. Mr Smith was supposed to second mark my scripts, but look at them, look at them!!'

'What am I supposed to be looking for? Is that his scrawl in green pen?'

'No, No! That is mine. His is in black. He has not marked the scripts properly.'

'In what way? I still don't understand.'

'He is supposed to put comments on the front page. He has not done so.'

'Okay, so he has made an error, but I see that he has made lots of comments on the essays themselves, so that is nothing serious. Just tell him.'

'He won't listen to me, you must tell him yourself. You are his line manager.'

Jenny was getting more irate as the moments passed. 'Gwen, you are my deputy. It is in your authority to correct junior staff members of minor errors.'

Gwen was persistent. 'That is not all.'

'What else is there? What would you like me to do Gwen?'

'Well, obviously I would like you to have a word with him. It is totally outrageous. That boy treats this place like a hotel. He comes in at three minutes past nine and leaves as soon as his teaching is over and sometimes before it is supposed to be finished! He says he can't concentrate on his research because I keep interrupting him.'

Jenny started to lose her temper with Gwen. 'Well Gwen, do you?'

'No, I just go in to check that he has the right notes and the right copy of the book, I really don't see that I have done anything wrong in doing that. After all, it is my course, and he should be grateful that I let him teach on it at all.'

'Gwen, I don't want to be too rude here, but you know Anglo-Saxon literature isn't everyone's cup of tea. I know that Percy is very keen on the more modern genres, so I think you, perhaps, should be a little more respectful of Percy's skills. It is out of his comfort zone, and he does do it quite well.'

'But if only that were it. The man is a libertine.'

'Really? That is news. What has he been doing?'

'The other day, I saw him grab Joyce's bottom.'

This was too much for Jenny. 'Which Joyce? A student?

'No, Joyce James, our teaching fellow.'

'Did she complain to you?'

'No, of course not; why should she?'

'Well then, are you complaining on her behalf?'

Gwen started to go red in the face. Never had Jenny been so dismissive of her. 'Really I expected better from you, Dr Jordan. You are the head of department. It is your duty to challenge poor behaviour. It's not fair! It should have been me! I should be the head of department; I should be flying to the Bahamas, not you! All the years that I have worked here; it's disgraceful.'

Jenny said calmly but through gritted teeth, 'Dear Professor Jones, I am so sorry that you feel this way. To be honest, I would be extremely grateful if you were to take over as head. In fact, I told Hardwicke to give you the post. He told me that you didn't want it.'

'Oh, that wicked, wicked, man! Of course I wanted to be head.'

Jenny's face looked like thunder. 'Well, make your protest to Hardwicke, but please don't grumble to me.

You have made a complaint against Percy, so I will have to waste the rest of my day, and Tom's, investigating it. Thank you very much Professor Jones, I will be grateful if you could leave now, so that I may get on with my enquiries.'

And with that, Jenny almost forced Gwen out of the door. 'Tom, come here will you?'

Tom ambled into the office. Jenny explained the problem. Tom was as impressed as Jenny had been.

'Bitch!' was all he could say.

*

Percy was duly summoned. When at first Jenny explained the situation to him, he was shocked.

'But what is her problem? I don't understand it. I did everything that she asked me to do with the marking. She specifically said do NOT write on the front cover.'

'Of course Gwen will deny that. Now, moving on to the alleged incident of Joyce's backside.'

'It was a joke. I said that she had a bum that was better than Beyonce's. You know that they are distant cousins, don't you? Joyce didn't mind; actually, I think she rather liked it, particularly as it made Shelley jealous.'

'Are you and Shelley an item now?'

'Well, sort of…'

'Crikey! I've missed that one. For God's sake don't let Gwen know or there will be another complaint! It's very boring but I will have to ask both Joyce and Shelley about it. In the interim, arrive at nine, do not leave until you have finished your teaching hours – no, don't look at me like that. I did see you bunking off early last week. Keep your hands to yourself, in the corridor, anyway. And for God's sake keep away from frustrated spinsters!'

CHAPTER 14
THURSDAY, 21 APRIL

The week had limped through until Thursday. Jenny had not spoken to Caldicott, or he to her since Saturday morning. She knew that he was now on annual leave, but she did not know where. She told herself to forget it and carry on with her work. That made things even more unbearable.

Her mother had once told her, "If you are happy in your relationship and unhappy at work, you can cope. Likewise, if you love your job and hate your partner, you will be fine. Only call your mother if you hate both your job and your man…"

Jenny would have loved to have spoken to her mother, but her mother was no longer alive. She had died some four years ago. Jenny felt her absence enormously. It was at times like this that she just wanted someone to talk to and listen to her. She would never follow her mum's advice, of course, but at least she could release her feelings.

Today she had a very good reason to phone her mum. She had been alerted to five poor essays, all allegedly written by the same student. These had been forwarded to her by five different tutors assessing five different areas of English, all with potential plagiarism marked on them. In fact, one comment written on the work from an examiner boldly stated, "If this isn't plagiarism there is no such thing." On top of this, the candidate's dissertation had also registered a warning mark in the Turnitin system. The most annoying aspect of this situation was that this student was one who had been flagged up as a potential first class candidate by Hardwicke.

'Huh,' Dryden had said, 'that is why she has first class marks to date; she is copying everyone else's work.'

Jenny knew that she had an unpleasant task ahead of her. She braced herself for the visitor by asking Tom to make her coffee. This was almost unheard of. At nine thirty, there was a knock on the door.

'Maya Dewley to see you,' Tom said.

'Come in Maya and have a seat. Would you like some water? Tom, be an angel and get some water and glasses for us, then please come and minute this. Otherwise I may not get it right. Right Maya. Do you know why you have been called into my office?'

'It's because I haven't paid my fees isn't it, miss?'

'Not precisely. You do have a problem with your funding, but that can be sorted out if you finish your course. What we do is withhold the classification and the award until you pay us in full. So in the short term that isn't an issue. The problem is that looking at all the information I have been sent by a number of tutors, you are unlikely to be graduating at all.'

By this time Tom had returned and was minute taking.

'What do you mean miss, I done all my work.'

'Well, now, that is a matter of opinion. Yes, you have submitted your assignments on time, including your dissertation which is worth 30 per cent of your final year's mark, but the trouble is that certain staff have informed me that they believe that you have not submitted *your own* work, but someone else's.'

'No miss, I typed it all myself, I done my research on the Internet.'

'Yes, we can see that, but the trouble is that you appear to have copied and pasted all your paragraphs from information that you found on the Internet. To make matters worse, a significant amount of it has come from Wikipedia.'

'That's a good site.'

'Um… yes, and no. It can be a useful quick referencing point, but has no academic credit. But regardless of where it comes from you can't just "copy and paste" your answers. That is academic theft. Let me show you. You submitted your essays through the Turnitin system, the anti-plagiarism software.'

'But that is rubbish, everyone says it doesn't get it right.'

'Well, it has its limitations, but on the whole, if used by staff appropriately, it will let us know where there are correlations in your work and the work of another. See, this is your Turnitin report on your Wordsworth assignment. It has a 95 per cent match with an essay submitted to the University of Leicester. Can you explain why that might be?'

'Well, my cousin goes there; she might have taken my essay and submitted it.'

'That was indeed a possibility, but unfortunately for you Maya, I have asked for the corresponding essay to be revealed, and the lecturer concerned kindly released it to me. Your cousin's essay was submitted over a year ago, long before you were even given the essay title here. What is more, although the Leicester essay is an excellent answer to the question set, it does not really answer the question that *we* set. Do you see my point?'

Maya looked at the essay. 'Oh, but that is the wrong one. I have submitted the wrong one into the system. I am sorry; my own essay must be on my hard drive still.'

'Maya, Turnitin asks you when you attach a document, whether the first page of the item uploaded is what you want to submit.'

'I didn't bother looking at that as I was near the deadline.'

'Yes, I see that you had seconds left before you were locked out of your account.'

'But I helped my cousin write it, so why should I get in trouble?'

Jenny did not believe one word of Maya's excuses but she had a ready answer to this one. 'Maya, did you know that it is also an academic offence to assist someone else in writing their essay? See paragraph 4 (b) (i) of the regulations on academic misconduct. It is the same for all universities. Now, coming back to your dissertation on Bacon, here is the Turnitin report for this.'

Jenny handed over several sheets of typed paper with distinct colour bandings on every page. In fact, every word on the page was covered in some coloured highlighter, indicating that none of the work was the author's own.

'Now Maya, what can you say about this?'

'Well, I done my research from different sites.' And looking at the match reports indicating various websites, she added, 'Yes, these are the sites that I used.'

'Yes indeed, but where are your references?'

155

'What do you mean?'

'You are supposed to acknowledge the source of your research – particularly quotes of which this is a composite piece.'

'I dunno what you mean about references.'

'Does the Harvard style mean anything to you?'

'That's a place in America isn't it?'

'Yes indeed and birthplace to a specific style of referencing which you have been asked to adopt for all your summative assignments.'

'But I didn't know – nobody told me.'

'Maya, we had a training session on this, during the first week of your first term.'

'Ah, but I started late, see.'

'We had a repeat session at the first week of your second term.'

'I was on holiday then.'

'We also sent round by email, information on individual training sessions for those that had missed the original sessions.'

'Oh, I never received my emails.'

'Okay, let us put it another way. How did you know what essay to write? You have put the question in your answer, so you obviously read the assignment title.'

'It was in a booklet with the module details.'

'Correct. In fact, a booklet like this?'

Jenny held up an A4 booklet stapled on one side, marked "Wordsworth – Third year assignment". She passed it over to Maya.

'Yes? And can you turn to page five please and read it to me.'

'Assignments must be fully referenced in the Harvard style. Any student unfamiliar with this style is requested to ask for help… Ah, but miss, this page wasn't in my booklet!'

'Nor in any other of the assignment booklets that staff gave out? Maya, you are beginning to try my patience. It is bad enough that you have been found out by the Turnitin software, but now you are trying to make up quite ridiculous excuses for not doing as requested.'

'But nobody told me what I was supposed to do. Why does this all matter anyway?'

Jenny exchanged glances with Tom. Never had either of them come across such blatant plagiarism. The concern was that it had proved extremely difficult in the past for students to get the punishment that they deserved, and the students knew it. Nor, on a pragmatic level, was it good to expel students if they were debtors, as then the university would never be able to retrieve its finances.

'I have gone through the evidence and you have not told me anything to assist your case. Ignorance of the law is no defence, and even if it was, before submitting each of your essays you signed a disclaimer saying that you had not plagiarised any submitted material. I am willing to accept that there have been some difficulties with attending classes due to your non-payments of fees, but I have no alternative than to find that the alleged offence of plagiarism has been made out on two of these six essays submitted. Regarding the other four essays, it does appear that you have attempted to do some of the work for yourself, so in that case I will send them back to the examiners, with the instructions for them to mark your work on what they believe to be your effort alone. I should imagine you will receive a mark in the range of 30 to 40 per cent.

'In regard to the two assignments that we have discussed today, your essay on Wordsworth and your dissertation on Bacon, you will be awarded a mark of zero. You have the right to resubmit your assignments by the end of June for a capped mark of 40 per cent. I can tell you now, that taking all these into account, and examining your previous marks, you will be graduating with a third class degree at best.'

'What, not a first?'

'No, definitely not a first.' Jenny handed Maya a booklet. 'You have a right of appeal. Here is the appeal policy; read it carefully. You have twenty-eight days to appeal to the dean of humanities, Professor Hardwicke. You must discuss this with Dr Lowry, your personal tutor, first.'

'Oh, they will be on my side; well, Hardwicke will.'

'I am sure that he will, but even he will find it difficult to justify your two pieces of work here.'

'I'm sure that I can persuade him otherwise; I did last year.' And saying that, she left with a shake of her hair in a mood of total defiance.

Jenny and Tom were left speechless. 'She doesn't think that she has done anything wrong Tom!'

'No, I saw that.'

'Well, if that is the message they have been receiving when Hardwicke was the head of department, then there is no way we can change this around overnight. I hope she doesn't get to sit the exams, it will be a complete waste of time for all concerned, and more to the point it will be another notch against us – a third at best. Tom, you've done the stats, where are we going to get any firsts from this year if they are all like that? I didn't realise that we had such a bad set of finalists.'

'There are one or two hopefuls: McClellan is a clear first, so is Chowdry, and then we have Webster and Roberts. They should all do it. In terms of upper seconds, we should have Doyle, Mitchell, Cody and possibly Browning, but then we will be struggling to get the others to the upper second level.'

'We could bring in reinforcement lessons for those on the 2:2 cusp. That might do it for Mantuwa and Khan, and possibly even Miller. How many does that make?'

'Ten at best, so out of our total of twenty-nine finalists, possibly twenty-eight if Bernice cannot sit the exams, that gives us in the region of 36 per cent good degrees.'

'That's nowhere near our target. We need to find a mechanism to intervene in their studies. We might be all right with some of the middling students if we could suspend their studies for a few months and ask them to take the exams as a first attempt in August. I think that could work for Eliot and Fitzgerald. It won't work for Bernice, but I have a cunning plan to send her to theatre studies, if she recovers, that is.'

'What about Lawrence?' Tom asked.

'Not a chance, his writing style is altogether too sloppy. Ideally, we need to stop the hopeless bunch sitting the exams altogether. I presume that the percentage is worked out on how many complete the course, not how many are in the year?'

'Yes,' said Tom, 'that is correct. So, out of the twenty-nine, we need to remove at least five.'

'Well,' said Jenny pacing her office by now, 'Bernice is probably one, but you can't count on it because she tends to do her own thing.'

Tom quickly did the maths. 'That would give us a chance of reaching a 50 per cent target.'

'That is just about okay for this year, but we will need to get the results up to 70 per cent next year, with even weaker students!'

Tom tried to calm Jenny down. 'One step at a time,' he said. 'We will worry about that next year.'

'Yes, if we still have a job, that is. In the interim, I wish that we could remove Maya and her pals completely. Tom, if you come up with any ideas let me know.'

'Am I your fairy godmother? I don't think that I can grant that wish for you.'

But, although Tom said that he could not grant any of Jenny's wishes, someone did. That following evening, perhaps in a continued act of defiance or perhaps as a result of a period of remorse, Maya took a dangerous combination of drugs and alcohol, and thinking that she was Wonder Woman and could fly, she ended the night, and her life, by falling off the multi-storey car park in Minehead. It should have been an open and shut case. Should have been…

CHAPTER 15
SATURDAY, 23 APRIL

On Saturday morning, Jenny was rudely awakened by a knock on her door. *I wonder who that is*, she thought to herself. She was in the process of finding her dressing gown when a shower of stones hit her bedroom window. 'Bloody vandals,' Jenny said. She was even more surprised, on opening the door, to find that the missiles were launched by a man in a trench coat and a woman in a police uniform. The man waved a card in front of Jenny's nose so frantically, that she was unable to read it.

'DC Stone and PC Swift. Now then Dr Jordan, we have a number of questions for you about Maya Dewley.'

Jenny may have been semi-comatose, but she had twigged that this was serious. Caldicott had never behaved with such urgency or indeed with such discourtesy. 'May I know why?' is all she could say.

'It would be easier if we were to talk inside, or you can come with us to the station.'

'Would you like to come in?' she said in a resigned fashion, knowing that she had no choice. Somewhat ironically, her cottage was in an immaculate state as she had made a real effort to ensure it was tidy before she went to the Bahamas.

She led them to the sofa and asked them to sit down. *But I am not making them coffee*, she thought.

'Right then, Dr Jordan. You may be unaware that at 00.43 hours this morning, Miss Dewley jumped off the multi-storey car park in Minehead and died of her injuries some three hours later. Can you shed any light on what might have been disturbing Miss Dewley?'

Jenny was shell-shocked. She had wanted to get rid of Maya, and the girl was no longer alive. It could be argued that retribution acts swiftly, but Jenny really did not think that she should express her opinions freely. She was pretty certain that it would not go down well with this clearly humourless policeman.

'Well, I am, of course, very sorry to hear about Ms Dewley's death, but I am surprised to hear that she might have been excessively disturbed by anything that took place recently. It is true that Ms Dewley was under investigation for academic misconduct, but she did not seem at all upset when she left my office.'

'I see; when was this?'

'When did the misconduct take place? Judging by her file, ever since she had started her course.'

'No, no, I mean what about yesterday might have made her, shall we say, susceptible to her actions?'

'Our discussions took place on Thursday. I know nothing about yesterday. Mr Stone, believe me, I had reason to find the case made out against her. I am more than happy to show you the evidence that she accumulated against herself. If you do not believe me you may ask any member of the teaching team, and additionally my administrator who was present during the enquiry.'

'No, that won't be necessary. Now then, did she feel persecuted by your conviction?'

Jenny thought, *what sort of language is the man using? It is like something out of the nineteenth century.* Jenny was beginning to feel victimised, herself.

'Mr Stone, I am afraid that you have this all wrong. If anyone felt persecuted then it was me. Miss Dewley was in total denial about the seriousness of her actions. Moreover, she alerted me to the fact that this was not the first time that such an enquiry had taken place. This was a third year student about to graduate using someone else's work as the basis for awarding them a degree. What did surprise her, this time, was that I said that I was intending to give her a mark of zero for her work. In other words, I was not prepared to let her off. I am sure that you understand that if you catch a thief, and plagiarism is academic theft, then you would want the perpetrator to be punished accordingly, would you not?'

'Yes, well…' This was clearly beyond Stone's grasp. 'Is there anyone who would benefit from her death?'

Only the whole faculty, thought Jenny. Out loud she said, 'Not that I am aware of.'

'Did she do drugs regularly?'

'I really have no idea, but her academic record to date was nothing short of atrocious, so that it would not surprise me if she did.'

'Where did she go after she left your office?'

'The University regulations specify that anyone initially found guilty of plagiarism has a right of appeal to the faculty dean, or in the absence of a dean, the VC, after a consultation with their personal tutor. Judging by her comment when she left my office, I would surmise that she went to make an appointment to see Professor Hardwicke, our faculty dean, in order to appeal, and in order to do that, she would have first had to see her personal tutor who is Dr Lowry. I gather that she was an expert at appealing, as she had had ample practice at it during the last two years. I do not, however, know if she did actually make one.'

'Very well. That is all for now. We will be in contact.'

Yes, unfortunately I think you will, said Jenny to herself.

'Oh, just one more thing, is this book yours?' Stone showed Jenny a copy of *Falling* by Elizabeth Jane Howard.

'Does it have my name inside?'

'Yes.'

'Then it must be mine. Where did you find it?'

'It was in Miss Dewley's pocket. Did you give it to her?'

'No, not at all, perhaps she took it when she was in my office.'

'Well, we will keep it for the moment. I will write you a receipt.'

In complete contrast with her previous dealings with the police, or more to the point Caldicott, who had started to alter Jenny's preconceptions of detectives in general, this one fell straight back into the thick delusional stereotype that Jenny had read about. Pompous, arrogant, bombastic, words failed to sum up the qualities she had just witnessed during the course of her interview. Jenny vowed to be of no further assistance in the matter.

Had Jenny been asked different questions, or, perhaps more to the point, had she been asked the same questions using a more open-minded approach, she might have been able to answer more effectively. Likewise, had it been Caldicott who had interviewed her and valued her acute observational skills, the case may have been solved at this point. But no, this heralded the start of the escalation of unpleasant incidents, all of which could easily have been avoided by appropriate action at this stage.

Jenny spent the rest of the day packing for her trip to the Bahamas. She was extremely angry. Angry that she had to go to the Bahamas; angry that her head still hurt her, angry that the time seemed to rush by and she had no way of accounting for it, and incredibly angry that her dopey students were constantly doping or worse. But most of all she was angry with herself for falling for a policeman who preferred older women and she was angry with Caldicott for letting her fall for him. She sat down and cried, frustrated in every single aspect of her life.

Once she came around, she telephoned Tom and Dryden and filled them in on her visitation. They said that they would tackle the monolith if he came to question them. (She did not contact Gwen, as she was still annoyed with her peevish behaviour from earlier in the week.) With that, she had to be satisfied that something would be done to stop the drugs culture taking hold of the English department in her absence. It was too much to hope for, she realised. As pleased as she was to remove an academic disaster from her lists, Jenny was exceptionally unhappy that a student had ended her life in a drug-induced state, and cursed Maya for being so stupid. In this, Jenny was unwittingly being unfair to Maya. On this one occasion, Maya had not been responsible for her seemingly foolish actions.

CHAPTER 16
MONDAY, 25 APRIL:
The Trip to the Bahamas

It was finally the day of the marketing trip to the Bahamas. Most of the staff were going to Heathrow by minibus the night before and were staying at the Marriott Hotel, but Jenny made an invalid friend an excuse for her non-conformity, and told the others that she would make her own way to the terminal on the Monday morning.

She decided to travel by coach to Heathrow Airport, which arrived at the horribly early time of half past seven in the morning. As the flight was not due until twenty-five minutes past ten, she had plenty of time to amuse herself. After checking in her luggage and undergoing the boredom of the security searches, Jenny arrived at the duty-free section and sauntered around the various shops. She decided that she ought to buy something to read to help her endure what was bound to be an excruciatingly long fourteen-hour journey, so she entered the branch of WH Smith to look for reading material. Out of the corner of her eye, she noticed Hardwicke, looking through a row of magazines. He seemed to be getting more and more worked up. He clearly couldn't find what he wanted. Jenny wondered if he was trying to find what is euphemistically referred to as a "gentleman's magazine".

Not that long ago it was relatively easy to buy a "lads' mag" to entertain the man in your life, or yourself. Now it was impossible to find these on the average supermarket shelf. Jenny knew, as she had tried to buy one to give to Tony as a birthday present the year previously.

Amused by Hardwicke's not-so nonchalant actions, Jenny positioned herself behind a nearby postcard stand, in the pretext of choosing a card. Oh yes, he was reading through every magazine to try to find something to titillate him, no doubt. She wondered if he would spend money on any of the magazines. *I can't imagine that man spending any money on something he invariably gets for free*, Jenny thought.

Hardwicke suddenly swooped on a magazine. She watched his face reach for it with the pure expectation of pleasure. She was not quite sure what magazine he had, but she could tell by the cover that it held scantily-clad females. As predicted, he did not intend to purchase the journal; he merely wanted to gaze through it to entertain himself for a while. Jenny soon reached her boredom threshold, and she was about to leave her hiding place, when she noticed a sudden change in the professor's demeanour. In a split second, this libertine had been tamed into a quivering wreck. He dropped the magazine that he was holding as though it was made of molten metal. He picked it up, shoved it back into the stand, turned and fled out of the store.

Jenny had a look around to identify what might have made him react in this manner. As she could see no obvious reason for his swift departure, she concluded that it must have been something in the magazine itself. She resolved to buy it, to see if she could work out what he was looking at. There were two journals out of place in the section for angling magazines. She picked them up and looked at the titles, *Sport's Summer Bikini Sizzlers*, and *Zoo*. *It has to be one of these* she thought. She started to look through them, but she felt an idiot standing there; supposing one of her students came up to her? She was pretty certain it was *Zoo* that Hardwicke had been looking at, but just to be on the safe side she decided to buy both magazines. *Well, in for a penny in for a pound*, she thought. She didn't want to be standing around for too long with her "hot" magazines, so she took them to the nearest empty till. The man serving her gave her an inquisitive stare whilst asking her if she would like to purchase a bag. 'Yes please,' said Jenny. She thought, *I am just going to have to brazen this out.*

Having her secret purchases safely bagged up, she then spent a longer time browsing in another store for the type of reading material that she really wanted.

'Oh darling, how wonderful. Isn't it simply marvellous that we are going to the Bahamas?' Dr Touchwood was at her side.

'Yes, indeed,' Jenny responded. 'I do hope that the university can pay for us all.'

'Of course it can, darling. Reg and I are going for a coffee; would you like to join us?'

Dr Touchwood was accompanied by a young man no more than twenty in age, sporting a hangdog expression. Every time he looked at Medusa, Jenny could hear him pant. The young man did not look like he wanted Jenny's company; neither did she want either of theirs.

'Thanks, but I want to make sure that I have all I need to work with on the plane. I will get a coffee later.'

'So dedicated, isn't she, Reg? So marvellous. Darling, see you later.'

See you in hell, thought Jenny.

It was only after they had parted that Jenny realised the young man was Reg White, one of her own English students, and one of several no-shows to her classes. Bahamian by birth, he was obviously promising to show Medusa all the sights of his home islands. *Goodness only knows what Medusa has shown him*, she thought. No wonder her students were all underachieving. If they were not "spliffed out" to the max, then they were being screwed to death by the theatre studies staff. Reg was destined for a third class degree; there were no redeeming features about his academic achievements to date.

If only Hardwicke was a reliable dean she could ask him to demand a modification in staff behaviour. But he was the worst of the lot. She was so shocked by this turn of events, that she completely forgot her mission to examine the Hardwicke magazines in the toilets, and leave them there. They ended up in Jenny's hand luggage boarding a flight to a destination some four thousand miles away.

*

The London to Bahamas flight took Jenny and her colleagues to Nassau International Airport, which lies just outside the capital city. Having deliberately avoided all university personnel until now, Jenny tried to identify some of the more reliable staff to share a taxi with. As it was, a shuttle van had been arranged for the whole university group. Soon Jenny was established in the Atlantis Hotel.

The hotel had shocked her with its magnificence. *This is ridiculous* she thought. *No wonder we have no money for essential maintenance at the university. This whole trip must have cost thousands of pounds.*

Looking at the price of the rooms in Bahamian dollars, she calculated that each room, including an additional single supplement fee, must have set back the university to the tune of three hundred pounds per night each. That was nine hundred pounds for her alone. The flights were over fifteen hundred pounds for a return ticket. Therefore, not including food, drinks and travel, each person on this trip would set the university back the princely sum of nearly two and a half thousand pounds. She had lost count of how many staff members she had seen, but thought that, counting all the student representatives, there were over twenty in the party all told. Therefore the minimum cost to the university was over fifty thousand pounds. Of course, if they managed to sign up three students, the expenditure would be worth it, but if they didn't… what a colossal amount of money down the drain.

At the last minute, Jenny decided that she would visit Dwaine's family in Long Island later that week, and attend a memorial service for him. That meant altering her flight back. This had cost Jenny over a thousand pounds of her own money. At first, she was going to pay for it out of her own pocket, but when she realised that this was a meagre outlay compared to the whole extravaganza, she asked the

VC if he would reimburse this fee and the cost of three further nights' accommodation and travel to Long Island.

'Good idea,' said the VC. 'It is important to be seen to do the right thing to promote the reputation of the care we give at this university. Finance will pay you back on your arrival home.'

Opinion was divided amongst her colleagues as to whether departmental money should be spent in this way. Dryden told her to go and enjoy herself. 'Let's face it; if you lose your job in a couple of months, at least you can say that you got a trip to the Bahamas out of it.' That was the pragmatic view that most of the staff took. Gwen, on the other hand, was furious that Jenny was allowed to go at all. Her face became more contorted than ever.

CHAPTER 17
WEDNESDAY, 27 APRIL:
Poolside Tragedy

From the minute that the university entourage had reached the Royal Towers of the Atlantis complex, Robert Wiley, the group organiser, had given detailed, one might say over the top, directives. He became extremely agitated if his instructions were not adhered to.

'Dinner at six. I repeat, dinner at SIX on the dot, ladies and gentlemen. We have our first public meeting at half past seven in the Atlantis Theatre. Yes, that is correct: 7.30 pm, not 7.32 pm,' he said looking at Medusa.

'I don't know why he is looking at me,' cried Medusa.

Someone near to Jenny said, 'Neither do I – that would be too punctual for her.'

Robert sensed that he was losing control. 'I say, do pay attention. This is followed by drinks in the casino, for those with a flutter in mind. This is not obligatory and the money must be your own, not the university's. We had a very unfortunate incident two years ago, when our then vice chancellor, decided that he would play roulette with money that the university had just been donated. Needless to say that his luck was out and this is why we have our new VC, Professor Everson.'

At this point the loud sound of clapping could be heard, coming primarily from the VC himself.

'Tomorrow we are going to the College of the Bahamas where we have an all-day conference. The coach picks us up at 9.30 am pronto. You will be returned safe and sound by 17.47. Students, where are my students? Oh, there you are. I am afraid that your presentation is the most important of all, so to accommodate you, if you don't make the coach, we will provide you with a taxi, to arrive in time for your talk at 14.21.

'Lucky buggers,' Hardwicke said. 'Hah! I was hoping to stay in bed!'

'How much longer is this man going to drone on?' Professor Hastings muttered.

A kindred spirit Jenny thought.

Robert continued, 'You will be free to do what you want on your return.'

'Have a good fuck, I hope,' Professor Silvanus Straw was heard to say. Hardwicke roared with laughter.

Crikey, who with? thought Jenny. *Nobody could be that desperate, surely?* He was truly the most repulsive specimen of manhood within a thirty-mile radius. If there was to be a murder on this trip, Jenny sincerely hoped that Straw would be the victim.

Robert continued, 'On Wednesday we are at Bahamas Baptist Community College to hard-sell our product, but as a special treat we will be returning by 14.00 to visit "The Dig", which allows us to wander through the streets and tunnels of the fabulous lost city of Atlantis. The display includes over five hundred piranhas. I know that Professor Carter will be looking forward to that.'

At this point the professor in question snorted very strongly. 'I've seen enough piranhas to satisfy me for a lifetime,' he said.

'Really Carter, that's not a very pleasant way to describe Christine Vincent,' Hardwicke retorted. Everyone who heard this remark laughed. The woman was universally detested.

Robert continued, desperately trying to cling on to control. 'And if you like you can take the Leap of Faith, the waterslide that takes you through a shark-infested aquarium.'

'Oh, is that where Christine is staying? That's why I haven't seen her today.' Hardwicke was in full form.

'Our final meeting, Wednesday, will commence at 19.50 back in the theatre. It is a plenary session where we can share good practice in terms of our student recruitment.'

'Fat chance,' piped up another jaded member of the party. Jenny recognised the voice of her English department colleague, Malcolm Lowry. How come she didn't spot him before? That was always the way with Malcolm; so easily forgotten.

The narrator carried on regardless... 'Thursday, most of us are returning to the UK. Meet in the hotel lobby at nine to be taken back to the airport in time for your eleven thirty flight. Those who are not coming with us,' and at that point he looked at Jenny, 'it is up to you to make your own way back.'

Jenny was planning to spend another night in Nassau, before catching a flight to Long Island for Dwaine's memorial service on Saturday afternoon. She had, however, booked a less flamboyant hotel for this night. *And I will go there a night early if I have any rubbish to put up with* she thought, looking in the direction of Straw and Hardwicke. Straw was all right, it seemed. He had already found a waitress to get his arm around, and probably his leg over at a later stage. That just left Hardwicke. For once, Simeon looked lost and uninterested in pursuing a shag, but Jenny wasn't taking any chances. She beat a quick retreat into her room every night.

*

To everyone's surprise, the itinerary went according to plan. There had been a slight hiccup on the first morning, when the coach broke down near the docks. The stench of oil mixed with the warm air made the unscheduled stop most unpleasant. Someone shouted something about watching out for the potcakes coming.

'Oh goody,' said Robert clapping his hands like a five-year-old, 'I'm hungry.'

'Potcake is the Bahamian slang for a stray dog, you moron,' Hardwicke had told him. Robert sulked for the rest of the day; he had never been so quiet before. As a result, for the first time ever, Hardwicke was everyone's hero.

After that, the group from Sedgemoor participated well and complimented each other. A number of new students were recruited for the following September, and some of them showed real promise.

On the final night, and in a celebratory frame of mind, a number of past students were invited to a farewell dinner. They were joined by some of the current Bahamian students, who had flown home to be at Dwaine's memorial event. The inevitable happened. A surplus of free wine led to a series of quarrels after dinner, and one excessively loud argument broke out between two female students in the entrance hall. Jenny wasn't listening too closely, but the dispute appeared to be over a male student. She was later informed that it was about Professor Hardwicke. There had been the usual accusations that Hardwicke was assisting female students with "exam preparation" in exchange for sexual favours.

Jenny had other things on her mind. A smooth-talking Bahamian businessman had taken a shine to Jenny, and was "giving it some", telling her to shake her "boungie" along the bridge connecting Paradise Island to Nassau to meet up with him later that evening. Jenny beat a hasty retreat into the toilets.

Whilst this was going on, the hotel security managed to escort those quarrelling out to the poolside but they were unable to stop the fight completely. Eventually, one of the girls was led away whilst the other stayed by the pool. As the cabaret entertainment had started, most of the students came back inside the building. What happened next was difficult to tell, but the girl who had been inside the building decided to go outside and reignite the argument and she pushed the other into the pool. The victim, unfortunately, was a non-swimmer. She tried to call for help. As no one was near, the other girl ran off to seek assistance, but by the time this had arrived, the victim had drowned. No amount of resuscitation could bring her back. The party atmosphere was frozen.

The local police was called and everyone gave statements, but no one had heard or seen anything extra to the statement given by the surviving girl, who, having sobered up instantly was wailing for all she was worth. Jenny, who by this time had escaped her would-be seducer, tried to comfort the student, but to no avail. The death was signed off as just an unfortunate accident.

Ted Murray sidled over to Jenny and with a very pragmatic attitude said, 'Well, it could have been worse, it could have happened on the first night before we had the new recruits. I gather she was one of yours.'

'Yes, I've just been informed by Hardwicke that was the case.'

Medusa slithered up to the pair of them and in her sugary-coated venom hissed, 'Another one for the English department. Dear Dr Jordan, we shall have to change your name to Dr Death from now on. All your students seem to be dying – who was she by the way?'

'To be honest, I didn't know her,' said Jenny. 'I've only just found out myself from Professor Hardwicke that she was an English student. I have never taught her. She has been in the Bahamas for the whole of this year, waiting to take her resit examinations. This was to be her final chance.'

'Not one of your finest then?' Even in the dark, Jenny could tell that Medusa was smirking.

'No, my finest are in England revising for their exams, not hanging around with women old enough to be their mother.' Jenny couldn't stop herself saying it. Medusa hissed away. A deep chuckle from her left meant that Medusa's place had been taken by Professor Hastings.

'Jennifer Jordan, what did you say to upset Dr Touchwood so much?'

'I just reminded her of her age, Mike. You wouldn't be happy if she picked up your students, would you?'

'No, indeed not, but then most of my students are females and I know she isn't interested in them.' There was a pause in the conversation at this point before Hastings changed his tone. 'Jenny, I understand that you are going to Long Island to Saunders' memorial service.'

'Yes. I am flying over on Friday and coming back to England on Monday. Thank God for bank holidays, eh?'

'Are you travelling alone over there?'

'Yes, why?'

'Take care, won't you?'

Jenny felt a cold tingling down her back at these words. 'Why are you telling me to do that?'

'I gather that Medusa might be going too. She won't put up with your comment. She never could stand home truths, so she will make life hell for you if she can. She cannot abide any female competition and now with you as head of English she has a rival who is younger, prettier and more intelligent than her.'

'Mike, you are very sweet, but I certainly don't meet all those criteria.'

'Rubbish, of course you do. If I were single I would ask you out myself, but sadly I am married. Been tied to the old bag now for twenty-two years. I don't think I can be bothered to change. It's like wearing a pair of slippers with holes in them. You realise that you should get another pair, but you also know they won't be as comfortable. Now, just do what you are told, and watch out for Professor Straw, an incarnation of Bacchus if ever there was one. Although between you and me he looks more like Goebbels.'

'Mike, this is not the time and the place for jokes.'

'My dear Jennifer, I am not joking. I only wish that myself or Carter could come with you to look after you. You haven't been looking too well as of late, ever since you were pushed down the stairs.'

'Mike, I wasn't pushed down the stairs, I just fell.'

'I would like to believe that, but I don't. No Jenny, you watch out for yourself. As a single woman, you will not be troubled too much on Long Island, but Nassau is a different kettle of fish: Big, fast moving and cosmopolitan. A number of drugs rackets also – although probably fewer than there are at Sedgemoor.'

'I'm sure that I will be okay, but thanks, I will bear what you have said in mind.'

'Make sure you do.'

*

Despite her tiredness, Jenny found it difficult to sleep that night. She did not want to spend another day in Nassau after the events of that evening, and she was deeply affected not just by her own unease, but additionally by Michael Hastings' warning. She went online to see if she could reschedule her flight to Long Island, and book an extra night at the hotel in Clarence Town, where she had planned to spend Friday and Saturday nights. As luck would have it, there was availability on the Bahamasair flight that was leaving at seven in the morning. She also secured a room on the island, albeit at a different hotel in the north of the island. *I might as well make a holiday out of it*, she thought. For good measure, she decided to hire a car, so that she could explore the island. It was ironic that only Ophelia's rent-a-car service had a vehicle available. *Bloody hell, I just can't get away from Shakespeare!* she thought.

Jenny left the Atlantis at five. Although the airport was close by, she did not want to miss the flight. She realised now that she had felt imprisoned during the whole marketing trip, and the thought of spending any more time with a group of people who she would only socialise with at work, made her feel miserable.

At one stage in her academic life, she worked with a number of good friends. Some of those were still in the English department, but none of them was with her in the Bahamas, and although Michael Hastings and Howard Carter were nice enough in their own way, she didn't experience a sense of relaxation as she might have done with some of her other humanities colleagues. Moreover, some of the other staff present she positively hated. It was also true to say that someone positively hated her.

Unbeknownst to Jenny, at eleven that morning, her former room at the Atlantis was suffering from a barrage of knocks and calls. The service staff had assumed that Jenny was still asleep and wanted to wake her up so that she would leave in order for them to clean the room for their next customers. They were not, however, the only people who sought access. Whilst Jenny was waiting at the airport in Long Island for her hire car to be delivered, a mysterious voice phoned the Royal Bahamian Police Force, to inform them that they had some information about the student drowning the night before. The voice explained that Dr Jordan had been seen walking away from the pool area, just minutes before her student was found dead.

CHAPTER 18
THURSDAY, 28 APRIL:
Long Island

The flight from Nassau left promptly at seven. As it only took fifty-five minutes to fly to Deadman's Cay Airport, Jenny barely had time to get accustomed to flying again. The memorial for Dwaine was taking place on Saturday. Jenny would attend that, and then stay on for the meal in the evening. She had booked to fly back to Nassau on Sunday afternoon and then to take a flight to the UK later that night. She dreaded the prospect of her long return journey back to the UK, and now wished that she had booked some additional annual leave. Not that it would have been granted, with the examinations looming; in fact someone, namely Gwendolyn, had complained about her staying as long as she was. It seemed that there was no chance of pleasing Gwen. Still, at least Monday was a bank holiday, so she would get one more day of rest, and one less day of Professor Jones for next week.

The car journey to the north of Long Island was the libation that Jenny so desired. She was alone. No colleagues, no students, nothing but beautiful views of sun, sea, and the sand. She had been shocked by the events of the previous night and even more disturbed at the thought that this was the third death of a student from the English department in such a short space of time.

If it carries on like this, we won't have any income, she thought. *Still, I suppose at least we will achieve a higher percentage of good degrees than anticipated at the end of this year.*

She immediately regretted her uncharitable thoughts.

She focussed on Dwaine. He had once told her that his mother had to work as a cleaner just to pay the fees. Is that why Dwaine appeared to have started dealing? She was certain that his mother didn't know and she wouldn't say anything to her. That would be unprofessional. As a cleric keeps his confessions to himself, so must a tutor keep a student's secrets. It didn't matter to his mother if he achieved a first class degree, nice though it might be; she just wanted him to do the best he could. Now she was left with the miserable chore of burying her son. Someone once said that there was nothing more wretched than having to say goodbye to your child.

Jenny experienced the emotional recall of her bereavement after her mother's death. Yes, she supposed that losing a son was worse than losing a mother, although losing a mother was pretty grim too. She thought of Caldicott. He had told her that his wife had died. She imagined that this was a significant reason for his, at times, reserved behaviour, although she liked that aspect of him. It made a change from being chased by various members of the humanities department, staff and students alike.

After driving carefully along the narrow road, she arrived at the Cape Santa Maria Beach Resort in the late morning. She hoped that she would be able to book into her room straight away. Luck was with her. The lady at the desk took pity at what appeared to be a lone woman harassed by life, and gave her the keys. Jenny hauled her suitcase into her room. She had a quick shower and decided to take a short nap. She fell asleep instantly and did not wake up until two thirty in the afternoon.

When she first woke up Jenny was somewhat dazed by the brilliant sunlight streaming in at her window. The heat of the afternoon coupled with the sound of the chirping insects disorientated her. She tried to remember where she was. And then she recalled the last twenty-four hours. Oh so slowly, the concern of the latest student death cast a shadow over her in the way that no Bahamian cloud could do. She felt rather selfish, but she sincerely wished that she had left Nassau the day before the accident had happened.

In an effort to shake off her gloom and make the most of this once in a lifetime trip, she packed a rucksack with bottles of water, collected her car keys and headed back on the road. She had wanted to go to Hamilton's Cave where, the guidebook told her, she could find several underground chambers – the former homes of the indigenous people. However, she noted that this was a foolish expedition as it meant doubling back on her tracks. A better plan would be to stop there on the way back to Clarence Town in the morning.

So, instead she decided to find the Columbus Monument, located in the north of the island. She was warned by the receptionist that the road was not very good. The receptionist was being modest; the road up to the top of the island was in desperate need of repair and driving along it was trickier than she had initially anticipated. She wished that she could have hired a jeep but the only vehicle available was an antiquated Ford Mondeo. It didn't want to go any further. On asking a kindly man how she could best get to the monument, she was advised to abandon her car where she was now and do the rest by foot, two miles to the track and then a mile up the hill, some three miles in total. Jenny was pleased that she had comfortable shoes on, as she was certainly going to need them.

After the best part of an hour, with the sound of the waves crashing against the cliffs as an accompaniment, Jenny finally reached the summit of her climb. A clump of palm trees swaying in the warm Bahamian breeze partially hid the memorial. She pushed through the foliage and stepped onto the base. The memorial itself was modern, being unveiled less than thirty years ago, but its significance was historic. The obelisk marked the spot where Columbus supposedly viewed the neighbouring islands on his arrival at Long Island in 1492. Jenny could easily see why the explorer might have stood on this spot. From here she beheld the stunning panoramic view of the jade inlets and sapphire seas that surrounded the island. The beauty of the place made Jenny feel lonelier than she had felt for ages.

Despite all her sadness, the root cause of Jenny's anxiety was the number of deaths that had occurred; a series of rather unfortunate accidents, but *were* they accidents? This was the question that bothered her the most. She was convinced now that there had been too many deaths to be a coincidence. It was back to that old scenario of George Joseph Smith, the man convicted of murdering his wives in the bath. As the saying goes, once is okay, twice is suspicious but three times is a definite pattern. Somehow, she believed that these students had been individually targeted and picked off, but why? They were not good students; no one could be envious of their talents. Neither were they rich; they all owed money to the university. She had heard that in the past, a number of students were deliberately failed for antagonising their tutors, but surely not killed?

The rule of three... everything relies on the rule of three: drop one plate, break two more, and she understood from Amelia that good rulings in seminal case law all had a three-part test. But weren't there *four* deaths with Henry Fielding? And if there were four, mightn't there be two more...?

This was not her only concern. Jenny now knew that someone was out to get her. Caldicott had warned her to take care. Professor Hastings had cautioned her only the previous night. Since the moment that she had been thrust into the position of head of department, she felt the sword of Damocles hanging over her. Not just that, that would have been easy to deal with, but there were a number of people waiting in the wings, either waiting for her to fail, or waiting with their knives poised for action.

"You have to get behind someone to stab them in the back," said Tom.

How right he was. Each time she walked into the English building these days, Jenny was reminded of Act III, scene I of *Julius Caesar* in which Caesar enters the forum and is promptly assassinated.

Et tu Brute? she thought.

Every member of staff could play Brutus, but Brutus would not act without the persuasion of Cassius. It was "Cassius" she must seek.

And who is to say that he or she is even a member of my department?

She knew for a fact that Dr Touchwood had hated the idea of another woman being a head of department. For all her promotion of equal opportunities, she was the first to stamp on any promising early career researcher who was female.

No, the whole thing stinks, she thought. *Perhaps I should just pack up and move away. But then they will have won, won't they? Still, if I find a genuine reason to leave, a different job, I will take it. I am not hanging around in a dying institution with a bunch of inadequates who are fighting for their lives.*

Trying to shake off her gloom, Jenny applied herself to the task of looking at the memorial. That did nothing to cheer her up either; in fact, Jenny found it a rather sad monument, due to the inscription it bore. It read, "This monument is dedicated to the gentle, peaceful and happy aboriginal people of Long Island, the Lucayans and to the arrival of Christopher Columbus on Oct. 17, 1492."

That was the end of the Lucayans' peace she thought. She found it easy to identify with the persecuted Lucayans. As though echoing her thoughts a young voice spoke to her. 'My dad says it was bad luck on the Lucayans to be wiped out like that.'

'Yes,' said Jenny, 'I think I agree with him.'

Jenny turned to look at the speaker, and was struck by his resemblance to someone she knew. Not so much a Samuel Taylor Coleridge, but more a young version of Samuel Coleridge-Taylor. He had a big beaming smile on his face.

'I recognise you,' he said. 'You're English, aren't you? You're staying in our hotel at the Cape Santa Maria Beach Resort. I saw you earlier when you arrived, but you didn't see me; I was eating an ice cream on the veranda; cookies 'n' cream, it's my favourite flavour. You looked really tired; did you go for a sleep? You look a lot better now.'

Jenny tried to answer but couldn't get a word in.

A completely different thought crossed the boy's mind. 'You've got a hire car. You've left it a couple of miles away; I saw it when we were on our way here. You should have left the window down a bit, or it will be too hot to drive...'

If this had been an adult saying all these things to her, Jenny would have thought that she was being stalked. However, because it was a child of about nine years of age, Jenny was amused. 'Well, I hope the car's still there when I get back to it, otherwise I shall have a very long walk back to the hotel.'

'Did you fly here from Nassau? They have a great place in Nassau called Frank's Ice Cream Parlour. Did you go there? They serve a Superman flavour. No, really! They do, but I can't tell you what it tastes like, as I had the rainbow sherbet instead.'

The cheery face suddenly looked very sulky. 'Dad said I couldn't have more than one ice cream as he wasn't paid enough.' As quickly as his face had turned sour, it brightened up again. 'But he said we could go back another day.'

'Where is your dad now?' Jenny finally had a chance to ask a question of her own.

'We've got our bikes. We left them at the bottom of the hill. I'm used to cycling but Dad's out of practice. I ran up here, but my dad is a bit slow. It will take him ages to get here, so I left him.'

'Are you sure that was a wise move?'

'Oh, I am quite happy on my own. I don't get frightened.'

'I was thinking of your dad, suppose he gets lost... ... do you think he might get frightened?'

'You are having me on,' said the boy, 'my dad isn't afraid of anything... except spiders. But don't tell him I said so.'

'Don't tell me you said what?' came a voice from behind her in the undergrowth. It routed Jenny to the spot. It was a voice that she had grown to miss during the last ten days. No, she must be imagining it. The fatigue of all the events had finally caught up with her. Nevertheless, she decided to turn around, just in case.

'Your son has just told me that you are frightened of spiders,' she said.

'And he is absolutely right; hate the things, particularly the big tarantulas you get over here. It's why I can't live here, isn't it Marcus?'

'They don't have tarantulas here, Dad! You are winding us up.'

'Well, they have black widows and they are even worse!'

If Caldicott had been as astonished to see Jenny as she had been to see him, then he was doing a very good job of covering it up. But then he would have less reason to be surprised than she did. He knew that she was flying to Nassau, on a marketing trip with the university. He also knew that Dwaine came from Long Island. His detective instinct would suspect that it was possible for Jenny to fly over for the memorial service, even if she hadn't told him she was planning to do so. They stood staring at each other for a few seconds, until his face lit up with a big smile, just as his son's had a few minutes earlier. It made him look as young as one of her first year students. She thought that she had never seen him look so handsome and relaxed before. The Bahamian weather had a positive effect on him; that and the fact that his hair had grown longer, its natural waves being allowed to express themselves. Both had a hundred questions for each other, and neither would be able to ask any of them for the time to come.

Sniffing out a mystery, Marcus broke the silence with a penetrating remark aimed at his father. 'Well, if you know each other perhaps you would introduce me to this nice lady.'

'Sorry, Marcus. Dr Jordan, I would like to introduce you to my son Marcus. Marcus, this is Dr Jordan.'

'Haven't you got another name?' Marcus asked. 'Dr Jordan is a bit stuffy, and I'm not ill.'

'I'm not that kind of doctor, Marcus. I am a doctor of English.'

'Does English need first aid?' Marcus asked.

'Some people would say that the English language needs considerable medical assistance,' Caldicott chipped in.

'Shut up Dad, you are always embarrassing me.'

'That's what parents are for, Marcus,' Jenny said.

'You still haven't told me your real name,' Marcus persisted.

'So I haven't. It's Jennifer, but my friends call me Jenny.'

'Then I will call you Jenny. My dad's name is Kevin in case you didn't know.'

Jenny, of course, did know, but she thought she would play along for the moment.

'That is a nice name,' Jenny told Marcus.

'That's not what you thought before,' Caldicott said, rather spoiling the charade.

This was too much for Jenny and she burst into giggles, 'Well, you are so much more like a Bobbie or a Nick.'

'Steady now, no need to be insulting,' Caldicott stated.

Marcus, not understanding the play on words, accused them of getting boring.

'You are absolutely right Marcus,' Jenny said. 'What can we do to make amends?'

'Let's have a drink and sit down. I'm tired now. Dad, you've got the bottles of water in your bag; get one out for Jenny too.'

'Yes, master,' was the reply.

'It's all right, I've got plenty of my own,' Jenny said.

They followed their young commander and bade his order to sit in the shade. Seeing Caldicott bossed about by his young son gave Jenny a fit of the giggles. She was told off in no uncertain terms by Marcus. That in turn caused Caldicott to burst into laughter. He then received a strong rebuke from his son.

'It is important to sit in the shade; I do not see what is so funny about it,' he said.

That was the worst thing that he could have said, as Jenny could not resist looking at Caldicott. They caught each other's eye and then fell into gales of laughter on the floor. 'Is he always like this?' she asked, once she had got her breath back.

'Always with me,' Caldicott answered.

'Dad, Jenny, control yourselves. Now, I want to ask you some questions Jenny.'

'Marcus, don't pester Jenny.'

'I'm not pestering you, Jenny, am I?'

'It's all right… Mr… eh… Kevin,' she corrected herself under Marcus' watchful stare. Jenny was used to dealing with her recalcitrant nephew, so she was not the slightest bit embarrassed at young children's questions.

'However, I have to warn you Marcus, that although you can ask me anything you want, I remain free to not answer if I so choose. Is that a deal?'

Marcus thought for a moment. 'Deal. Okay Jenny, question number one: Are you married?'

'No, absolutely not.'

'Don't you want to be married?'

'Only if I find someone nice.'

'Have you got a boyfriend?'

'Not at the moment.'

'Have you got any children?'

'No, but I have a fifteen-year-old nephew. His name is Matt.'

'Where does he live?'

'He lives in England with my sister and her husband.'

'What is your sister called?'

'My sister is called Katie. Her husband is called Sacha.'

'Isn't Sacha a girl's name?'

'No, but I can understand why you think it might be.'

'What football club do you like?'

'Well, it has to be Leicester City at the moment; although I used to support Bristol Rovers when I was young.'

'So why change your teams now?'

'I like winners.'

'Yes, so do I, that's why I support Man U. What films do you like?'

'I don't know, I haven't seen any for ages.'

'I like James Bond. I want a car like that when I grow up.'

'You'll have to save up a lot of money.'

'What's your favourite food?'

'Toast, no, probably chocolate.'

'Why do all girls like chocolate?'

'Do they?'

'All the ones that I've asked.'

'Do you like chocolate?'

'I'm supposed to be asking the questions.'

'Don't you think that it's about time we swapped?'

'Well, okay.'

'Good. Now tell me your full name.'

'That's not a question. That is a demand.'

'You are correct, I will try again. What is your full name?'

'That's better. My name is Marcus Samuel Rolle.'

'Where do you live Marcus?'

'I live on Cat Island, with my mum.'

'What is your mum's name?'

'Marguerite Rolle but everyone calls her Meg.'

'Is she in Long Island as well?'

'No. She is hospital at the moment in Nassau, but she is coming home soon, isn't she Dad?'

'Yes she is,' answered Caldicott. 'At least we hope she is, don't we Marcus?'

Marcus had already moved on to a new thought.

'Jenny, why don't you go out with my dad? He needs a girlfriend.'

At this point Caldicott dropped the bottle he was holding. Water splashed everywhere.

'See, I told you he needed a girlfriend. Look what happens to him if he isn't careful. He's made a mess now.'

'How sharper than a serpent's tooth it is to have a thankless child!' Caldicott retorted.

'And don't spout that old-fashioned stuff at me!' Marcus said in disgust. 'You know I don't understand it.'

'Oh Marcus,' said Jenny laughing, 'I have to be honest with you, I'm afraid that I am in a lot of trouble and it wouldn't be right for your poor dad to have to put up with me.'

Caldicott looked at Jenny intently and realised that something serious had happened since he last saw her. He tried to catch her eye, but she was very keen to make light of it all. She had yet to realise how much trouble she was in. As quick as a wink the moment was gone, and Marcus had resumed his interrogation. Caldicott quickly interrupted him.

'That's enough Marcus. Dr Jordan is quite worn out by your questions.'

'No she isn't. You're not worn out are you, Jenny?'

'Not yet, but I may be soon.'

'Well, I will just ask you one more question. Have you seen the Green Flash?'

'Is he a superhero?'

'No, silly, you are thinking of the Green Lantern. The Green Flash is something that we often see in the Bahamas but Dad says that you don't see it in England. It's when the sun is setting. For some reason, which I don't really understand, it suddenly changes colour from red to blue or green. It's great fun to look for it. But of course you have to be really careful not to look at the sun for too long or you might go blind. We are going to do that tonight, aren't we, Dad?'

'Yes, if you say so.'

'You can come with us! Jenny can come with us, can't she Dad?'

'Yes, if you say so.'

'So, that's settled. Jenny, we will meet you back at the hotel in the lobby about seven and we can all go down on the beach, all right?'

'Yes Marcus,' said Jenny, 'if you say so.'

'Dad, you will have to pedal faster than you did earlier as it is nearly five now. Come on, the last one down to the bikes is a…'

Neither Jenny nor Caldicott could work out what Marcus said at this point as he had run on several metres ahead of them.

'Wow, he is amazing, so much energy. I wish half of my students were so industrious,' Jenny said.

'Yes, he is a great pleasure to be with, but I think that

Meg gets fed up of how he behaves in front of me,' said Caldicott.

'I believe that boys like to show off to their dads, at least that's what my nephew does.'

'You were very good with him.'

'I enjoy intelligent company. Heaven knows I see little enough of it at work.'

Caldicott stopped walking. Her change of tone had alerted him to her misery.

'Jenny, what has been going on?' he asked.

'I don't want to bother you with it all, you are on holiday.'

'Not for much longer. I would rather be braced for the worst. Have there been any more deaths?'

'Yes, why do you ask?'

'Call it premonition; tell me all before we catch up with Marcus.'

So Jenny explained about Maya's death in England and of the death the previous night.

Caldicott surprised her by asking her if anyone knew that she was in Long Island at the moment.

'No, I was so shocked by it all, and by what Professor Hastings said, that I think I just flipped out and booked the earliest flight over here. They knew that I was planning to stay in Nassau tonight, and come over here tomorrow for Dwaine's memorial service.'

'Then you will be safe for tonight. We will have to think about tomorrow. I don't want to let you out of my sight, for more reasons than one, but primarily at the moment, because I am really concerned for your safety.'

'But I'm not a student, why should I be a target?'

'I don't know, but think about it carefully. I suppose that you haven't remembered anything else about your fall down the stairs?'

'No, nothing… I… sorry.' She was about to tell him that she had difficulty remembering numerous things these days, but she stopped herself just in time.

'Never mind.'

By this time, they had caught up with Marcus, so all work conversation had to cease.

'I bet I can get back to the hotel faster than you do, Jenny.'

'I expect you can, but you have a head start. I still have to walk a way to the car. I will see you at seven.'

Caldicott and Marcus were about to cycle off, when he turned to say something to Jenny. To his horror, she had collapsed on the ground.

'Marcus, quick.' They stood over Jenny wondering what to do. Luckily, she came to quite quickly. When she came around two anxious faces were staring at her.

'Oh, did I faint? How stupid.'

'I was going to pour water over you, but Dad said you wouldn't like that.'

'Your dad is absolutely right,' was all Jenny could say.

'Marcus, see if there is any rope around here. I am going to get our bikes to Jenny's car, so that I can drive us all back, but I'm going to have to tie up the boot.'

'No, I'm fine,' said Jenny.

'No, you are not fine, and you will do what you are told!' father and son said in unison.

'This has happened before, hasn't it?' Caldicott asked Jenny.

'Blacking out? Well yes, a couple of times since I fell down the stairs. But up to now it's been okay.'

'I'm not so sure,' said Caldicott. 'Remember when I met you at the church? You nearly collapsed then!'

'But that was the day after I fell down the stairs, it was to be expected.'

'But you should have got over that by now. Either way, I will drive us back.'

'You're not insured,' said Jenny.

'Let me remind you that neither are you if you are ill.'

Jenny wasn't in the mood to argue, so she acquiesced. They walked back in silence to the car. Marcus, to Jenny's amazement, had managed to find some rope from somewhere.

'He can always find things that no one else can,' Caldicott laughed.

Jenny smiled wanly.

Caldicott unclipped the bike wheels and threw them and the frames into the boot.

'Marcus, you are going to have to sit on the frames I'm afraid.'

It was clear from Marcus' expression that he was unhappy about that. 'Are you sure that it is safe, Dad?'

'Yes, if I go slowly.'

The journey back to the hotel was conducted in silence. When they finally arrived, it was approaching half past six. A somewhat doubled-over Marcus asked Jenny, 'You'll still come to the beach with us, won't you?'

'Yes, of course,' Jenny sighed. 'I'll just go to my room and be back down in a few minutes.'

Caldicott didn't say anything.

CHAPTER 19
THURSDAY, 28 APRIL:
Evening

Jenny collected the keys from the hotel receptionist and went to her room. There she sat on the bed and cried. She was not in pain, but she was exceptionally embarrassed and the embarrassment made her miserable.

Up to the point where she collapsed, she had been overwhelmed with happiness. The delight of seeing Caldicott again was only enhanced, not diminished, by meeting his son, who was an absolute joy to be near. He was relaxed, confident and most of all free, all those things that Jenny so longed to be.

But then she had collapsed. It was not the first time it had happened since her fall down the stairs but it was the first time that it had occurred in public, and more pertinently it was the first time that it had taken place in front of Caldicott to such a significant degree. In all her dealings with him, since their first meeting on the university's forbidden grass, she had been desperate to create a good impression on him. She now felt that the fainting episode must be a deterrent. She had already worked out that Caldicott didn't deal with illness very well.

And then there was the mystery of the son. Marcus had told her that his mother lived on another island. How had Caldicott and she met? What was their relationship now? And what of the woman he was holding hands with in Taunton?

The fact that Marcus said that Caldicott needed a girlfriend led Jenny to believe that Caldicott was no longer in a relationship with Marcus's mother, but Marcus would not know who his father was seeing in England. Jenny would have to try to find a way of asking these questions without appearing overly nosey. Well, that had been her thinking, before she fainted, but now she didn't think it was worth the effort. Still, she had promised Marcus that she would go down to the beach with them, and so she must. She couldn't let the boy down. She knew how miserable her then seven-year-old nephew had been the day she had to cancel her visit to see them all. She had no idea that would be the case until her sister phoned up afterwards and said that Matt had been crying for an hour. Jenny had been stunned at the time. She certainly wouldn't do that to Marcus.

She made an effort to get changed, and it was a real effort, as she was still feeling very sick and tired. When she had finally composed herself, she walked slowly and carefully down the stairs to the lobby once more. She arrived in plenty of time, as was witnessed by the big beam that Marcus wore on his face.

'See, I told you Dad! I knew she wouldn't miss it!'

'No, I said I would come, so here I am,' Jenny smiled back, 'but please don't challenge me to a game of leapfrog; I don't think that I would be up to that.'

'What's leapfrog?' Marcus asked.

His father intervened. 'Marcus, let Jenny sit down.' Concern was written all over Caldicott's face.

He spoke quietly to Jenny, 'You know, you really shouldn't have come down if you are not up to this.'

'I'm all right,' Jenny replied. But she could tell by Caldicott's expression that he didn't believe her.

They walked onto the sand with Marcus holding both their hands. It was a glorious evening, and Jenny tried to make the best of it. As the sun slowly slipped down below the horizon, Jenny felt that her happiness was sliding out of view. Tomorrow she would be going to Clarence Town to stay in the hotel there ready for Dwaine's memorial service on Saturday and then on Sunday, it was back to England. Not that she wanted to go back. What was the point?

No, she didn't want to go back to dreary old England, to Sedgemoor, with backstabbers and bitches, druggies and rakes, no thank you. She was not even sure if she was up to the journey. She was extremely concerned that she would collapse again whilst on her own. She had probably over exerted herself walking up to the monument, and that was the reason why she had fainted when she did. But suppose that her fits were getting worse? She was terrified that they might be. Ironically, Jenny had been warned that the fits were most likely to reoccur if she became stressed. She must try to relax.

She would have loved to have stayed out all night with the father and his son, but she knew her own limitations and made her excuses. In her mind, she had turned into that insipid heroine Fanny Price, from *Mansfield Park*, but nothing could be done about that. She must get some sleep, she had told them, but not before Marcus had extracted a promise from her that she would come down to breakfast before she left the hotel.

*

Whilst trying to enjoy himself, Caldicott was deeply troubled. He was delighted to see Jenny. He knew, of course, that she was coming to Nassau, and had half a suspicion that she might attend Dwaine's service on Long Island, but he didn't expect to see her by the Columbus Monument. He had not witnessed her arrival at the hotel that morning, nor seen her drive off in the car. Marcus had mentioned an English woman had arrived, but he wasn't really listening to his son. He was too busy wondering whether his son would be happy in England if he needed to take him there, if Meg's operation was not successful. But it had been, so there was no cause for alarm after all.

Although Caldicott had kept in regular contact with Meg and Marcus, the agreement had always been that Meg would bring him up. She had a large family in the Bahamas and so Caldicott thought that the child's quality of life would be preferable to moving to England. Besides which, he hadn't worked out how he wanted to spend the rest of his life. At the time, he was still in mourning for his wife and he felt it impossible to look after anyone else until this was done. Time had elapsed, and he still hadn't felt ready to move on. Then he met Jenny.

Caldicott had been shocked at finding that the seemingly controlled Dr Jordan had collapsed, even though he had noticed her blanking out on more than one occasion previously. He was certain that she had not realised that she had, but this time it was serious. It was also an all-too-vivid reminder of Lucy's illness; he really didn't want to experience that again. Did her illness now mean that she qualified as a "vulnerable" person? That was of concern. He would have to be even more careful in his dealings with her. Jenny had assured him that this was a temporary side effect from the concussion. She had said that it was called a non-epileptic seizure. He looked it up on the Internet when he got back to the hotel. The condition was said to be brought on by fatigue and stress. Dr Jordan had been under a considerable amount of stress in the past month. The advice also stated that the sufferer was not to drive until given medical clearance. That was going to be tricky to discuss.

He was annoyed that he hadn't been able to close the university cases before coming to the Bahamas, giving him a free run to ask Jenny out when he returned to England. No, to make matters worse, Jenny had told him that two more deaths had occurred. No wonder Jenny was unwell – and didn't she look ghastly tonight. He felt impotent. He decided to break his annual leave and phone up his superintendent later that evening.

CHAPTER 20
FRIDAY, 29 APRIL:
Cape Santa Maria Beach

The phone call to the UK was worse than expected. It appeared that Jenny was now the prime suspect in Maya's death. Only that day, someone had phoned the Minehead police telling them that Jenny had been seen arguing with Maya in the car park on the night of her death. The UK authorities had already informed the Bahamian police that she was wanted for questioning. That put things in a completely different perspective. On top of this, her quick departure from Nassau appeared highly suspicious after the pool death. Caldicott was informed that the Bahamian police intended to interview Jenny on Saturday after the memorial ceremony, or beforehand if they could locate her. He was instructed to contact the Bahamian force, to inform them of her whereabouts.

Then there were Jenny's fits. Was she, whilst during her blackouts, killing her students? It was entirely possible. She was under so much pressure to increase her percentage of higher degrees, that the easiest and quickest route to achieve this was to remove the students who were likely to obtain only a third class degree. Jenny had said that herself. She had even joked about bumping them off.

Perhaps she was enacting her supposed joke without her knowing it, or even worse, with her planning it.

Caldicott did not believe for a second that she was responsible for the deaths, but he had to view the evidence with an impartial eye. It did look particularly damning for Jenny. His main concern was that she was being used as a scapegoat for murder, and whilst it could not be proved that she had not committed the acts, there were likely to be further deaths. Someone had taken care to plan the killings. He was now certain that these were murders rather than accidents, but he would not tell Jenny this. She did not need any further worries.

Would there be another death before she left this island? Caldicott was exceptionally concerned that there would be. He decided that he must escort her every minute that she had left in the Bahamas, but he couldn't tell her so to her face. It would annoy her. In fact, he thought that she would be mortified, and probably wouldn't forgive him. He would have to think of a different plan. He thought of Marcus.

The next morning at breakfast, Marcus said to Jenny,

'Jenny, why don't you stay here for another day?'

'Well, I could do I suppose, but perhaps your father would like to spend some time with you without another person around.'

Caldicott called out from nearby, 'His father has had quite enough trouble from Marcus in the last day or two, and would be grateful for someone to help him share his burden!'

'I will have to ask if I can extend my room booking, here.'

'Why don't you let me do that for you, Jenny?' Caldicott asked. 'After all, it is you who are doing me a favour.'

'Okay Kevin, but only if you are sure.'

'I'm absolutely positive.' By this time Marcus had wandered off out of earshot so Caldicott continued, 'You don't know how good it is for Marcus to have someone to take his mind off his mum's illness. Also, as you found out yesterday, I can't leave Marcus for very long on his own. He starts talking to the strangest people.'

Jenny laughed, 'Yes, thank you very much.'

At this point, Marcus returned and asked Jenny if she wanted to go swimming.

'I didn't bring any swimwear, I'm afraid,' she replied.

'Why ever not? The water is perfect for swimming here.'

'To be honest Marcus, I didn't think that I would get the chance to go swimming at all, and for certain reasons, I've gone off pools recently.'

'Come on Jenny, you can hire a bikini from the desk!'

Jenny was horrified. 'Marcus, I absolutely refuse to wear a bikini anywhere!'

Caldicott was laughing at the pair of them; he seemed particularly amused by the idea of Dr Jordan in a bikini. Something that Marcus had said made her feel that she had forgotten something that she should have remembered. She told Caldicott that.

Caldicott went to see if Jenny could stay on in her room for another night. When he came back he had a wry smile on his face.

'I have some good news and some bad news; what would like to hear first?'

'Let's have the bad. Tell me it will cost me five hundred pounds, right?'

'Wrong, I'm afraid. There is no room availability here tonight. The good news is,' Caldicott started to laugh, his grey-green eyes twinkling, 'the concierge tells me that she can put an extra bed into our room, so you can share with Marcus and me…!'

'Is that the good news?' she asked.

'Well, perhaps not… Sorry, it is the best that I could do,' Caldicott explained still laughing.

Jenny smiled; she was certain that Caldicott was having her on, but, when she had finally checked this with the concierge herself, it appeared that he wasn't. A nice idea, in some respects, but she hardly knew the man. Not that that would stop her if Marcus wasn't there, but she was certain that Meg would not approve. This potential arrangement was all too awkward.

As she had no room to stay in, her mind was made up to go on to Clarence Town.

'I'm not sure,' she said. 'Besides I snore,' she added trying to lighten the tone of the conversation.

'Oh, you don't need to worry about that,' Marcus said overhearing this, 'Dad snores like a hurricane.'

'Thanks for that Marcus,' his dad said.

Jenny laughed but felt confused. Why did the man want her to sleep in his room with his son there? It would have been pretty obvious what his motives were if Marcus wasn't around, but Caldicott did not strike her as a particularly licentious person.

Caldicott knew that Jenny would not like the arrangement. Secretly, he was pleased that she had refused, but he also thought it a pity, if for no more reason than he could make sure that she would not be targeted this evening. Putting his job to one side for the moment, he certainly had no plans to seduce Jenny with Marcus around; what sort of a father would he be if he did that? He was very fond of his son, but for the first time since his arrival in the Bahamas, he was wishing that Marcus could entertain himself a little more. He needed to talk to Jenny, but could not work out how to approach her. Every time there was a potential opening, Marcus would intervene. That is ever the way with children, he had been told.

'Well, if she won't stay with us she won't, and who can blame her?' He decided to contact the hotel in Clarence Town where Jenny had her room reserved, to see if they had any availability for the night. He somehow doubted it. He then remembered that Marcus' Aunt Liz lived in Clarence Town. She was certain to put them up if they needed her to. That would also offer him a solution in respect of giving Marcus some fresh entertainment. Feeling much better about the possibility of being able to keep a watch on Jenny, Caldicott changed his approach.

'No, I quite understand, I wouldn't want to share a room with Marcus if I could avoid it.' Caldicott ignored an indignant yelp from Marcus... 'Tell you what Jenny, why don't you hang around with us today and go to Clarence Town later? You can leave your bags in our room and change there if you need to. Spend some time with us on the beach before you go; it is by far the nicest coastline that you will see.'

'Yes, all right. I'd like to stay put for a little while; I

feel that my feet haven't touched the ground since I left Heathrow.'

The three set out to the beach mid-morning. The Cape Santa Maria, lying on the western side of the island, was protected from the Atlantic waves, and was instead bathed by the gentle Caribbean Sea. Caldicott was right; it was an absolutely beautiful stretch of white sand. Jenny thought that it was the closest to heaven that being on Earth could be.

Not wishing to look completely out of place on a beach, Jenny had put on her shorts and T-shirt and was prepared to go swimming in these if she decided to. The sun danced on the water's surface and invited everyone to walk into the sea. Jenny paddled into the water up to her thighs. As tired as she was, Jenny couldn't help noticing how toned and tanned Caldicott's tall, thin body looked in his Bermuda shorts now he had removed his T-shirt. Marcus by comparison was on the rounded side. They looked like Laurel and Hardy when standing together in the water. Jenny hadn't noticed that before and it made her laugh.

'What's the joke?' Caldicott called over.

'Nothing,' Jenny laughed.

At that moment, Marcus splashed into the water, completely soaking Jenny. Caldicott was about to make a comment about liking wet T-shirts, but decided to keep his thoughts to himself. That didn't stop him smirking though. As though reading his mind, Jenny gave him a playful smack on his arm.

'Feisty, aren't you?' he said. 'That's a criminal offence.'

'So go on, arrest me,' she retorted.

'Jenny, I never mix business with pleasure,' he replied; although on balance, he decided that that was exactly what he was doing. It was killing him.

The morning quickly vanished into afternoon. The heat made Jenny aware that she should seek some shade. Besides, she was hungry. She hadn't eaten much for the last three weeks, and suddenly she found her appetite. She told Caldicott that she needed feeding. So they all went back to the hotel. Once there, the concierge informed Jenny that they had received a last-minute cancellation, and would Jenny like to stay on?

If Jenny felt relieved, it was nothing to the feelings evoked in both Marcus and his father, when she relayed this news to them. Marcus had become bored with his father this week, and wanted to watch YouTube. If his dad was talking to Jenny, he could have a go on Dad's laptop. Caldicott was relieved as it would make it much easier to look after Jenny for this night at least. He had not had an opportunity to talk to her about his phone call the night before and was anxious to do so, without Marcus present. As it turned out he had no opportunity for the rest of that day either, as Jenny spent most of the afternoon asleep.

During their evening meal Marcus asked, 'Can I come with you to Clarence Town, tomorrow?'

Jenny was surprised, 'Well yes, but… your dad…'

'Oh, well he can come too, if he wants to…'

Jenny was pretty certain that Marcus had been set up by Caldicott, so later, when Marcus was out of earshot she tackled him on the subject.

'What's going on?' she asked him.

'Jenny, I need to tell you something, but not in front

of Marcus. I will take him to visit his Aunt Liz in Clarence Town whilst we are at your student's memorial service, and hopefully I can talk to you then.'

The subject of the conversation popped up in front of them. 'Are you talking about me again? My ears are burning.'

'Yes, of course, Marcus,' he was told.

For once, Caldicott was glad to change the subject so quickly. He was concerned that Jenny might challenge his company to the service. But she didn't give it a second thought. She was glad that he was going to be with her.

CHAPTER 21
SATURDAY, 30 APRIL:
Clarence Town

Despite Caldicott's protestations, Jenny drove them all back to Clarence Town. On the way, they stopped to look at Hamilton's Cave, but Marcus beat a quick retreat when a bat scooted over his head.

'I hate bats!' Marcus cried.

Then, as planned, her escorts accompanied Jenny to her new hotel, and watched her check in. Jenny laughed, 'What have I done to deserve the bodyguards?' She received no answer.

After Jenny's luggage was safely stowed in her room, and Marcus had been dropped off at his aunt's house, Caldicott and Jenny made their way to St Paul's Anglican Church for the service. As they were now late, Caldicott did not get a chance to warn Jenny, other than to say that the police might want to speak to her about the pool accident. But Jenny wasn't really listening. Her attention had been drawn to the white marble building, which she thought, combined with the blue Bahamian skies, gave a romantic setting to a less than romantic occasion.

An elderly man in the congregation looked at Caldicott and Jenny together. 'Couples come over from the UK to get married here,' he added helpfully. 'You only need to be resident in the Bahamas for a day to apply for a licence.' Jenny decided that no reply was the best strategy; she didn't dare look at Caldicott.

Jenny was surprised to see so many people at the service. She hadn't appreciated until then that Dwaine's grandfather was an elder in the community – the whole town came to pay their respects. She noted some of her students in the multitude of people, including Dr Touchwood's latest toy boy, the appalling Reginald White. She wondered if Dr Touchwood was there as well. The Bahamas Police Band played some of the hymns, and other members of the Royal Bahamian Police Force joined in with the songs. A number of young females were crying, even the stone angels appeared to be weeping. She was reminded of the final scene in *Hamlet*, "Good night sweet prince: And flights of angels sing thee to thy rest!" Dwaine, albeit far from the most industrious or talented student, was certainly very sweet. She hoped that he had found peace wherever he was now.

After the service, Jenny ensured that she spent some time talking to Dwaine's mother. Mrs Saunders thanked Jenny for taking the trouble to attend, and asked her to stay on for the supper. Jenny had originally planned to do this, but she still felt unwell and she did not want to risk being with strangers, so she made her apologies. It was at this point when she realised that Caldicott was stuck behind a group of wailing women. Jenny waved to him and signalled that she would meet him outside. She had just walked into the soft sunshine, when she heard her name called.

'Dr Jordan?'

'Yes?'

'Clarence Town Police. I wonder if you would mind coming down to the station with us, we have some questions for you?'

'What is this about?'

'You are wanted in connection with the murder of one of your students in Nassau on Wednesday night.'

Jenny froze in horror; she really couldn't understand why anyone would think that she was responsible. She suddenly felt sick and dizzy and very, *very* tired. She turned to where Caldicott was. 'Kevin…' She tried to call him, but it was too late, she had collapsed again.

When Jenny came too she heard Caldicott rowing with one of the police. 'I told you not to approach her on her own,' were the words that she made out. She felt angry, furious. She thought that she and Kevin, as she had finally come to call him, were friends. Now she knew that she had been mistaken. He had deliberately led her into, as she saw it, enemy hands. So that miserable, no-good, conniving bastard had set her up. That was the last time she was going to speak to him!

Only too late did Caldicott realise that she had heard his conversation. Yes, he knew that she was wanted for questioning, he had tried to tell her so earlier, but he admitted to himself, he had messed it up. He didn't think that they would arrest her on the spot. He was angry with himself; he would have made every effort to instruct her, if he had known what they were intending to do.

Having had the opportunity to get to know Jenny better, he was certain that she, herself, could not have carried out the crimes. Was she being set up? If that were the case, all he could do whilst they were in the Bahamas was to provide a twenty-four-hour alibi for her. That chance was ended. He could tell by the anger on her face that she would not trust him again. He had failed. He would have to rely on Marcus, alone, to protect her. But Marcus, of course, was at his aunt's house, just when he was needed the most.

CHAPTER 22
SATURDAY 30 APRIL:
Evening

Jenny was taken to the police station where she had to wait over two hours to be interviewed. During this period Caldicott was nowhere to be seen, so she had ample time to consider his duplicity. How dare he let his son befriend her, when all along he had been planning to arrest her. Not that she had been formally arrested as such, she was merely being questioned. She laughed at herself for being a fool. Up until the moment when she was accosted by the police outside the church, she had been thinking that she had finally met someone who she could genuinely relax with. But, oh foolish woman to think along these lines, it was perfectly clear now that Caldicott had been interested in her purely as a lepidopterist is interested in a new species of butterfly. She felt pinned to the spot.

Finally, she was taken into a police interview room. Could she tell the officers of her exact movements of two nights ago? Had she been down by the pool? Had she seen anyone fighting near the pool? What had she been drinking? Was there anyone with her during the time of the accident?

Jenny, answering as truthfully as possible, could only

say that did not know where she was at the time of the accident. Yes, she had gone to the pool at some point. Yes, she had been aware of an argument going on inside, but was not paying much attention to it. No, she was pretty certain that she had been on her own. She couldn't say if anyone had seen her at that time. No, she had most definitely not been drinking.

One of the police waved a book in front of her face. 'Is this yours?' It was a copy of *Drown* by Junot Diaz.

'I do have a copy of that book in England.'

'Wrong, it is here. This has your name in it. Is this your writing? We found it by the poolside this morning.'

Jenny was staggered. She knew she had not packed that in her luggage. She had absolutely no idea why it might appear in the Bahamas.

Then finally a voice cut in on the questions, a voice that she suddenly detested.

'Jenny, is there any chance that you blacked out at any point during the evening in question?'

Jenny was miserable. 'Yes, it is possible that I might have done so at one point. I remember sitting down in a chair near the pool and the pool lights were on, but when I looked again, the lights were off.'

'What time was this?' Caldicott asked.

'I really have no idea, I'm sorry.'

She was then left in the room, alone. By now extremely angry and wishing death on Caldicott, she couldn't stop herself from listening to his conversation even though she wanted to.

'Well then, as far as I can see there are no grounds for keeping Dr Jordan any longer. It is possible that if she blacked out she would not know what she was doing, but having seen her fall down, and you have witnessed it yourselves this afternoon, I would say that she would not be active in her fits. I really cannot see that she would push the student under the water… No, I don't think that she is a danger to anyone else, but I do think that she is a danger to herself. The more stress she is under the more likely she is to collapse again… No, there is no one here to look after her, and I am certain that she won't trust me now after you moved in before I could talk to her. Your chief agreed to let me bring her in when she was ready; you have set this enquiry back a number of hours by your pre-emptive action.'

The next part of the conversation was inaudible to her. She fell asleep.

*

It was a little while later that she came back to consciousness. She probably would not have come to at that moment, as part of her brain had decided to go into "power off" mode, but a little voice had a large effect. It called her name. It was Marcus. 'Dad said that you are not going to speak to him anymore. Is that true Jenny? Because he does like you, and I like you and I thought that we were friends.'

Jenny continued to be furious. She thought it typical that a grown man could use his own child to get to her. But when she opened her eyes, and turned to face Marcus, sporting a look of blazing wrath, she heard a small sob escape from him. Tough as she was trying to be, she felt that it would be wrong to take her anger out on a nine-year-old. That was the action of a bully. She wasn't one of those, even if his father was.

'*We* are friends, Marcus, but I am not your dad's friend at the moment.'

At that moment the subject matter of their conversation came into the room.

'Marcus, I told you not to disturb Dr Jordan, she is very tired.'

'She is not tired,' said Marcus, 'she is merely tired of you! You have let us both down. You were supposed to take us to a party tonight but instead poor Jenny has been stuck here. No wonder she doesn't like you anymore. No wonder you don't have a girlfriend. You are really horrible to nice people. You are horrible to Mum. You hardly ever come to see me and when you do, you mope about as though you have lost your teddy bear. You are supposed to be my dad, but you behave like a child. All you are interested in is tracking down bad people and arresting them. Why don't you protect the good people from harm instead? Why can't you protect Mum? Why can't you protect Jenny? When are you going to grow up and take responsibility for your friends? No wonder Jenny doesn't like you, I'm not sure that I like you any more either!'

And at that point, to both Jenny's and Caldicott's utter amazement he burst into tears and flung himself into Jenny's lap.

'Marcus, what on earth is the matter?' Jenny asked when she could hear herself talk above Marcus' sobs. Neither Marcus nor Caldicott answered. Caldicott was too

219

dismayed to even move, and Jenny could not get Marcus to answer. It was a good five minutes before anyone spoke, and that was only in answer to the police telling Jenny that she was free to go, but to make sure they had her full home details before leaving.

Having signed everything that was required of her, Jenny spoke to them both. 'What party have we missed, and can we still go there?' It has to be said that Jenny had absolutely no desire to go to a party, but felt that she had to say something to cheer up Marcus. Something terrible had happened that evening to him, of that she was certain, and it had nothing to do with Jenny herself.

'You were invited to Marcus's aunt's house,' said Caldicott, 'but I think it is too late to go now.'

'Nonsense,' said Marcus. 'You know they party all night there. We could still go. Come on Jenny!'

'Well, I…'

'Look Marcus,' Caldicott cut in, 'Jenny really isn't too well, don't be bossy.'

'No Dad. I've told you before not to interfere. Let people decide for themselves. Jenny?'

Jenny found it hard to work out Marcus' relationship with his father; it was pretty clear that he was the one in control. Jenny presumed that Caldicott just acquiesced to keep the peace. That surprised her because she had initially thought him somewhat cold and aloof, and more to the point, in control of everything he did. She now saw that she was wrong. He was as much a victim of himself as she was a victim of herself. It was the case of the great double-bluff. She was attracted to him because he appeared to be thoughtful and calm, whereas he liked her because she seemed to be straightforward and composed. Inside they were both a mess! In fact, the only person present, who, despite his recent outburst, was naturally in control of himself, was Marcus.

'Marcus. What has happened? You have stopped smiling, it is not like you!'

'I just want you to come with me to Auntie Lizzie's party; that is all.'

Jenny recognised the petulant boy for what it was. She had been his new toy, but the toy was broken. She would have to do what she could to please him.

'I don't know Marcus,' she started. 'Of course I would like to go but your father is actually right that I am not feeling very well. However,' she added seeing his crestfallen expression, 'I would be happy to go for a little while…'

'That's settled then,' said Marcus. 'Dad!'

'All right Marcus, but I need to speak to Jenny first, if she is prepared to speak to me?' He gave Jenny a questioning glance.

'Can it wait?' she said. 'I don't feel up to much…'

And so it happened that an extremely reluctant Jenny, much against her better judgment, was forced to enter into Caldicott's company once again.

CHAPTER 23
SATURDAY, 30 APRIL:
Late Evening

The party was a lively affair and was likely to go on all night, but Jenny just wanted to sleep. After an hour, she decided to head back to the hotel, but was told by everyone in the family that was not to be heard of. She must spend the night as a guest, she was told. A row of camp beds had been put up in one room for "girls", and another room for "boys" to accommodate what was destined to be a large sleepover. No one minded that Jenny was the first to retire onto one of the camp beds, but as soon as she had, three of the daughters of the house were also sent to the room. As for Jenny, she had lost the will to argue about whether she could go to the hotel on her own or not. Everyone in the house was against it, and truth be told, she could not care less where she slept, as long as it was not dangerous to do so. She knew that in this house, she would not be pestered by unwanted attentions. In fact, although virtually everyone was a stranger here, she felt safer now then she had felt for ages.

Back home in her own cottage, she was frequently disturbed by the sound of the wind rattling the front door, or a cat meowing. This would cause her to spend most of the night worrying about whether there was someone prowling about outside. Likewise, when she was in the Atlantis, she couldn't properly fall into a deep sleep for fear that her room would be invaded by an oversexed professor. Even in Santa Maria, when Caldicott and Marcus were nearby, she still could not fully relax. And when she did finally nod off, most of her dreams were invaded by statistics of degree classifications and threats of redundancy. 'Oh well, bring it on!' she said. In Liz's house, she entered into a deep sleep that was not disturbed for hours.

Whilst Jenny slept, a female sauntered into Jenny's hotel. When the concierge was not at his desk, she detached Jenny's room keys from their resting place on the hook above the letter tray, behind the reception desk. She returned to the party and addressed Caldicott.

'I've done what you asked me to do. Here are the room keys. The concierge goes off duty at eleven, so you will be able to get in at that point unnoticed. Do you think Jenny will be safe tonight?'

'Yes, as long as she stays here.'

'Don't worry; the girls have been primed not to leave her side. If she moves, then one will give the alarm and everyone will wake up.'

'Thanks Liz, you are a true friend.'

'Why couldn't you ask her if you could search her bags? It would have been so much better to ask her directly rather than all this sneaking around.'

'Yes I know, but thanks to those clowns in the police station, I have managed to lose any goodwill that I had with her. Up until then I thought... well, it doesn't matter, but I am pretty certain that she has something of importance on her. It is a chance that I have to take. If I don't find anything, then the police won't either, should they decide to search her belongings tomorrow.

'You must tell her what you have done as soon as possible. You need to tell her what you suspect to be going on.'

'It's going to be tough to explain it all.'

'Is that any excuse not to do it?'

'No, you are right.'

At midnight, secure in the knowledge that Jenny was fast asleep in Liz's house, and assured of the fact that Marcus was finally asleep in the boys' room, Caldicott dressed in the dark clothes that Liz's husband had given him, and taking a torch with him, went over to the hotel. Using the keys that Liz had collected, he entered the building and Jenny's room. He secured the shutters by torchlight then turned on the main light. He pulled a pair of disposable gloves from his pocket, and looked for Jenny's bags whilst he put them on.

As Jenny had only planned a short journey to the Bahamas, she had very little luggage: one small wheelie suitcase and the handbag that she had with her at Liz's house. Of that he was thankful. He knew of several women who managed to pack the entire house including the kitchen sink into their luggage when they went on holidays or on business trips. And invariably, if he was in that sort of relationship with them, he was the one who had to carry it all. It would make a change to go on holiday with someone who travelled light. Not that he would have much chance of that now, he thought ruefully. Still, he would have to work on reconciliation if that was what he really wanted to do. All these bloody deaths, why couldn't they have happened at another university?

And then he laughed at himself, he was so stupid sometimes, he thought. If they had happened somewhere else, he wouldn't have met Jenny. What was worse? Meeting her and losing her before their relationship had had a chance or not finding her at all? He carefully opened Jenny's suitcase and methodically set about emptying it, ensuring that he knew exactly where to replace it.

There was nothing of any particular interest in the body of the suitcase, except for Jenny's underwear, which he restrained himself from investigating in too much depth, except to note that it was practical in nature. For some reason, he found this to be reassuring. Then he carefully repacked every item as he had found it.

He then turned his attention to the side pocket on the case. This was far more interesting, and surprising. He pulled out the glamour magazines that Jenny had bought in Heathrow. For a second he was stunned. Perhaps that explained why, at times, Dr Jordan seemed aloof. Did she prefer women to men? Then he shook himself. No, that wasn't true, well not entirely true; even if she did like women she also liked men, as evidenced by her relationship with Carstairs. And so what if she was bisexual, wouldn't that make it more interesting? He laughed. That was the appealing aspect of Jenny, it was impossible to predict what she was going to do or say next. He liked to be kept on his toes.

By this time, fascinated as to why Jenny might want to buy men's magazines, he decided to look through them for himself. Here was another surprise. When he looked closely at them, he realised that Jenny had not opened them at all. Why buy a magazine and not read it? He supposed that she could hardly read them on the plane, sitting by other people. But why not read them in her hotel room in Nassau? Perhaps she had forgotten that she had even bought it in the first place. He had now witnessed Jenny blacking out a number of times, and he was aware that she was having memory lapses alongside them. Did she buy these for her own sexual satisfaction, or for another reason? Perhaps she hadn't purchased them at all. He would have to investigate.

*

The mixture of jet lag and emotional stress in Nassau had ensured that Jenny had forgotten that she had bought the magazines in the airport. She had meant to examine them at the time, but hadn't had the right opportunity. By her second night in Nassau, she thought of nothing but sleep. Had she remembered to look at them, she would have discovered the reason for Professor Hardwicke's reaction.

*

Caldicott had selected *Zoo* as his first choice. He carefully turned each page. His mystification for Jenny's purchase prevented him enjoying the "read". In fact, sexual excitement was the last item on the agenda when he reached the centre, despite the view of a stunning body in the more-or-less raw.

In the middle of the magazine, underneath the caption "English Rose", lay a naked Bernice Pye, with the *Complete Works of Shakespeare* lying over her bikini area, and rose petals partially covering her breasts. The effect was a cheap version of the DVD cover of *American Beauty*. The simple text in the far right-hand corner of the photo told the viewer that this month's main course was Bernice who was currently reading English as a first degree (no university mentioned). It further stated, and this was the significant point thought Caldicott, that she liked older men, and was currently dating a lecturer. *Which one?* Caldicott asked himself.

Caldicott made a note of the issue number of the magazine and put it back in its place. So this was the reason why Jenny had bought them, or at least *Zoo*, but why the *Bikini* magazine? He found nothing of interest in this. And then he remembered their conversation about bikinis only the day before. She said that she had forgotten something. This must be it. She had forgotten that she had bought them. He was pretty sure that she would have shared the joke with him, unless she didn't want to discuss it in front of Marcus. What a shame, he would have loved to have had that conversation. And there was something else for her to tell, of that he was certain.

The only other item of potential interest in Jenny's luggage was a bottle of iron tablets. He wondered if Jenny was suffering from anaemia, which might explain some of her fainting episodes. Caldicott opened the bottle to see how many tablets were left of the initial one hundred. The bottle was about half full now. He poured some out on his hand. They looked like iron tablets, at least most of them did, but amongst the pills that lay on his palm, a couple seemed to be subtly different in colour, although he admitted to himself that it was difficult to tell under artificial light. He decided to take a selection of the tablets for analysis, and worked out how many he could take without alerting the owner to their loss.

Having settled on a selection of eight tablets of different shades, he replaced the lid on the bottle and repacked it where he had found it. He then turned off the light, closed the door and crept quietly down into the hall, where he hung up the room keys on the appropriate hook. He walked back to Liz's house, still mystified about what he had found, but believing that something, at least, had been explained.

*

It was particularly curious that, later that night, a car collided with a lamp post, on the Queen's Highway in Clarence Town. On inspection it was found that the driver had been shot at close range. The driver was one Reginald White who was studying English at the University of Sedgemoor. The bullet had penetrated a copy of Dostoyevsky's, *Crime and Punishment* that was found in his pocket. Despite the violence that the book had suffered, it was still possible to read Dr Jordan's name inside the front cover.

CHAPTER 24
SUNDAY, 1 MAY:
The Journey Home

The next morning Jenny woke up to find that she was in a strange room crammed full of women. For a brief second, she thought that she might have been captured by white slavers. Then she realised that she had been invited to a sleepover party in the Bahamas. In the room there were twenty other females of all shapes, sizes, colours and ages. Some were awake, some asleep, but all seemed to be focussed on Jenny. Boy, was she suffering from a persecution complex, she told herself.

At the same time that Jenny was waking, Caldicott had been summoned into the Clarence Town Police Station.

'What do you think you were doing removing the witness from the hotel?'

'Sir, Dr Jordan is not the culprit. She is a potential victim.'

'You are not thinking rationally, it is easy to see that you are emotionally involved with the woman. You have not behaved in a professional manner.'

'Now hear me out,' Caldicott continued. 'You have informed me that you suspect Dr Jordan to be involved in the death of Reginald White. You are insinuating that he was shot at close range by Dr Jordan, and that you will be searching her luggage soon. No, you are the one who is mistaken when you think my activities are illogical. I have informed you that I removed her for her own protection. She has been surrounded all night by numerous friends and family members. There are in the region of ten to twenty women who are prepared to give her an alibi.'

'She might have an accomplice.'

'You are clutching at straws, you need to find out the real culprit, but I can guarantee that it is not Dr Jordan. I do not want you to question her any further. She is more unwell than she realises. Since I met her on Thursday, she has had at least four fainting attacks. They are increasing in frequency and strength. I am sure that it is because she is becoming more stressed. Her travelling so far in such a short time has added to her underlying health difficulties. You must let her go. You know where you can contact me. If she remembers anything else then I will make sure that she relays the information to you somehow.'

'I understand that she is not speaking to you.'

'That is not strictly true. She will speak to me in a professional capacity I am certain of it. That is all that you need to worry about.'

'Very well, but it is against my better judgment. Who is escorting her back to England?'

'That, I can't answer. Even if she would let me, I cannot go back yet as I have to stay with Marcus. She might let us escort her back to Nassau though.'

'Escort her to Nassau and I will ask for an undercover officer to join her there to watch over her on her way back to the UK.'

*

Caldicott arrived back at Liz's house in plenty of time to talk to Jenny before she would have to collect her luggage and catch her flight. He knew very well that she would not want to see him, but she hoped that she would still speak to Marcus. He had to find a way to explain about the suitcase, and Reg White's demise. But would she be prepared to listen to him at all? He very much doubted it. He had taken a high hand with Dr Jordan, and he was preparing himself for the biggest smack-down of his life.

As it happened he found Jenny in a more compliant mood than he had expected.

'Jenny, I have lots to tell you.'

'Well, get on with it then, I have to get back to Nassau this afternoon for my connection to the UK... Kevin... I don't think I am up to it.'

At least she is not referring to me as Mr Caldicott, he thought.

'Is there any chance you can cancel your flight?' he asked her.

'To be honest, I don't think that I can afford to. Anyway, I just want to go back to my own house.'

'Yes, I understand that, I feel the same way.'

'But it's different for you, you have Marcus.'

'Yes and no,' he said. 'Yes, he is my son, but I don't have the day to day care for him. I'm not sure that I am up to that.' *I might have to be soon, but that's a different issue* he thought.

Caldicott continued. 'Jenny, why don't you let Marcus and I escort you to Nassau. We can visit Marcus' mum in hospital. She was supposed to be out yesterday, but they decided to keep her in for further observations. This is not good, and Marcus is missing her terribly. That was the main reason for his outburst yesterday, I believe. I can't come back with you to the UK, but if I get you to the airport, I will feel a lot happier. I should be back in England on Thursday, and then I will sit down with you and explain it all carefully.'

'I am so sorry that I have been such a trouble to you,' was all that Jenny could say. 'I think I overreacted yesterday.'

'You had reason to.'

'Don't tell me any more now,' said Jenny, 'but if you want to escort me to Nassau I would like that.'

During the flight to New Providence, Marcus talked all the time to Jenny and she responded warmly to his questions, just as she had two days before. Caldicott wanted to tell Jenny about Reg White, but he didn't get the chance. In retrospect he thought that was probably just as well.

The flight was on time and landed just under an hour later. When they arrived in New Providence, Caldicott and Marcus escorted Jenny to the international terminal where she checked in her baggage.

'Jenny, can I visit you if I come to England?' Marcus asked.

'Yes, of course you can,' she responded.

'It might be soon, mightn't it, Dad?'

'It is possible Marcus. We will see,' was the reply. Caldicott wanted to kiss Jenny goodbye, but on reflection he thought perhaps he had better not.

*

The flight to the UK was uneventful. Jenny went to sleep, or perhaps passed out, she wasn't sure, several times on the way back. The combination of the two meant that her mind was refreshed and focussed. At one point she thought that someone had put an object into her bag, but on consideration she decided that this was just part of her dream-like state. She went through passport control and customs without a hitch. She arrived at her house on Monday evening.

For all the stress of the previous few days, she carefully inspected her small house in case there was a predator waiting for her. There was no one, except a note from DC Stone telling her to phone him on Tuesday morning. 'Huh, that is something to start my week off well,' she said to herself.

She had promised Caldicott that she would email him, to tell him that she had arrived home. Despite his deception, she wished that he was with her, but she was unsure of where she stood with him. He had been very loving towards her on Long Island before she fainted, but after that time, it was natural that he wouldn't want to get involved with a person suffering from what might appear to be psychotic episodes. Anyway, it would be completely out of the question for him to have a relationship with a potential murder suspect. Even if that was all sorted out, what of Meg and Marcus? More to the point, what of the unknown stranger who held his hand in Taunton? Where did she figure in Caldicott's life, and how could a boring English lecturer compete?

Back to work tomorrow, and...
       ... tomorrow, and tomorrow,
    Creeps in this petty pace from day to day,
      ... Out, out, brief candle!
    Life's but a walking shadow, a poor player,
    That struts and frets his hour upon the stage,
    And then is heard no more...

Never had she felt so akin to Macbeth. He was a murderer. Was she? Did her blackouts occur in order for her to kill? In other words, were these psychotic episodes brought on in order to commit a crime, or perhaps excuse the crime? Amelia had told her about a legal case from Northern Ireland, Bratty was the name, in which a girl was strangled by a sexual-psychopath.

Eurgh! Time to change her thoughts. No, she would not do any work tonight. Nevertheless, she had promised to email Caldicott. She only had a work account, so no doubt that there would be many unread emails waiting for her, having not bothered to log on all the time that she was in the Bahamas. She promised herself that she would not read any of the emails unless they came from Caldicott.

To her horror, she noted some 1,987 emails waiting for her. Thinking about it, that was not unreasonable, as every day at work she constantly received in the region of two hundred. She quickly trawled through to get rid of obvious spam.

She was delighted that one of the most recent emails sitting in her inbox was marked up as Marcus Rolle. She knew that Caldicott had set up an account specifically for his son, and was planning to use this to email her, as his only other account was his work email. The message was short and to the point. "Missing you already." It was signed Marcus and Kevin.

She was just about to answer it, when to her annoyance, another email entered her inbox. The subject matter was "Emergency". She made the fatal error of clicking on it, it read:

"Jenny." *No "Dr", no "Dear" she thought.* She continued reading.

"Is there way I can appeal mark for my essay? I don't think my works has been marked properly. The marker says "you could done this" or "you could said that". But I got all the main points in with a wide scope of research and, i could have done many things but we were only given 1,500 words and I believed I utilised this well, with a variety of sources and many views and points of discussion.

Can you guide me through the appeal process? If not, then I am deeply and surprisingly shocked by an unfair mark. Franz Kafka"

Jenny had to read it through three times before this made any sense to her. She eventually worked out that Kafka was disappointed with his mark for the Wordsworth assignment. She remembered now that it was awarded a mark of 30 per cent. *And that*, thought Jenny *was extremely generous.*

Kafka was in debt to the university library to the tune of over one thousand pounds, and therefore had no access to books or to lessons. How he had got to the third year, she had absolutely no way of knowing. *He must have done his number on Hardwicke*, she thought.

As a joke, she forwarded this email to Marcus and

Caldicott, and said, "As you can see I am enjoying myself enormously back in Sedgemoor. Here is a student who I would happily see buried alive!"

She signed off just after she had forwarded Kafka's email to the "boys" account. Had she stayed online for just a few more minutes longer, she would have received an email signed "Kevin". In it, he had casually mentioned that one of her students, Reg White, was not going to return to the UK.

As she did not respond to this email straight away, Caldicott rightly concluded that she had gone to bed. He hoped that she read his message before someone had the chance to tell her to her face. He did not like the thought of her passing out in the university at the shock of yet another death. He hoped that White's death would be the last. It wasn't.

CHAPTER 25
TUESDAY, 3 MAY:
Morning

The last few days had been stimulating, if not always enjoyable, but now she needed to brace herself for another spell of boredom. Thanks to the May Day bank holiday, work started this week on the Tuesday. Regardless of whether the week started on a Monday or a Tuesday, the week always started on a low note as far as Jenny was concerned. As disinterested as some of her students were, she would much rather have been lecturing them Shakespeare, than face the challenge of the morning ahead of her. Instead of doing, as she saw, her job, she had the somewhat dubious pleasure of attending the weekly heads of department meeting. The fact that this was always held in Bridgwater made the gathering even more inconvenient and time consuming. She was rarely back to *Kubla Khan* before twelve. On top of that, today the weather was ultra foul, with rain flying at her from what seemed to be every direction, on her journey there and on her journey back. She did not make it back until two fifteen.

The meeting was, as usual, dull and tedious, and achieved nothing to positively improve the university. There was no debrief on the Bahamian trip, and Jenny was firmly of the opinion that the trip had been set up to be nothing more than a management jolly. Not even the death of the suspended English student was referred to. Jenny certainly wasn't going to mention it. Nor was she going to raise the issue of Reg White. She had checked her emails during the meeting, and read Caldicott's message three times to ensure that she understood it correctly. No, she would keep that to herself.

Halfway through the meeting Jenny called DC Stone as requested. The meeting was so bad, that for once her conversation with Stone was positively uplifting. Jenny was secretly hoping that Stone would come to arrest her, so she had a valid excuse to leave it!

With this in the forefront of her mind, she paid little attention to several new strategies, introduced by the management team, which seemed to the more alert around the table, to be poor for both student and staff morale. In fact, the majority of the heads from Sedgemoor were in agreement that this meeting saw an all-time low in administrative planning and functionality. Amongst the more incomprehensible policies issued, was the desire to only admit students with three A*s at A level – a sure-fire way to close down the university. That, however, was nothing compared to the most ludicrous policy of the planned introduction of a rigorous attendance register, which included the requirement that students should sign in every three hours, even if they had no lectures or tutorials on the day in question. This flawed policy was guaranteed to ensure that no one would have a good word to say about the university to potential students, A* or not.

To add to the misery, staff were also informed that the signing-in lists were applicable to staff. In future, staff were to be issued with swipe cards, which they had to use to swipe in and out of every teaching session. If they were not teaching on that day, they would also have to swipe in every three hours. When one member of staff had the audacity to ask if signing every three hours also meant signing in during the weekends and the middle of the night, he was shot down in flames for being facetious.

It was made clear to all concerned that with or without staff support these plans were going ahead. In an effort to minimise the rest of the meeting, the staff duly said "Yes" to new strategies, with everyone really meaning "NO". Well, nearly everyone… Medusa was up to her old tricks, standing up and saying 'What a marvellous idea, how magnificent, how fantastic that you can think of all these things.'

For once, the normally complacent Professor Carter turned to Jenny, who was sitting on his left and said, 'Look at that woman! She'll be asking if they would like a blow-job next!'

'Howard!' Jenny exclaimed in unison with Michael Hastings, sitting on Carter's right. Even Hardwicke looked at Carter with surprise – the old professor had never said anything like that before. At this point, it was obvious even to the rhinoceros-skinned management that dissention was starting to brew in the ranks, so the meeting was drawn to an abrupt close.

At the provided lunch afterwards, and out of earshot of the management, the staff swapped ideas as to how to get around these new plans.

'Well, I think we just give the students the attendance sheets in advance for the whole term and ask them to sign in,' Ted Murray said. 'As for the swipe cards, I happen to know for a fact that an IT whizz-kid can manipulate the data. I suggest that we all employ a new IT specialist, whose job is to crack the code, so as to speak. If we have one complete week of this bollocks, of signing in, then we can just re-siphon the same information and send that to the management.

Jenny said to Murray with some surprise, 'Ted, you are lawyer; you are supposed to do things lawfully.'

'Supposed to, but not planning to,' he replied.

The head of business, who was allegedly partially sighted, but who invariably found his way to a lone woman, sidled up to Jenny. 'My dear, how is it that your department has got away with a significant number of student deaths?'

'What are you inferring Professor Andrews? That our staff are responsible?'

'I am merely surprised that you were not challenged by the Management this morning, that's all.'

'Well, I will let you into a little secret. They were all failing students, and on top of that, each one had student debts… so you see they were expendable. Management are pleased that they are no longer with us.'

'Oh,' was all that the head of business could reply.

'Ignore him,' said Ted, 'he's just sore that his retirement fund isn't building up as nicely as he hoped.'

'Don't get me started on that one,' said Jenny. 'Is it just me or does our pay go down every month?'

'It does appear to be the case. We have been informed

that the pensions fund is the cause, but it wouldn't surprise me if the finance department was feathering its own nest.'

On that note, Jenny stormed back to her car, in a particularly foul mood.

*

Back at *Kubla Khan*, Jenny walked into a bitch-fest led by Shelley and Percy. They were complaining bitterly because along with the Reverend Dr Clifford Martin, they had been summoned to a meeting with the Quality Assurance Officer in order for her to explain to these reprobate academics, how important it was to complete the paperwork.

Percy moaned, 'That dreadful QAA woman. Don't you think she looks like a raccoon?'

'More like a skunk!', Shelley answered.

'I say,' Clifford had joined in, 'that's a bit much. The woman doesn't smell.'

Shelley expanded on her favourite theme, 'She may not but her job does. Bossing us around like that, bloody administrators. I mean, her whole role stinks; it's not a personal odour problem.' At that moment Shelley turned to Jenny, 'I hope that you are going to fight in our corner against the whim of the QAA office?' But Jenny wasn't in the mood to play those sorts of games today.

'Oh, for God's sake Shelley, just do your bloody paperwork as we have requested countless times.'

And with that she marched off, to a chorus of 'oooOOOooohh!' coming from her junior staff.

Finally reaching her office, she slammed the door shut

and locked it from the inside. 'No one is going to interrupt me for the rest of the day!' she said. She applied herself to her ominous pile of marking that had been left abandoned on her desk during her week in the Bahamas.

She picked up the paper sitting on the top of the pile, and as if trying to cast a spell on it, she said, 'You are worth at least a 2:1, at least a 2:1. I repeat you are going to get a 2:1.' That was before she had read it. Within three minutes, all her expectations were dashed onto the rocks beneath. 'No, fuck it! It doesn't even deserve to pass!' She felt considerably better for adding a whole novel in red pen on the hapless student's essay. 'Thirty-five per cent and be grateful!' she snarled at it and threw it on the floor. 'Next!'

This process was continued for over one and half hours, with none of the essays being up to scratch. Jenny was so frustrated that when a banshee-like wail emanated from the corridor, she thought for a split second that she had made it herself – it echoed precisely how she felt about the essays that she had just been marking. When she finally realised that it was not her own voice, she rushed out of her office in case someone had been taken seriously ill, or was being attacked by a disappointed student in the corridor. It was neither of these dramatic events. It was, in fact, Percy, back from his meeting with the "QAA Woman", doing his best impersonation of Victor Meldrew.

'I don't believe it! Someone has stolen my printer.'

'I say, Percy, you are not the only one. Someone has taken mine too.' The Reverend Dr Clifford Martin was on the verge of uttering forth some further ungodly expletive, but his soul was preserved in time by the voice of reason, who uttered it for him, 'Damnation, you disturbed my sleep. What is all the kerfuffle about?' Dryden shouted out.

A series of disgruntled academics stood in the corridor swearing their heads off much to the amusement of the passing students. When the theft was explained to Jenny she just shook her head sadly.

'I am afraid that it is worse than you think. They have not been stolen, merely removed by IT services.'

'What? Why?'

'Oh come on, you know the drill by now...

> *Theirs not to reason why,*
> *Theirs but to do & die...'*

'Buggeration! This really takes the biscuit.'

Jenny tried to calm the waters, 'Come into my office, out of earshot of the students and I will explain. Tom, can you summon all the staff and we will have a quick debrief about all this? Now hear me out,' she started when all available staff were collected. 'The Powers that Be have made possibly, but only possibly, the most stupid decision in terms of IT support, to date. I only heard about it this morning, but I gather that it has previously been sanctioned by our dean, and therefore we have no muscle to challenge it. No amount of grimacing, whingeing, swearing or bullying is going to change his mind. He is totally in agreement with the VC on this one – you know the spec. Anyway... someone came up with the bright idea of saving our budget, by removing our printers...

Hang on…this was supposed to happen later this week. By Thursday we were all to have links to the printer in the English office, and that is where from now on we will be sending our documents. Yes, I know it is a stupid idea… I tried to argue that we should be linked up only when our working printers have died, but I'm afraid that was too efficient for them, so no! Our printers have to go.'

'But that's preposterous,' said Joyce James, 'we will have to walk miles each day.'

'It's not so much the miles, it's the time,' Percy chipped in. 'It takes me on average a good seven minutes to leave my office, lock my door, walk to the English office, talk to a wandering student on the way, collect what I need and return. My God, if I have to do that ten times in a day that is over an hour wasted.'

'Thank you Percy, we can all do the maths.' Malcolm Lowry had entered the fray. 'I have just been kicked out of my office so that the IT guy can steal my own personal printer! I told him to F**K OFF. If you get a complaint from IT services, you will back me up won't you?'

'Of course,' said Jenny. 'But if I were you, anyone here with a printer still attached to his computer, should hide it. By the way, I was very firm that IT should not disconnect the computers before we are set up to the office one. Has anyone tried printing to here yet?'

A general murmuring of "no" could be heard. 'Let me try mine.' Jenny went over to her desk. Her printer had gone. She looked for a printing facility on her computer screen – none was to be found. 'Well, that's it then – What a bunch of… Tom, are you still connected?'

'Yes.'

'I'm afraid that if we have anything urgent to print off we will have to email it as an attachment to Tom and he will print it off for you.' Tom looked apoplectic at the thought.

'Yes, Tom, I know you will be inundated, but what else can we do? Tell you what, phone up IT and tell them to get back here now.'

The staff all shuffled off in a discontented fashion. She had yet to tell them about the attendance policy… perhaps that could wait for another day. She could justify that inaction, as she couldn't print off any instructions to give her crew! Oh… but Tom could.

'Oh sod it!' she said.

This was unfortunate timing as Tonya Fitzgerald, one of her more able students, walked in at that moment.

'Sorry Tonya, I wasn't meaning to offend you, we are having an IT crisis.'

'So are we Dr Jordan, not one of the English department printers is working for us, and the second years have an assignment due in tomorrow.'

'Oh great. Today is going from bad to worse… Tom…? Can you tell IT they have disconnected the student printers as well…??'

The reply uttered forth by her administrator cannot be printed here…

And it was only Tuesday… surely the week couldn't get any worse, could it?

CHAPTER 26
WEDNESDAY, 4 MAY:
Morning

It *could* get worse! It was eight o'clock when Jenny arrived at the university car park. A mist hung over the ground on this morning giving an ethereal quality to the Nether Stowey campus. 'So much for spring,' Jenny said to herself. She was missing the Bahamian weather that she had enjoyed so much during the previous week.

"At least you will be able to guarantee sunshine in the Bahamas," one of her students had informed her. "I'm so sick and tired of the cold... and it rains all the time too. My friends didn't warn me about that when they recommended this university."

Yes, it really did seem to rain all the time in Somerset. Nor did she see the sun in Nassau. Except for the days on Long Island, Jenny had spent the rest of her time attending boring talks on why the students should come to Sedgemoor.

"And I would like to know the answer to that one myself," she had told Caldicott. Was she unprofessional? Perhaps, but he seemed to enjoy her anarchic attitude.

All of these thoughts entered her head as she walked from the car park to the English building. Was it less than a month that she had met Kevin for the first time? She was still cross with him for the whole "high-handed Bahamian treatment"; nevertheless, she was aching to see him again, but was afraid that she shouldn't. She was concerned that he was too involved with her to do his job efficiently. The last thing that she wanted was to get him into trouble.

In her office, Jenny opened up her newly set-up personal account, to be able to correspond freely with "Marcus", even though she suspected that they shouldn't communicate at all. Marcus' emails were always signed off "Take Care"; why did she need to take care?

For her part, she wrote back an account of her day. She informed "Marcus" that he would be pleased to learn that with the exception of (yet more) poor management decisions, nothing untoward had happened since her arrival back to England. She hoped that this status quo would remain. It didn't.

Jenny had made the mistake of arranging to see all her remedial students on the Wednesday after her return from the Bahamas. Tom had duly organised the list, and the students had duly ignored their summonses.

'Really, what more can we do with these students? This is ridiculous!' she said to Tom. It was now half past ten and each of the three students that had been asked to attend so far had failed to do so. She cast her eye on the list of student names that she was destined not to meet that morning. Kafka was next. No, he wouldn't show up, of that Jenny was certain. She noted that Reginald White's name had been scratched from the eleven thirty slot. That left only one potential student to interview before lunch. Jenny then looked at her list again.

'Why have we got Ashley Roberts scheduled in to see me at eleven, Tom? She isn't on our hit list, is she?'

'No, she asked to see you, not the other way around.'

'Oh. Right. Have we got her file?'

'On your desk with the others,' Tom said.

Whilst waiting for Ashley to arrive, Jenny turned her attention to her work emails. Much to her annoyance she discovered a whole raft of them from the VC, Hardwicke and just about every other middle manager going.

She took great delight in deleting five emails from the VC, without even reading them, knowing full well that they would merely be repeating the same mantras that had been issued every day for the previous term. If she could be bothered to read them they would say "Numbers, Higher Classifications, Finance, Distinction, and Staff Morale". It was a great pity that there was too much emphasis on points one to four and not enough on point five. "Numbers...what are you doing about numbers?" it would ask. "How are your numbers? How do your numbers compare with last year? What about your good degrees? Are there going to be more good degrees this year?"

Jenny had to hold herself in check from replying, "Bad, very bad, very, very bad, losing students by the score, more student deaths... Results are appalling but getting better thanks to the killings... keep the murders coming... but forget having any students here next year."

No one is going to come here now, she thought. She would like to tell the VC that to his face, but she knew that he wouldn't listen to her. After all, a man who listens to Hardwicke will not bother to listen to a mere underling as herself. Underling – that's it! A word that Cassius used to describe himself to Brutus, a speech that started to change Brutus' mind:

> *The fault, dear Brutus, is not in our stars,*
> *But in ourselves, that we are underlings.*

Perhaps it was she who was Cassius after all. But no, that wasn't right. She may like to kill Hardwicke when he annoyed her sufficiently, but she had no cause to kill the students. Saying that… when you summoned them to attend your office for their own good, and they ignored your emails, it was enough to make you want to shoot them.

On reflection, she could understand why Caldicott had behaved as he did. It was obvious that she was a suspect, but she had not realised that from an outsider's point of view she was the person who appeared to have the best motive. Each death had significantly increased her chance of obtaining the minimum 65 per cent of good degrees, and securing her job for another year. People had been murdered for less.

If she had been teaching at a larger university, two or three student deaths would have minimal impact on overall classification averages. But there again, these universities were likely to be on target for a good percentage of higher degrees without resorting to underhand tactics. Not only that, but they need not worry about student recruitment now that the cap of their admissions figures had been lifted. 'And so the rest of us are made redundant thanks to yet another great Government policy.'

She wondered if Oxford and Cambridge used step marking. 'Step marking, I ask you,' she said out loud. Kangaroo marking was a more accurate description. Let the students bounce from one classification to another, without any cares in the world. Kevin understood her dilemmas…

She was so lost in her own world that she hadn't even realised that Ashley had come into the room.

'Dr Jordan?'

'Ashley… hello, have a seat.' Ashley sat herself down on the uncomfortable pine chair. 'What can I do for you?'

Ashley looked extremely ill-at-ease. 'I was wondering how my classification was shaping up. I know that I am not your best student, but I don't want to be your worst…' Jenny phased out momentarily. When she came to she realised that she had only caught the gist of what Ashley was saying, something about the fear of being picked off…

'Sorry Ashley, can you repeat that to me, I'm afraid that jet lag has eaten my brain.'

'I was saying, Dr Jordan, that I don't want to find myself at the bottom of the exam results. It seems to us, that whoever has been killing the students has started at the bottom of the aggregate list and is working his or her way slowly upwards.'

'That's an astute comment.' Jenny sat still in contemplation for a few seconds. 'Ashley, how do the deaths make the students feel?'

'Well, nervous, but it has given most of us an incentive to study more. Dr Jordan, I have been trying my hardest since I started at Sedgemoor, but I really feel that I have been let down by staff and students alike.'

'In what way?'

'Some of the students are lazy. They want to copy everything out of a book. Some try to copy my work, and submit it under their name. In fact, I know that one person stole my notes and photocopied them, as he told me so himself.'

'Did you make a complaint to Professor Hardwicke about this?'

'That takes me on to my second point. Some of the lecturers here are crap.' Jenny sat upright in her chair. 'I mean someone who is called a professor should know their stuff, right?'

'Yes, they are supposed to know it, Ashley.' *This is going to be tough*, thought Jenny, *she is about to complain about Hardwicke.*

'Well, everyone knows that Hardwicke is a bit thin in knowledge and his book isn't correct.' *Ahh, here we go*, thought Jenny... 'but,' Ashley continued, 'nobody minds that. He is quite upfront about it. "If you spot a mistake let me know," he says. "I will reward you with extra marks on your exam!" Well, I mean, that obviously isn't right, but no one is unhappy about that and he is so funny, nobody takes him seriously.'

Jenny thought that this was not the appropriate way for a student to talk about the dean, but as it mirrored her own opinion of him she could hardly condemn her.

'Okay,' said Jenny, 'go on. I take it you are not here to complain about Professor Hardwicke. Can I add that if you were, you would need to make an appointment with the vice chancellor, rather than me?'

'Thank you, Dr Jordan. No, I am here to make a formal complaint against Professor Jones.'

'Would you mind explaining why?'

'Well, I don't mind failing an assignment if my work is poor, but I studied really hard for the last assignment on *Beowulf* and I was only awarded 30 per cent for my final mark. What is even more annoying is that the person who might have "borrowed my notes" was awarded 70 per cent. I am sure that he just copied out everything I had written. I can't understand it except that Professor Jones obviously doesn't like me. Can I get my assignment re-marked?'

'I'm sorry but our policy is that every script is marked once by the main assessor, then second-marked by an independent member of staff. Then, the two markers sit down and discuss each script. Where there is any disagreement between the two, our process is to send the script to a third marker. This all occurs before you are given back your scripts.'

'There was only one marker's writing on my paper, not two as usual. We were given our papers back briefly, and then we had to hand them in again. I pointed this out to Professor Jones at the time, but she became very angry and accused me of troublemaking. I didn't tell her to her face, but I suspect that she kept my assignment away from the usual second marker, just because it was me, and she wanted to fail me.'

'But Ashley, even if a paper had, in error, failed to be second-marked the original mark should be accurate. Furthermore, all the marking is anonymous; we do not know who you are. We award the marks we do purely on the quality of the paper we have received. What makes you think that you were failed because it was you? That is an exceptionally serious allegation.'

'Dr Jordan, I am sure that you do not waste your time checking up on each student number, but I am afraid that I know for a fact that this is what Professor Jones does. She finds out which student the student number refers to and marks from there.'

'Why do you think that Professor Jones doesn't like you?'

'I caught her doing something that she shouldn't have been doing fairly recently. I didn't say anything at the time because I wasn't sure. But now it all fits together. She suspects me of knowing something that she doesn't want me to know, and so she is punishing me with my work.'

Jenny was struggling to keep up with this cloak and dagger speech.

'Well, Ashley, I don't quite know what to say. I will ask Tom to bring me all the *Beowulf* assignments, so that I can look through them myself. Then I can ensure that they have all been second-marked. If your paper, or any other paper for that matter, has not been seen by two markers, I can hand it to another member of staff. When I have examined them, and where appropriate asked another colleague for their opinion, I will invite you in to discuss your paper. If I feel that there is something amiss with the mark awarded we can discuss it then. At the moment, that is all I can do. I suggest that as we are so close to the exams now, you forget about this, and concentrate on your revision. I will not call you in during your exams week, if I can help it. We can discuss this afterwards. In the meantime, I will ask Professor Jones in a roundabout way what she has thought about this year's classes. It is just possible, *just* possible, that your paper has been incorrectly graded.'

'Thank you Dr Jordan, I know that I can rely on you to sort it out.'

After Ashley had left, Jenny stopped to think for a while. Was it possible that Gwen was operating a system of favouritism in her marking? Some staff had been known to do such a thing in the past, but Jenny thought that time had long since gone. Jenny's largest concern was that, at a time when the department were being whipped to produce more 2:1s or better, Gwen was preventing good students from getting good degrees. That was unacceptable. If Jenny found out that Gwen was being vindictive in her marking scheme then she would have her on disciplinary procedures. Jenny would enjoy every minute of it, too.

With malice in her thoughts and revenge in her heart, Jenny dreamt of taking Gwen out to an empty field, tying her to a stake, and leaving her there, to let the crows peck out her eyes… No, that was too light a punishment for the woman, and damned hard luck on the birds!

Jenny shook herself down and focussed on Ashley's conversation. She phoned Tom.

'Tom, would you mind being an angel? Two things, I need you to retrieve all of Gwen's third year assignments on *Beowulf*… Yes, the ones that you put in the archive room last week… Yes, I'm sorry I know that it is an inconvenience… no, no need to rush on that. However, secondly, and this is to be actioned straight away, I want you to send out an urgent email to all our students and staff alike, calling them to an emergency assembly in Wordsworth Hall at two this afternoon. Yes, this afternoon… Yes, you bet we will take a register – of the staff as well. It is important that staff are there to set an example. Oh, but Tom you had better check that the room is free first… Thanks Tom. I owe you a drink!'

*

Jenny addressed a sober and responsive assembly of students that afternoon. Nearly everyone was there, only Franz Kafka remained *in absentia*.

'It will have come to your attention that we have had a number of student deaths in recent weeks. I do not want to alarm anyone unduly, but I do need to let you know that all the students concerned were students who were struggling with their studies. There were several reasons for their poor performance here, but they broadly fall into two categories. Firstly, these students failed to attend classes and failed to put in any extra study. Remember, you are supposed to be full-time students. That means thirty-six hours a week, minimum. Secondly, and I would suggest that this was an even more significant factor, the students were all taking narcotics to a lesser or greater extent. Please, can I impress upon you, how vital it is that you do not squander your academic potential by indulging in drugs? Your exams start next Monday week. Do not, I repeat, do not take drugs before, during, and indeed after the exams.

'Additionally, make sure that you DO get enough sleep. Three hours of sleep a night is not enough to achieve a high grade for your examinations. Nor do I recommend that you spend the night in a cupboard, as a previous student did, because her bed was uncomfortable. I implore you; think of what it means if you leave here with less than a 2:1. To be blunt, you have wasted your money, or perhaps I should say your parents' money.

'If you have been emotionally affected by any of the deaths, to the detriment of your studies, please ensure that you fill in a mitigating circumstances form before your examinations start.

'Most importantly, if you need help with your revision ensure that you ask us. Every single one of us is here for you. Email us and we will help you out if we can.'

At this point, Jenny was distracted by the sound of Professor Jones hissing. She was literally foaming at the mouth. 'Won't we Professor Jones?' Jenny asked pointedly. This so-called professor was earning over twelve thousand pounds a year more than any other member of the English staff, yet she seemed to get away with just turning up two days a week.

Jenny continued, 'But at the end of the day it is up to you. Only you can make it happen. Only you can do the work required. Remember, your lecturers do not fail you, you fail yourselves. Now, on Friday we are heading for the archaeological dig. This is where you can "dig up" really top class marks, so make sure that you appear on time and have all the right equipment for the weekend…'

And with that she left the hall and headed back to her office to complete another round of email deletion.

*

Caldicott had finally arrived back in England late on Wednesday night. The last two days with Marcus had been tough. Marcus was extremely upset that Meg was still not well. Caldicott would have stayed longer if he could, but he had been summoned to report back to work on Friday. This did not strike him as good news. He presumed that he would be removed from the university cases completely. Well, perhaps that was just as well. He wanted to see Jenny, and if he had a choice between Jenny and his employment, then his job would have to be sacrificed. He had had enough. It wasn't just Jenny, he hardly knew the woman. He was living in cloud cuckoo land if he thought that it would work out for him. His main concern was Marcus. He wondered whether Jenny would like to live in the Bahamas. He would ask her the next time he saw her.

CHAPTER 27
FRIDAY, 6 MAY:
Morning

Friday had arrived. It was the first day of the department of archaeology's field trip entitled "The Arthurian Digs". Jenny was pleased as it gave her a legitimate reason to miss the day's Friday meeting.

Due to budgeting issues, the department of archaeology was confined to the employment of one full-time member of staff, the notable Professor Howard Carter. Carter was not left entirely on his own. He was assisted by Dr Aisha Baigum, a part-time teaching fellow. In addition, numerous PhD students assisted with the teaching and the more laborious marking. Jenny thought it was a great pity that no one wanted to study archaeology here, mainly for the reason that unlike virtually every other professor in the university, Carter really did know his stuff, and what a sweetheart he was. Every Christmas he had made it a habit to send all the female staff a box of chocolates, until a feminist do-gooder, Ms Anne Bagshaw, the lecturer in gender studies, complained that he was being sexist. In an effort not to offend anyone, he then sent *all* the staff a box of chocolates for Christmas.

'Ah, good on Carter!' exclaimed Dryden. 'That's one

in the eye for our voice of feminism. It is the only time it has done *me* any favours.'

'Yes it's women like that who give us a bad name,' said Percy.

'Percy, you are the limit!' Joyce laughed. 'But I have to agree with you. I am rightly behind the campaign for equal pay – or at this university perhaps one should say, *any* pay, but some people go too far!'

The hapless Ms Bagshaw sulked past at that moment, and headed straight away to the then Mr Hardwicke's office, to make a complaint. She came out two minutes later in tears, and with vengeance in her heart.

Since that time Carter had been heralded as the true Man of Sedgemoor, but that did nothing to improve his student numbers. In an effort to encourage students, it was suggested by one of the English staff, that they did a combined project on Glastonbury and the Arthurian legends, a sort of excavation of the Knights of the Round Table. A great programme was launched, the most exciting for a significant number of years, and although the student recruitment did not rock the world, it certainly maintained the department sufficiently to keep it open. The highlight of the programme was a simulation dig, set up in advance by all the PhD students in the faculty of humanities, near sites such as Burrowbridge and Glastonbury Tor. This year a field in Glastonbury was to be the host site. A "dig", or to be more correct, a series of digs, had been specifically prepared some weeks previously, and had been given time to settle before allowing the artificial site to be excavated in the name of archaeological practice. There were various pits that replicated famous archaeological finds; the Arthurian legend was only one aspect of the dig.

One pit was the host to a Roman coin hoard, an imitation of the hoard of some two thousand coins that was found locally in 2006, during excavations started by Wessex Water. The pottery container was carefully created by Dr Baigum, to give it the appearance of a third-century Roman pot. It took her eight attempts on a potter's wheel to get the desired effect; the other seven attempts ending up either in Dr Baigum's hair or on the clothes of any unwitting passer-by, including Jenny who had been struck by a flying lump of clay on more than one occasion.

Another part of the field had been moulded to give the appearance of a Bronze Age round barrow in the vein of Wessex Culture. Inside this simulated grave lay artificial (that is plastic) stone battleaxes and daggers with elaborate hilts, decorated in precious jewels. To give a further element of authenticity, a replica Mycenaean golden cup was embedded in the centre of the earth. When questioned as to why this chalice should be buried, Carter replied that it was to remind his students of the trading that occurred across Europe at this time.

All of these beautiful treasures had been secured, during the run up to Halloween, at the noble price of one pound each from the local Poundland store. Therefore, because the mere sum of twenty pounds had been spent on these princely items, the faculty decided that they really didn't want the artefacts to be returned, cleaned and stored. This meant that for the students, it was a real case of finders' keepers, which made the work all the more exciting. As these digs formed the vast majority of students' classification marks, it was easy to see how the archaeology department alone, managed to maintain its enviable conversion rate of 93 per cent of higher classifications.

The most outlandish part of the dig was the simulated Egyptian antechamber some twelve by twenty-six feet, the type that Professor Carter's namesake entered in 1922. This burial chamber came complete with an imitation stone sarcophagus. It would have been impossible to have created an underground chamber, so some artistic licence was applied and it was built by virtue of installing a Portakabin on the field, and then building up layers of soil around the Portakabin to cover it. The assembly of the Egyptian tomb required intricate workmanship to stabilise the surrounding ground. On previous occasions, due to an inadequacy of the construction, a number of students had suffered minor bruising when some of the earth had fallen on them during the excavation. Additionally, the site was a target for some of the local idiots, of which there were plenty, stumbling into the tomb. To prevent anyone from accidentally incarcerating himself, the entrance to the tomb was protected by a modern-day lock. All of the PhD students held a key to this lock, as did most of the staff. As this was the most obvious construction, it was the "dig" that was always attempted first. This fitted neatly into the historical timeline that Carter wanted to adapt, the idea being that the digs were excavated in order of their dates, ending up with the crème supreme of the weekend – the finding of the Holy Grail.

This Friday morning, the combined studies group

met at the Sedgemoor car park at half past seven, to be transported to Glastonbury by the university minibus to take part in the simulation dig. They would be camping out on the field for the rest of the weekend, and had been given detailed instructions of what to bring. Needless to say, getting students to arrive so early in the day was next to a miracle in itself, and invariably some of the students wouldn't make it. The plan was for any late arrivals to find their way to Dr Jordan's office so that either she could drive them over to the site that morning, or if the numbers were excessive, she could phone for the minibus to make another journey.

At half past eight Jenny sat in her office secretly hoping that she would not be called upon to drive to Glastonbury. She hadn't seen any stragglers left behind in the car park, but perhaps there were some who were still asleep. She would wait until Howard phoned to let her know who was missing. The call duly came through at nine.

'Hello, my dear,' Carter started. 'Oh sorry, that is sexist, I should say hello Dr Jordan.'

'Howard, I have told you a thousand times that I do not and will not take offence at being called "my dear". "Whore", "slut", "slag", "fuckwit", "c**t", yes, but "dear" – no!'

'Jenny, really, where did a lady like you learn those words? Sorry, being sexist again. Now then, where was I? Ah yes, missing persons... well, you will be shocked to find that most of the students made it! Yes, for half past seven. Perhaps there is some hope after all for the faculty. McClellan was absent, but he phoned us beforehand to say he would drive himself over. He has yet to arrive but at least we know that he is on his way. So the only people we are missing are Faye Goddard, Josh Miller and Franz Kafka.'

'Hold on Howard, someone is here now, let me check.'

Jenny looked outside the door, but it was only Tom coming in to start his work.

'No, sorry Howard, none of those has turned up yet. Well, they have been given enough time really. Why don't you start the morning session when you are ready, and if any of the others roll up in the next hour, I will drive them over – otherwise, they can forget it for today; it will be too late to participate by that stage, won't it? They can catch a bus at their own expense.'

'Good idea Jenny. It's a lovely day here, I can't wait to start. Ah, here is Miller now, so there are only two to look out for.'

'If I am not with you by eleven thirty then you can assume that I am not coming,' she said to Howard.

'Perfect. I'll phone you tomorrow with the results.'

Jenny laughed when he mentioned results. All the staff knew what the students were going to find, as they had all been involved in the prop-making sessions. Still, it was a bit of fun, artistic licence, and it really did help the students achieve higher grades. No one begrudged helping Carter out, primarily because no one was told they had to.

It is a well-known organisation miracle that staff will work flat out if they like their job and feel empowered to do it, but as soon as management tries to take unnecessary control, all goodwill evaporates. And talking of which, Jenny had settled down to an email battle with the finance director, one she vowed she would see through to the death, when an ominous knock on the door interrupted her.

With a deep sigh she called, 'Come in.' It was one of the missing students.

'Ah Faye, you're late.'

'I'm really sorry Dr Jordan, but I have been sick and had stomach cramps all night.'

'Then for goodness' sake don't come near me, go back home again.'

'No, it's not that, it's just my time of the month; I always get ill then. It's so unfair. I want to go to the dig. I am not going to get my degree if I don't.'

'Tell you what,' said Jenny, 'I am still waiting for one more of you. Go to the cafe and come back in twenty minutes. If you feel better I will take you myself, but mind you, it's quite a way to go. You will be staying there until Sunday; have you got everything you need? They won't have sanitary wear available, not if the men have been organising it. They might have some paracetamol for their hangovers, but make sure you have your own. I can't rescue you once you are there, so I will take you home if you still feel ill.'

'Thank you Dr Jordan, I will get some breakfast.' Faye left the office and went to the student cafe.

'Bollocks! Bollocks! Bollocks!' exclaimed Jenny. 'Just when I thought I might get a day to catch up on my work.'

At ten o' clock precisely, she told Tom that Kafka had missed his opportunity and that she was going to collect Faye from the cafe and take her to the dig.

*

264

The journey took longer than anticipated and when Jenny finally arrived at Glastonbury, all the students had embarked on lunch.

'Good morning Howard, I've brought you Faye.'

'Ah, Jenny, come and stay with us for the afternoon, we are just about to break open the seal on the tomb. What do you say? You must come and see. It really is the most wonderful thing. The PhD students did a fabulous job. I anticipate that it will take about another thirty minutes till we break into the chamber, then you can go back to Sedgemoor happy in the knowledge that no one has been hurt.'

'Thanks Howard. By the way, has McClellan arrived?'

'No, I'm afraid that he has not. He promised to be here by eleven. Perhaps his car has broken down again.'

Jenny had not noticed any stationary cars with hazard lights flashing on her way to the field. There again, she probably was not paying full attention. Nevertheless, it was odd.

'I tell you what,' she added seeing how crestfallen the professor looked, 'I will pop off for an hour to town, I have to get some supplies for our female students. Whilst I am away, I will see if I can find out what has happened to McClellan.'

'Perfect. Thank you very much Dr Jordan, as always a gem.'

Jenny was disappointed that she was not to get any time to herself, but it was important to assist her colleagues. The entire faculty needed to push up the numbers of good degrees awarded, and besides, most of the students on the dig were her own English students.

Those who participated well invariably ended up walking out of the university with at least an upper second class degree, *and goodness only knows, we need as many firsts and 2:1s as we can get this year, they are a particularly lack lustre bunch.*

Jenny was genuinely surprised that McClellan had not turned up. He was a potential first class student, and one of the reasons being was that he usually turned up to classes on time. Jenny had a strange foreboding that his car had not broken down, but she was not going tell Carter that.

*

Caldicott had been relocated to the Street Police Station office on Friday morning, just at the time that Jenny was setting off on her journey to Glastonbury. Caldicott was told in no uncertain terms that he was now deskbound at Street for the next two weeks, and was taken off the university cases completely. These, he was told, were in the process of being handed over to a higher authority. That suited him fine. He had to admit that he had failed spectacularly to find anyone responsible. The only link to all the crimes appeared to be Dr Jordan, and he had ruled her out of the killings. That was the trouble. His bosses seemed to intimate that he was too emotionally involved with the suspect to make a rational decision. In this they were doing him a disservice. He would have happily arrested Jenny if he felt the evidence was compelling, but, although he was working with an incomplete set of jigsaw pieces, he was certain that the picture created would not be of her.

He had offered to hand in his notice, but this was not accepted. Instead, he was told categorically to keep away from Dr Jordan. This concerned him for two reasons: Firstly, he needed to let Jenny know that he wasn't ignoring her on purpose, and secondly, he needed to ensure that she would be safe from harm. He knew from their email exchange that she was normally home on a Saturday morning. He would go round then, and explain this to her in person… just in case their emails were being intercepted.

It was while he was fixed to his desk in Street, that he received an emergency call out to a place on the outskirts of Glastonbury. No further details were given to him. He was instructed by the superintendent to attend at once, and take the only available PC. That, he thought, was odd.

*

When Jenny arrived back at the dig, armed with painkillers for Faye, she found that the professor had been over optimistic with his time estimate. In fact, the students appeared to be nowhere near to breaking into the tomb. She found a folding chair and sat herself in it. She pulled out an article on Priestley, which she wanted to read, and applied herself to the task in hand.

Halfway through the article, a shout was heard from the professor, 'At last I have made a wonderful discovery in the Valley; a magnificent tomb with seals intact!' *Howard really does get into the role*, thought Jenny.

Another voice piped up, 'Can you see anything?'

The professor responded, 'Yes, wonderful things.'

Jenny had to laugh at this. Well, if it made the professor happy acting out his little scene, why not? This meant that the door would be breached imminently and Jenny could go home. She strolled over to the tomb, but was struck by a standstill in the excavation.

'What's that smell? It's very authentic, isn't it?'

'Probably just some sewage has leaked in, that or someone left their lunch behind.'

When the grave door was finally opened, the smell became overpowering. The PhD students looked at one another. 'This isn't how we left it,' one of them said.

Jenny asked Carter, 'Has someone been tampering with this?'

'Quite possibly, my dear; perhaps the undergrads should wait outside.'

'Yes, I will keep them back,' she said and deftly arranged it so that all her students were sitting on a bank some thirty feet away. Then she went back into the grave, with a searing pain inside her skull.

'Just where is the stench coming from?' Dr Baigum asked.

'It's in one of the four Canopic jars,' said Nigel Downs, the lead designer. 'We put plastic body parts in them, they shouldn't smell like that. We had better open them up.' Nigel opened up the Canopic jar bearing the head of Duamatef the jackal, the guardian of the stomach. Duamatef had failed to protect his contents from necrosis. Nigel opened up the other three jars. All contained real organs in various states of decay.

'My God,' Carter spluttered, 'this is sacrilege. If this is some kind of joke it's not funny.'

'No!' said Jenny. 'But that's not the only place where the smell is coming from.'

'I think it is the sarcophagus,' Tammy Smith, one of the PhD students, replied.

The PhD students attempted to prise open the sarcophagus. It was not sealed as such, but the lid was very heavy, and needed more than one person to move it.

What with the overpowering stench and the oppressive atmosphere of the tomb, it was entirely understandable that Sophie Bellinger fainted, but neither the smell nor the room had distressed Sophie. It was the site of a real mummy in the sarcophagus which had caused the upset. Franz Kafka had magically appeared, holding a copy of Jacqueline Wilson's book *Buried Alive*.

CHAPTER 28
FRIDAY, 6 MAY:
Afternoon

It was impossible to say whether anyone was more stunned to see Kafka in the sarcophagus, or Kafka in any shape or form, so elusive had he been. Either way, this was the end of the field trip as far as the university was concerned.

Professor Carter was beside himself with rage. 'Whoever has done this to my dig? I will kill them myself!'

By this time, someone had contacted the police.

'Now Professor, you need to be a little more circumspect in your use of language,' Jenny said, 'otherwise you will find yourself under arrest.'

Everyone was shocked, but the undergraduates shook with fear. "Not another death?" ; "Who was it?"; "What were his results like?" They whispered questions to each other.

In an attempt to calm some of the sobbing students and prevent what was becoming mass hysteria, Jenny felt it best to take charge and talk to all the students in one go. She summoned everyone to follow her to the furthest part of the field so that she could address them all, away from the, now real, tomb. This happened to be near the entrance to the field. She stood on a small mound of earth, waving her arms around so that everyone could see and hear her. From a distance she looked like an ancient goddess. It was whilst she in this pose that Caldicott arrived. If Jenny had turned around at that stage she would have seen Caldicott looking first, shell-shocked, and then mesmerised. This was awful, he told himself, he had been forbidden to speak to Dr Jordan, but at the same time, he had not been instructed not to watch her. He was fascinated. For the first time in their acquaintance, he saw her working a crowd. He thought that she must be an inspirational lecturer if this was anything to go by. He wanted her more than ever.

'I understand how saddened you must all feel. The staff are truly shocked at our findings in the tomb today. To make matters worse for you, I'm really sorry to say this but we cannot go ahead with any further activities, I suspect, for the whole weekend. Do not worry about your classifications. We will find a way to ensure that you are not treated harshly for events beyond your control. I appreciate that a number of you, and myself included, would like to go home now. I am so sorry that will not be possible. I am fairly certain that each and every one of you will need to answer some routine questions when the police arrive. Please be as accurate as you can with your answers, this will ensure that we leave here as quickly as possible, and more to the point, that we may be able to apprehend the person or persons responsible. If anyone knows anything, anything at all, can you please see me straight away? I will draw up a list of those who should be interviewed first.'

Someone asked, 'Who was it?'

271

'We think we know but we would rather not say until the identity had been verified.'

'How did he or she die?'

'I really can't say. These are all questions for the police, not me. They should be along here very soon.'

Caldicott stepped up to the challenge. 'Thank you, Dr Jordan, for organising your students so well. I'm afraid whoever contacted us did not tell us that there were so many people here, or that it was the university who were carrying out a field trip. This is going to take quite a while, but as Dr Jordan has already asked, I will ask again. If anyone has any specific information then please make yourself known to Dr Jordan. Dr Jordan will draw up a list for me. I will need to speak to Dr Jordan first, and then I will cordon off the area.'

Jenny walked over to him.

'Why are you here?' she asked quietly. 'This isn't your normal territory.'

'What, no "it's lovely to see you again, Kevin"?' he asked half smiling.

'Yes, of course it is, but… uh… this is the freakiest of all…'

'What am I going to see?' he asked.

'A modern mummy in a modern sarcophagus.'

'Ah.'

'Do you remember my email saying that I wanted Kafka to be buried alive?' Caldicott nodded. 'Someone appears to have granted my wish.'

Caldicott stopped. 'Jenny, I have been forbidden from acting in the university murders and I am not even supposed to be talking to you. However, I have been sent here as I was redeployed to the Street station and no one else was available to come out. Isn't that ironic? I will have to phone for backup. I will come and see you at your house in the morning. Don't tell anyone else that I am planning to do that.'

'Of course not. Let me introduce you to Professor Carter, a genuine professor, by the way. Poor Howard, this will break his heart.'

'Is there anything else that I need to know urgently?'

'Well, I'm not sure but another of my students appears to have gone AWOL.'

'Is he a good student?'

'That, my dear, is an astute observation. Yes, he is one of the best – Donald McClellan.'

'I met him in one of Dryden's classes. Good with cars.'

'That's the one. According to Professor Carter, he set off this morning to get here. He was supposed to catch the minibus with the others, but his car was not running smoothly, so he was late. But he should have been here by eleven. Kevin, I'm worried. I was concerned before we found Kafka, but now… What are we dealing with here?'

'I don't know. I wish I did. Let's discuss it tomorrow.'

And with that they went their own ways for the day. As soon as Stone arrived Caldicott left the site. He did not dare look for Jenny.

It took a long time, but finally the questioning was over. No one was surprised that the site was formally cordoned off by the police. All the students were sent home whilst forensic experts tried their best to gather clues from a site trampled on consistently during the earlier part of the day. Finding a killer was going to be a nigh-on impossible task.

CHAPTER 29
SATURDAY, 7 MAY

It was eleven when Caldicott arrived at Jenny's cottage. He had a feeling that he was being shadowed, but he didn't care. Much to his surprise, he saw that Jenny had made an effort to tidy up her cottage. He hoped that she hadn't tired herself out.

It was less than a week since they had been together in Long Island, but a year might as well have lapsed. Despite the flow of emails, they appeared to have become strangers again. He wondered how she had felt during these seven days, and whether she had remembered any facts that might help solve the murders. Jenny for her part was concerned that Caldicott had turned up at all. He had given the impression that he wasn't supposed to be seeing her, so why was he risking his job? She was cross with him, for that. Under these strained conditions it was impossible for any conversation to be intimate. It was very practical and businesslike; at least it commenced that way.

'How's Marcus?'

'Not too bad; he is obviously concerned about his mum. We all are. I might have to go back over there shortly. Can't say that I relish the idea of flying there again so soon. Did you survive your journey back?'

'Yes, it was fine, I managed to sleep through most of it. That's probably what I needed all along – just lots of sleep. Kevin, why are you here? I mean… don't get me wrong, I am pleased to see you but shouldn't you stay away from me?'

'Probably, but I needed to ensure that you are safe. Honey, have you remembered anything, anything that might help us work out what is going on?'

'No, in fact everything seems to have merged into a horrible blur. I just feel depressed and utterly useless.'

'I'm sorry to hear that.'

'Well, you weren't supposed to, it slipped out unguarded,' she said.

'That's what I love about you, Jenny, the fact that you are so straight. It's why I have always thought that you were not responsible for any of the deaths. I am pretty certain that you would tell me if you were.'

'Yes, I probably would.'

'Look Jenny, I have something to tell you. The night in Clarence Town… I should have asked you at the time and I'm sorry that I didn't, but you were so angry that you would have said no.'

'No to what?'

'I had to search through your bags. No, don't get mad at me please. Let me explain.'

'WHAT?'

'Your bags in your hotel… when you were sleeping at Liz's house.'

'But… you mean you went into the hotel room and searched my bags…? Why?'

'Jenny, I had to be sure, you need to see it from my

point of view. I was certain that you were not responsible for any of the crimes, but all the circumstantial evidence said otherwise. Believe me I did not want to do it.'

'Then why the hell did you?'

'I was informed that the police were going to do the same thing. One of the local lawyers told me that over there, the police can search for firearms or dangerous drugs without a warrant if they have reasonable suspicion, to do so. And they did have reasonable suspicion. Someone informed them that you had a gun in your bag.'

'Did you think I had a gun?'

'No, of course not, but I thought that you might have another book in there.'

'What? Why couldn't you have asked me directly rather than sneaking around like a… like a… No, it's outrageous. God, I thought that you were on my side, but I can see that I was wrong…'

'Okay, so report me to my superiors if you feel like that. I am quite happy to face disciplinary proceedings.'

'As if I am going to do that, Kevin! I'm not a monster even if you are! No, not a monster, duplicitous! I didn't know until I met you that "doing paperwork" was a euphemism for screwing older women! You have behaved completely appallingly to both of us. No wonder… ah, well, never mind!'

'Jenny, what the hell are you talking about? Yes, Meg is older than me but what has that to do with anything? I mean, we were never really together and it was many years ago. I haven't been in that sort of relationship with Meg since Marcus was born. I'm sorry if I didn't make myself clear.'

'I'm not talking about Meg. I understand your

relationship with her perfectly. You are just trying to evade the subject again. You should have retrained as a barrister! They always dodge direct questions. You know what I mean. The last time you were around here, you stayed for barely ten minutes, and then said that you were off to do paperwork. Well, after you had left I went to Taunton. I saw you there myself with an older woman. You were holding her hand. Now don't tell me I was mistaken, although I am sure that that is what you are going to do.'

'Jenny, what are you talking about? Where did you see me? And if you saw me why didn't you come to speak to me?'

'I saw you in Starbucks, and obviously I didn't want to interrupt your tête-à-tête with an attractive older lady! God, how foolish would that make me look and perhaps her as well? No, I've had enough arse-holes to deal with in my lifetime. I don't want any more of that sort of relationship, again. Oh and another thing…'

Their conversation was interrupted by a knock on the door. It was DC Stone.

'Sorry sir, you are not supposed to be here. We will deal with that later but we have come to ask Dr Jordan some questions. Dr Jennifer Jordan, you are wanted at Minehead station to answer questions about the murders of Franz Kafka and Donald McClellan.'

'McClellan?'

'Yes, his body was discovered at 19.05 last night in his car, which was parked in the sea-front car park at the Blue Anchor. He was holding your copy of Anthony Horowitz's *Point Blank*.'

CHAPTER 30
SUNDAY, 8 MAY

Jenny reached her cottage late in the evening, but couldn't settle down to sleep. Her head was still pounding from her words of fury at Caldicott and of the rather ferocious police questioning. She was exceptionally angry with the police, predominantly because they ruined a perfectly good argument. Jenny knew that she would have calmed down fairly soon, in fact she had almost done so. If they had not been interrupted by Stone, Jenny was pretty certain that she and Kevin would have sorted everything out, worked out who was behind the killings, and even settled on what to do with each other. But thanks to DC Plod, the couple had been ripped apart. Honestly, it was almost like a scene from *Romeo and Juliet*.

Stone had let her go of course, well he had to. She was innocent, so why were they wasting her time and theirs taking her in? Jenny was certain that they were trying to intimidate her into confessing. No, try what they wanted the police could not make her confess to something that she had not done. The only link to her that they had was that her books appeared to find themselves by the victims. That was easily explained, she told them. Some of the students, including McClellan, had helped her to pack them up when she moved offices. It would have been easy for McClellan to take books of his choosing, she wouldn't notice. But, and she had kept this to herself, to choose specific titles meant that the series of deaths had been planned for over a month. That was extremely worrying. Perhaps she should go to work to unpack the rest of her boxes to see if she could identify any other missing titles.

Eventually, the results of Kafka's and McClellan's post-mortem found their way to Stone. McClellan had died sometime in the early afternoon, the time when both she and Caldicott had an unsinkable alibi; the time, in fact, that they had been standing in front of fifty students and lecturers. That brought a look of vicious delight to Jenny's face. As McClellan had been executed in the manner of the book (shot at point-blank) there would be no significant gap in time between the act and the death, unlike a poisoning. Stone reluctantly let her go, but not before trying to pin Kafka's death on her. Kafka had died some four days previously. She pointed out that she could not lift the sarcophagus lid on her own. "McClellan could have helped you," she was told. Next, they decided that Caldicott might have assisted her. Were they mad? He wasn't even in England then. Stone ought to get a medal for that idea.

They could throw anything that they wanted at her; she was not in the slightest bit worried. She was, however, concerned that she had flared up at Caldicott. 'It was a misjudgement, an error, I should not have lost my temper like that,' she said to no one in particular. In doing so, she had managed to rip out the only silver lining in the vast array of dark clouds above her. God, she was a fool!

But then he had been a fool too. Why didn't he tell her that he wanted to check her baggage? And more to the point, what of the other woman? He had denied any wrongdoing. Perhaps it was a something or nothing. Perhaps she had been mistaken after all. She would have to apologise, but she couldn't bear to speak to him just then and more to the point, she was pretty certain that she should not contact him at all.

She looked at the time; it was now half past eleven. The Bahamas was five hours behind. She sent an email to Marcus asking him to pass on a message to his dad to the effect that she was sorry she had got cross. Marcus emailed back instructing her to visit a cafe called "Toast" (chosen, he said, because she had told him that she liked toast) in Honiton the next day (Sunday) at 2.45 pm. She was told not to drive there.

For his own part Caldicott was bemused. He was not at all concerned that Jenny was angry that he had searched her luggage, particularly as she had some semi-pornographic magazines in there. It was only natural that she would be annoyed. His concern was that she appeared to be labouring under an illusion that he was seeing someone else. No, that would not do! He was unlikely to embark on two romances at once at his age, and come to think of it, he had never done so when he was younger, unlike some of his friends. Yes, he had been in Taunton on the Saturday in question, and yes he had a coffee in Starbucks, but he wasn't seeing anyone.

And then the penny dropped. Yes, he had seen someone, quite by accident, an older woman. And now he came to think about it no doubt she did hold his hand as she often did. Caldicott roared with laughter; Jenny would see the funny side of that too when she knew. He would have to let her know, but how? He had been strictly forbidden from contacting Jenny in any shape or form by his superiors. But he had to tell her this… he didn't want her to think badly of him, quite the reverse.

Just then his phone rang. It was Marcus. Marcus told him to have "Toast" in Honiton the next day at 2.45 pm.

*

In the early afternoon, Jenny set off to Honiton. It was a place she used to visit when she was a girl. She parked her car in the car park and was heading to Lace Walk when Caldicott appeared from out of nowhere. Although she was expecting to see him, the abrupt meeting in the car park struck her as being in a fashion akin to Mr Darcy's arrival at Pemberley. The opening conversation was as equally tense as the Darcy-Bennet affair, particularly as Caldicott was not on his own…

'Kevin, where have you got to? Oh, there you are!'

The other woman had appeared at Caldicott's side and linked arms with him. The shock of seeing him attached to this beautiful but obviously older woman gave Jenny a stabbing pain in her solar plexus. Of all the insults! For a second, Jenny thought she was going to be sick. Caldicott, misreading the signs and thinking she was going to collapse, broke free from his shackles and went over to catch her if he needed to.

Jenny felt nothing but utter confusion, which was not helped by seeing the woman give a knowing smile.

'Well, go on! Introduce me to your friend!'

By this time Caldicott's arms were firmly around Jenny's shoulders.

'Dr Jordan, let me introduce you to my mother… Mum, this is Dr Jordan.'

Jenny looked at Caldicott in bewilderment for a second, and then a smile of recognition lit up her face. She said to the other woman, 'You don't look old enough to be Kevin's mother!'

His mother replied, 'Pleased to meet you, Dr Jordan. Now Kevin, you have been very unkind to Dr Jordan. Dr Jordan, my son had described you as average looking, but I can see now that he was doing you a disservice. Either that or he did not want to let me know just how serious this was.'

It was difficult to assess who was the most embarrassed at this point, Jenny or Caldicott. His mother was enjoying herself enormously at her son's expense.

'Oh for goodness' sake, Mum! You always complain that you don't meet any of my friends, and this is precisely the reason why! I can't rely on what you will say next.'

'Rubbish, I don't meet your friends because you don't have any time to make any. When you are not working, and goodness only knows how many hours you spend doing that, you are too busy looking after me, or my grandson. You never get a chance to enjoy yourself, I know that is the case, and… stop pulling that face at me, Kevin… I'm speaking to you! You better behave yourself Kevin, or I will cut you out of my will! Dr Jordan, do you have a less formal name I can use?'

Jenny had been trying not to laugh. The woman was a

tyrant, or was it just an act? Either way it was easy to see that Marcus took after his grandmother. Grandmother? She only looked late forties, but she must be more than that surely…

'Your name, please?' Jenny was asked again.

'Jenny,' she managed to say without laughing.

'Yes that's better, and you may call me Stella.'

Caldicott cut in. 'Why on earth would she want to do that? Your name is June!'

Stella turned to her son, 'Yes, well Kevin, I'm a bit bored with June, I thought I might have a change,' and to Jenny she said, 'and I don't suppose that he has even spoken about me, has he? No, I thought not, typical man! Anyway Jenny, Kevin has told me that he is not allowed to talk to you, some stupid work rule, so *I* won't allow you to either, at the moment. Tell you what Kevin, I have some shopping to do and it would bore you senseless. Men hate shopping. I know that for a fact, as I've had any number of them! Go in Warren's Bakery over there. Jenny, you are coming with me. I need a woman's touch on this. Kevin, we will come and get a drink when we are finished. We should be over in twenty minutes. I haven't got all day, and the shops shut soon anyway. In the meantime, have a look around. You know what I mean.'

Jenny hoped that Caldicott knew what Stella meant because she certainly didn't. As soon as Caldicott had gone, his mother continued, in a completely different manner, and in a very low voice.

'Right then Jenny, come into this shop with me, we are going to assess whether you have been followed here today. Kevin brought me here from Taunton, and at one point we were definitely being tailed, but I think they backed off. Were you followed?'

By this stage, Jenny was completely nonplussed by the whole "Stella" experience. 'I really didn't think to look.'

'Never mind. Let's try on shoes. It's a great cover. I always find it helps to try on the most ridiculous pair possible in these situations, as you know that you are never going to buy them, and no one in the shop can expect you to. How about these?' she said pointing out a toeless shoe in red leather with pink tassels on the side. 'They are grotesque. Go on. Try them on.'

They were in the shop for at least ten minutes trying on footwear, and laughing at each other's choices, before turning their attention to the handbag selection. Stella told Jenny that it was time to exit with dignity. 'Just watch and learn,' she said.

Stella pointed to the highest pair of stilettos ever designed, and in a loud voice called out, 'Jenny, I am going to try on these.' She did so and immediately fell over. Whilst winking at Jenny she cried, 'Oh dear, that was stupid, I think I've sprained my ankle. Jenny, I need you to help me get up. Oh, how bad I feel! Take me to the cafe over there.'

And so Jenny and Stella limped over to the cafe opposite, only to find Caldicott eating a Cornish pasty. 'Look at my son. Isn't that just typical?' Stella said. 'Did I tell you to order food? You were supposed to wait for us!'

'How the heck was I supposed to know that? Caldicott retorted. 'You just make up the rules as you go along.'

'That's what mothers are for darling, you should know that by now.'

Caldicott surrendered. 'All right, what do you want? Jenny?'

'Scone with jam please, and a cup of tea,' she said to the hovering waitress.

'Mum?'

'Tell you what, I don't want to be a gooseberry for the rest of the afternoon. I am going to go elsewhere and come back and have something later... that is if it is safe to leave you two alone. Is it?'

'I was hoping that you were going to tell us that.'

'Well, I think that I will just wander to the High Street. If your phone rings and it is from me, then go back to the car.'

Stella exited the cafe leaving Caldicott and Jenny alone. They looked at each other. Caldicott was smiling at Jenny. She, in her turn, was trying to work out what had just happened. 'This is like working for MI5,' Jenny started. 'Is your mum always like this?'

'Sorry, Mum can be a bit of a joker at times. It is what keeps her so noticeably young. Not that she is that old, but I will tell you about her another time. I thought it best to bring her with me. I presume that she was the woman that you saw in Taunton?'

Jenny nodded, looking somewhat ashamed. She concentrated on spreading jam on the scone that the waitress had just placed in front of her.

Caldicott asked her gently, 'Why didn't you speak to us then?'

Jenny continued to look at her scone. 'I didn't want to make a fool of myself, I guess. I mean, I didn't know anything about you really, and I was... perhaps still am... your main suspect.'

285

Caldicott's whole manner changed abruptly. 'Dr Jordan, you were specifically instructed not to drive here. I'm sorry I have to do this.' He sounded so stern that Jenny looked up at him in alarm, only to find herself being kissed. It took her breath away.

'Jenny, you are adorable. I've been dying to do that for the last month ever since I first met you by the bloody birdcage.'

'Sorry I've been a bit slow… I've been…'

'Preoccupied, and quite understandably too,' Caldicott added. 'We both have for a variety of reasons.' They looked at each other, without speaking for a good three seconds, before the waitress broke the spell by banging Jenny's tea down in front of her. Caldicott switched into full work mode. 'Right, now that is out of the way, drink your tea before it gets cold.'

Jenny laughed at this ludicrous change of personality. He had obviously inherited something from Stella himself.

Caldicott added in a low voice, 'In all seriousness, you shouldn't be driving. Typical of Marcus to choose a place miles from anywhere… never mind. Now, I need you to explain what happened yesterday. I can still try to assist you, even if I have been suspended.'

So Jenny talked Caldicott through her interrogation by DC Stone, '… and Kevin, he seems to think that you and I are working as a team to bump off my students.'

'Christ!' Caldicott exclaimed, spitting out his coffee. 'The man is more of a moron than I thought. If this wasn't so serious it would be funny. Now listen, and please don't flare up at me when I ask this question… was there any reason, apart from the obvious, as to why you had *Zoo* magazine in your bag?'

Jenny first looked astounded, then enlightened, and then laughed. In doing so she nearly choked on the scone that she had just bitten into.

'Oh my God! Yes, I had completely forgotten, and no I don't like women like *that*, if that is what you want to know... well, not very often,' she added giving him a cheeky smile.

'You know, I will have to kiss you again if you smile at me like that,' he said, and promptly did so.

Jenny had a sudden thought. 'Kevin, you don't seem to be upset at being suspended.'

'That's because I'm not.'

'Why not?'

'Think about it, I couldn't kiss you if I was still working on the case.'

Jenny playfully smacked him lightly on his arm. 'Ouch!' he said. 'I'm not into pain. I would much prefer you to kiss me, you know.'

'Oh for goodness' sake!' Jenny said. She reached up to put both her hands around his shoulders and pulled him towards her to kiss him.

'That's reassuring,' he said when they had finally broken contact. 'I thought that I might be wasting my time when I found your magazines.'

Jenny stifled a giggle. 'I had better tell you what happened.' And so Jenny explained the history behind the purchase. 'What was in it?' she asked. 'I presume that *you* have looked through them?'

'All part of the job, I'm afraid. There was a very

interesting centre piece. One Bernice Pye, sporting nothing but *The Complete Works of Shakespeare*. The caption told us that she is dating a lecturer.'

'Really…? Ohhh… so no wonder Simeon dropped it, if he's the man in question, which I'm pretty certain he is.'

'Lucky devil.'

'Are you trying to make me jealous?'

'Is it working?'

'No. You wouldn't like Bernice; she would bore you in ten minutes of talking to her.'

'I don't think that I would have planned to *talk* to her, but there you go.' Jenny grinned at him. He added, 'Poor girl, she won't look the same again, not that she was ever as beautiful as you.' Jenny gave him a look as though she didn't believe him.

'Rubbish,' she said. She received another kiss for that.

Caldicott recommenced in work mode. 'Did you get any further with the handwriting on the letter?'

'No, but I will make every effort to investigate it this week.'

'It would be extremely useful if you could match it up. Jenny, this is the most important question, how long have you been taking iron supplements?'

'Since the end of March; why?'

'Did you happen to notice that some of your tablets were slightly different to others?'

'No, should I?'

'I think that someone has been tampering with them. Do you normally carry them on you?'

'Yes, they are in my handbag most of the time, in case I forget to take them, which I frequently do, why?' On saying this she started to rummage in her handbag for them. She pulled the container out of her bag and placed it on the table.

'Someone has replaced some of your tablets with ones that are five times the strength of your normal dosage.' Caldicott opened the container to show her. In the broad daylight, it was easy to distinguish the subtle colour differences in the two types of tablet. 'It might explain your fainting fits,' he added.

Jenny looked astounded, 'Why would anyone want to do that?'

'Presumably to make you ill. Adults don't usually die of iron poisoning, but children can. That might have been the intention. I've told you all along that I thought that you were being targeted for some reason. Did you start this container in March?'

'Yes, I bought it around the same time that I received my demotion.'

'Don't you mean promotion?'

'That's not how I see it.'

Caldicott half smiled at Jenny, but he was more interested in confiscating her tablets. 'Give me your pills and buy a fresh lot. Besides, the high strength ones have got gelatine in.'

'Yuck,' she said, rolling the bottle over to him. 'What are you going to do with them?'

'Send them to Stone and give him something tangible to concentrate on.'

'Kevin, I have a question for you. On the day that we first met, Tom told me that after I had left for Bridgwater you came back into my room to look for something. What were you looking for and did you find it?'

Caldicott's whole demeanour changed. 'No, I didn't find it. I had lost a photo of Lucy, my wife. I kept it in my wallet, but somehow it had fallen out that day. I thought it might have got mixed in with your paperwork,' he smiled ruefully. 'It doesn't matter now,' he added.

Jenny observed how his body tensed up when discussing his wife. She would have liked to have discussed her further, but she could sense that it would be a difficult conversation. It was not the right time. Besides, his mother had just come back into the shop.

Jenny said, 'I will have a look for you. I expect I can find it if you dropped it in my room. The cleaner never does her job properly.'

She squeezed his arm and finished her scone.

'Jenny... I...' Whatever Caldicott was about to say was interrupted by his mother.

'Well, have you two made it up? I hope so because judging by the people I have just seen down the road, it is time for Dr Jordan to leave.'

There was something about Stella that was impossible to disobey. Jenny stood up and picked up her bag.

'Oh Jenny,' Stella continued, giving her a piece of paper, 'here is my mobile phone number. Please feel free to call me if you need to chat,' she added looking at her son. 'I apologise in advance if Kevin answers by mistake.'

'Thank you,' said Jenny. She turned to Caldicott and kissed him. 'Goodbye for now,' she said. 'It was nice meeting you, Stella,' she called as she walked out of the door. She felt that she had just been enacting a version of *The Thirty-Nine Steps*.

CHAPTER 31
WEDNESDAY, 11 MAY

During the week after Jenny had met Caldicott and his mother in Honiton, a disquieting stillness covered the university. There were no more deaths, no threatening letters, just the sound of pens frantically scribbling away on paper as all the students undertook their final revision for their exams. This was the time of year that Jenny usually loved the best, despite the impending arrival of an inordinate amount of scripts to mark. It was the gentle lull after teaching; a time when one could hope for the best and that ever-elusive target of good classifications. But this year was different. Jenny was depressed.

This year, not only was she promoted to head of department, without her ready agreement, but she was under suspicion of murdering a number of her students, and was suffering daily visits from the likes of DC Stone. On top of that someone had been attempting to poison her.

Albeit that only a couple of days had elapsed since Caldicott's warning about her iron tablets, Jenny was starting to feel better. It was clear that although the concussion had led to some of the dizzy spells, the introduction of a significantly higher dosage of ferrous sulphate than required had affected Jenny's wellbeing. It might have been the cause of the initial accident on the stairs. It staggered her to think that someone would do that. Still, at least she hadn't been killed – yet.

However, none of this was the cause of her depression. It was the absence of Caldicott that brought the sense of early autumn to her week in May. She would not meet him again until this was all over. She felt guilty enough as it was for his suspension; she knew that she would feel terrible if he had to undergo disciplinary action over his relationship with her.

If only she could work out what was going on, find the person behind all these crimes, then this oppression would lift and they could be free to meet up. She had absolutely no faith in Stone's abilities to find the solution. That flat-footed fool had ruined every opportunity that he had been given. She was convinced that his trouble lay in his jealousy of Caldicott. It was clear that this man wanted promotion, and if he could step over a better person, so what? Yes, it was exactly the same modus operandi as in her work.

Well then, if Caldicott was not allowed to investigate, then she was determined to employ her research skills to good use and track down the culprit herself.

How to start? Having no formal training but having read detective stories by the score, she decided to "look for clues". In particular, she wanted to revisit the issue of the handwriting on Bernice's note. She knew she had seen its match somewhere in the English department. Once she had discovered the identity of the author, then she would tackle Hardwicke about his relationship with a student...

that ought to be fun, she thought – but dangerous. Suppose Hardwicke was being blackmailed about his relationship with Bernice; mightn't that be a reason to murder? Jenny realised that she may well be putting herself in danger; so be it. She would have to protect herself as best she could.

She started with the most obvious place to look for clues, a place that no one would suspect that she was even looking for evidence – her own office. This should be safe enough. Jenny thought it unlikely that she would discover who the killer was here, but if she could find the picture of Lucy that Caldicott had lost, she might be able to make amends, in a small way.

She cleared her desk of correspondence and painstakingly hunted through every single remaining piece of paper on her desk. No, there was nothing there of interest, merely her own old lecture notes and various minutes of the hundreds of weekly meetings she attended. Jenny took great delight in recycling all of these.

Next, she tackled the Hardwicke legacy, most of which had been left in the desk. This turned out to be various back copies of the *Sun*. These were recycled too. Then she remembered the newspaper cuttings on Henry Fielding. This was a likely place for Caldicott to have lost his photo. But it wasn't there. There was a picture of Fielding with his arm around Hardwicke, though. *Very odd*, she thought. *They look like lovers*. She put that in a folder, on which she wrote "Kevin" on the front. She decided that nobody would guess what "Kevin" entailed.

Her next action was to conjure up in her mind where Caldicott had been sitting when he first came to the office. She sat herself in the chair that Caldicott had placed himself in to get an understanding of where the photo might have fallen. She stood up and took off the cushions to see if anything had been buried there. Nothing had, except some loose change – a pound coin and a twenty-pence piece. She presumed that they were Hardwicke's. 'Ah well, mine now…' She put them in her purse.

Her next mission was to look underneath the chair. Here her efforts drew a blank, but she was rewarded by turning her attention to the bookcase close by. She discovered the old brown envelope that had prevented her drawer from closing, not so long ago, and which she thought she had assigned to the recycling bin. She was about to throw it in when something clicked in her brain. She smoothed out the envelope and had a really good look at the writing. It looked familiar.

She hunted in her desk for the copy that she had made of Bernice's poison pen letter. Then she compared the writing on the envelope with that on the letter. No, that was not the match… but both specimens of writing had partners in the English department, of that she was certain.

She put both of the letters in her "Kevin" folder, and then she had a change of heart. She decided to hide the material in her bookcase. She reached down her copy of *War and Peace* that was on her shelf, and slotted the envelope at the front. 'No one is going to look at that,' she said. She repeated the procedure with the copy of the poison pen letter into James Joyce's *Ulysses*.

She was at a loss as to where Caldicott's photo had disappeared if it wasn't near the chair. Then she remembered. When she first met him in her office she hadn't seen him initially. This was because he was standing in the window recess. Perhaps he had been looking at the photo. She did a sweep around the bottom of the shabby curtains and eventually, lodged in the back of the radiator, she found what she had been searching for: The picture of Lucy… with Caldicott.

She spent some time examining it. She hardly recognised Caldicott, he looked a different person. She was even more surprised to see that Lucy was Chinese, or partially Chinese. But why was she taken aback? Caldicott clearly liked exotic women, after all Marcus' mother was Caribbean. It depressed her to think that she might be too traditionally English for him. More significantly, looking at the photo she felt that she was intruding. The photo said, "We are complete, now leave us alone". But that, she recognised, was a stupid thought; obviously the relationship no longer existed since one of the partners had died.

Jenny suddenly felt envious. She had never been in that sort of relationship. How she wished she had. But then it didn't have the fairy tale ending did it? Perhaps for Lucy, she died with her partner still in love with her, but for Kevin? No. She appreciated that he had been at a loss for several years. She felt sad for the pair of them.

And what now? What, if she and Kevin became a couple, would that do? She was not taking one away from the other as in so many relationships these days; that, in itself, would be a help. But, it would never be the "chocolate box" dream that she had wanted for so many years. The man that she loved would always compare her to his first wife, of that she was certain. Suppose she wasn't up to the mark? And as for Jenny herself? Too many men, too much water under the bridge to ever live in constant bliss, for fear of some impending betrayal. For both of them it would have to be a compromise…

But wasn't that what life was about? A compromise… finding the right compromise, one had to live as best as one could. And why not? Better to try and fail… What was it that Bobby Kennedy had said? "Only those who dare to fail greatly can ever achieve greatly."

She didn't know whether she dared to fail greatly, but she knew that she was prepared to try. Finally she could bear it no longer. She texted Stella, 'Please tell Kevin that I have found his photo.'

CHAPTER 32
THURSDAY, 12 MAY

Despite this week being Jenny's favourite week of the year, there was always one black spot in it, namely the faculty board meeting. This meeting, which was held in the boardroom in the English department, should have been purely an exercise in rubber-stamping decisions taken by various committees throughout the term. Unfortunately, due to poor organisation, it was, without fail, a day for receiving new ideas for the first time and then having endless debates on the merits of these "novel techniques". Do they "inspire"? Are they "innovative"? Will they increase student numbers? As one might guess, the final outcome was that nothing was ever agreed upon, but by one of the miracles of life, the meetings' minutes said otherwise. It was clear to all present that Hardwicke, the chair of the board, was either in cahoots with the secretary and/or that he bullied her to death to produce a set of minutes that bore no resemblance to the actual meeting that took place.

Of course, any one of those present had a right to challenge the minutes at subsequent meetings, but to do so required another five hours of discussion, and then there was doubt that the minutes would be changed at all.

Jenny had made the fatal error during her first year of employment at Sedgemoor of challenging a minute connected with personal tutors. She disputed this at three consecutive meetings. Nothing had been altered, merely precious research time lost. By the fourth meeting she had learnt her lesson and didn't bother to challenge them again.

The one saving grace in this was that it usually meant that it was possible to fall asleep during the reports, or start marking exam papers without anyone else either noticing or caring. Unfortunately for Jenny, today a number of other staff from the other departments in humanities, wanted to know how the police enquiries were progressing.

'I'm sorry, all I can say is that enquiries are ongoing and we will be informed if there are any further developments,' she replied.

The enquirers let it go at that. Jenny rushed to the toilets to have a final cry before composing herself. She stopped by at Tom's desk for a tissue.

'Oh dear, Cupid misplaced his arrow again?' Tom asked.

'Something like that,' she said.

'Never mind, this will cheer you up,' Tom added, handing over a pile of papers to her. 'This is what you wanted me to get you last week – you know, the Ashley Roberts case. It will give you something to do rather than listen to our dean for five hours.'

'Thanks Tom,' she said, collecting these papers and taking them back to the room.

She took her place seven minutes late, just after the

minutes had been agreed. Hardwicke had moved onto his favourite item – Chairman's Business.

'Ah Dr Jordan, there you are. Now, I have some closed business for this afternoon, but I must tackle some difficult issues here. One – recruitment or lack thereof; two – our minimum target of 65 per cent 2:1s or above, are we on track? Three – I met with the VC last week, he is exceptionally keen that we recruit at least five hundred students in September…' At this point near pandemonium broke out from the staff… 'Yes, well we have to try. I shall ask for our recruitment report in a minute. Finally, I feel it only my duty to mention those English students who will not be sitting the exams this year.'

Professor Jones piped up. 'Oh yes, I do think that we must have two minutes' silence for the fallen.'

'Well I don't!' said Hardwicke to a number of shocked faces, particularly as other students were present.

There was an audible gasp from Gwen, 'Oh you wicked, wicked man,' she said snivelling into a tissue.

The sad truth was that although everyone agreed with her comment, no one thought that she meant it sincerely. Someone had once said that a more disingenuous person than Professor Jones was impossible to find. The false bonhomie, the "oh you must", constantly. Everyone hoped she would retire and, as bad as he was (and my word, he was bad) everyone preferred Hardwicke to Jones. This made it impossible to support her in anything she said, no matter how just.

'Now, moving on – Finance, over to you Ron.'

A bald-headed man stood up, and quickly sat down as his braces got caught on his chair. Guffaws of laughter permeated the room. This release was much needed after the somewhat abrupt exchange in regard to the student deaths. He tried to stand up again, and this time was successful. His report brought any laughter to an end.

'Unfortunately, due to the demise of several students, our numbers are down and so consequently is our budget. This means no pay increase but pay decrease for this year.'

At this point a number of staff grumbled. It was hardly surprising – all the staff had been promised a pay rise by the end of the year. Was this just a nasty trick to get the staff to work hard for nothing? This seemed to be the new strategy adopted in other institutions.

'Thank you Ron, or perhaps I should say, no thanks to you Ron. Now, QAA, we have that scheduled for closed business today, so moving onto our next item: Examinations. It has been agreed that the final examination timetable needs to be produced at least three days before the exams take place to allow students to fully prepare. Up to now this hasn't happened.'

Dr Martin attempted to be heard, 'I say, wouldn't it be better for all the students concerned if they had this for three months before the exams rather than three days?' A number of voices whispered 'Hear, Hear.'

Hardwicke sharpened his claws ready to pounce on the novice, 'Dear Rev Doctor, it is clear that you are a newcomer to our flock. In an ideal world, students would be given their examination timetable a year ahead, but this is Sedgemoor not Cambridge. You can't expect miracles from the centre here, I am afraid. We just have to thank the Lord that we are given three days' grace. Now, onto departmental reports: Let's have the report from head of English.'

Jenny gave her report slowly and succinctly. She reiterated what she had said to staff earlier, that she had no news to report on the student deaths. She discussed as far as was appropriate to go with student representatives present as to how the final grades might look, taking into account the fatalities. No one questioned it afterwards.

'Excellent; short and, well, not so sweet. On with theatre studies.'

Medusa took control explaining in great depth and great animation about how brilliantly her department was doing and no deaths to report. Someone muttered something to Jenny, was it bitch or witch? Jenny had zoned out. This was the most appalling meeting ever. What was the point of it all? It wasn't just the students, it was the whole faculty that was dying and everyone knew it. Really it would be a merciful release if they closed the place down. Jenny could try and get a job elsewhere away from this miserable place, a place that had given her so much promise in the early days, but that had brought her nothing but disappointment during the last year.

She remembered the first time that she taught at Sedgemoor. The students were bright and eager to learn. They did the prep and always came to classes with notes by the ton. Today, if they had opened the book before the class, it would frankly be a miracle. She had tried all sorts of techniques to engage them; sadly, the only thing that seemed to work was watching a YouTube video of David Beckham reciting a poem in his underpants. Her thoughts were finally interrupted.

'Thank you, we are doing well today. Now onto Student Business. Can we hear from our English representative first – Sebastian?' Sebastian was a nice lad but not the brightest star in the sky. Jenny held her breath.

'Yah well like, the students think it is unfair that we have to sit exams.'

Hardwicke responded, 'I hear what you are saying Sebastian, but some of your modules are assessed totally by coursework. I know, as I teach on them if you remember. Are you asking for all your modules to be assessed by coursework?'

'No, what the students want is, well, yah… I mean we think that you should just give us a first regardless, yah.'

Hardwicke was having fun at Sebastian's expense, 'Regardless of what, precisely?'

'Whether we do the exams or coursework.'

The staff around the table started to chuckle under their breath. Ever since the students' fees had been massively hiked up to nine thousand pounds a year, the students seemed to think they automatically qualified for a higher class degree, but this was the first time that any student had had the audacity to demand the award of any type of degree without the submission of a single piece of assessed work.

'So let me get this straight,' Hardwicke continued, deliberately attempting to catch the eye of all the staff present. 'You are informing your English tutors, all present here today, and that in itself is a first, let me tell you, you are informing us that all of the students believe that you/they should not have to sit exams, am I correct?'

'Yah.'

'In addition, they also believe that they should not have to do any coursework?'

'Yah.'

'In fact, the students just want us to give them a degree regardless?'

'Yah.'

'So… with no exams to sit and no coursework to take, you still think you should get a first? I'm sure that every member of staff here would agree that that is the most excellent idea, don't we staff? But unfortunately we just can't do that, as other universities will complain and cause us problems. Please inform your colleagues that they have no option but to do some work this year, but we will try to make it as painless as possible. Thank you for that Sebastian. Moving on to Sonia, our History rep.'

'Yes, we asked the students what their concerns were, and they said they were unhappy about the coffee here, isn't it? They also agreed that the price of the toast was too dear and that we should get free toast if we arrive before nine thirty.'

'Morning or evening? Thank you Sonia; that will be investigated. Anything else of concern? No? Right then; moving on to archaeology – Bill?'

'Umm… About these deaths? Are we likely to get any more?'

'Why, are the archaeology students hoping to excavate some more graves as part of their practical assessment?'

'Really, Hardwicke, that is going too far!' Carter exclaimed.

Hardwicke was all smiles. 'I do apologise everyone. Over to you Dr Jordan.'

All Jenny could say was, 'The police are still making enquiries, and rest assured we are doing everything we can to make the campus safe.'

Hardwicke continued, 'Any other business? No? Good. Let's break for lunch for forty minutes and we will tackle closed business. Thank you student reps, you are free to go.'

Jenny wandered out into the sunshine; the contrast with the dark gloomy meeting hall was startling. What should she do? She was on the verge of handing in her notice before all the deaths occurred, now she felt more alone and useless than ever before. If only there was a way to make amends.

She decided that the only thing that she could do was to get on with her job to support her finalists and she resolved to tackle the marking issues raised in the "Ashley Roberts" affair. She returned to the room and to all the coursework papers that Gwen had marked. To ensure parity, she decided to evaluate every paper to see if any discrepancies occurred.

Looking through them briefly, Jenny remembered, these were the very same papers that Gwen challenged Percy Smith about. Percy, she knew, was a fair marker, and would have been quite meticulous in his assessment… if he had come across Ashley's work. Perhaps Gwen gave these back to the students to look at briefly, before the pile was forwarded on to Percy. She would see…

*

The forty minutes were soon up. Hardwicke restarted.

'Right then ladies and gentlemen, let's begin the Reserved Business, and for Doc Martin, who, like a virgin, is experiencing the full penetration of this event for his first time, this is the real meeting where we discuss the important items that students shouldn't hear. Luckily for us our Professor Straw, the DVC, is ill. That means we can conduct a really useful meeting without a stool-pigeon in place.' At this point, Hardwicke turned to a thirty-something bleached-blonde on his right-hand side who was frantically writing notes. 'Don't minute that last comment.' He continued.

'Now, today we have some papers sent to us from the University Network of Teachers' Committee that I have the misfortune to attend every month. They, as you know, hold themselves out to be experts on what we can all do better, i.e. teach. The fact that they have never taught a thing in their lives is, of course, by the way. However, we have to pretend to listen to their advice so here it goes. Don't minute that Holly,' he said.

He continued to the rest of the board, 'In their infinite wisdom, they comment on how poor our feedback is for classes.' A number of staff muttered severely under their breath. 'No, no, I don't mean that the students have given *us* poor feedback; that is always very good. I mean that it appears that we have not given enough detail in our feedback forms about the modules we teach.' Even more mutterings were to be heard.

'Yes, well I think it quite acceptable as your dean to receive a module report that only consists of four typewritten sides of A4 paper. However, the UNTC seems to think that a twenty-page document is the minimum requirement. In this document you need to cover how you taught your module this year, the results of your module and what you could do to improve it. If I may suggest, ladies and gentlemen, they are wanting you to send eighteen out of the twenty pages commenting on how you could do your job better. This is to be avoided at all costs. I have spoken to Ted Murray, the acting head of law, and mind you this is not to be put in the minutes anywhere…' He bellowed at his secretary, 'Holly! Stop that writing straight away!' With that he snatched up her pencil, broke it in two and threw it over his left shoulder whilst continuing to shout at her, 'Now, that is enough of your useless scribbling, I defy you to take minutes, hear me?'

At this point it might be suspected that Holly would burst into tears, and that several members of staff would complain about Hardwicke's outrageous behaviour, but such were his long-established antics, that all the board knew that Hardwicke was just acting, except for the somewhat confused Rev Dr Martin, who was about to offer his assistance. Holly, well prepared to deal with Hardwicke's vicious acts of criminal damage, whipped out another pencil from her handbag and placed it firmly down in front of her as an act of defiance. All the board members clapped at this scene.

'All right, now that I have your attention, listen up. And mind, Holly, keep that pencil where it is until I tell you that you can start writing again. Ted is firmly of the opinion that the less you, as module co-ordinators, put down on paper, the better. In short, he seems to think that if you write down too many of your own errors, the powers that be will use this as an excuse to start competence proceedings. He suggests that we spend the vast majority of the twenty-page document explaining what material we have covered, and what books we have used, etc. This, he argues, looks like we have written loads, but in reality we have admitted nothing to our own personal detriment and given no analysis on where we could do better. Ted further adds, and this I quote, "Where the statistics indicate that there is a unit value of less than 65 per cent of firsts and 2:1s we need to look for an adverse condition which affected the whole cohort. Such as a storm, illness or dare I say it, a murder.' Several members of staff gasped at this point.

'Ladies and gentlemen, you may rest in peace for this year. It does not matter how bad our results are; we can argue that the number of untimely deaths in the department of English, has severely affected the morale and stamina of all the humanities students. This will give us, as a facility, the ability to push up student marks to meet the 65 per cent minimum quota.'

'But some of the students are utter crap!' squawked Percy.

Hardwicke continued, 'Yes, we all know that. There are some absolute shockers out there, well you heard from Sebastian earlier, thinks we should give them a degree without even attempting to do any work. Unfortunately, he is the rule, not the exception, and it is the same in every department. In this faculty there are bound to be one or two who will fail, let's leave it as that. As long as we have one or two scapegoats, who cares if the rest get 2:1s?'

Dryden spoke, for the first time that day, 'So Simeon, are you suggesting, and not for the minutes of course, that even if the students are not affected at all, the very fact that deaths have occurred means we can go for a ridiculous grade inflation?'

'Yes, brilliant isn't it? Ted only wishes they had a few deaths over there.'

'It can be arranged,' Dryden added.

All the theatre studies staff laughed heartily. Little did they know of what was to befall their department in the following months. As for the English department, most of them thought it was in extremely poor taste, but for once they did not blame Hardwicke for this macabre state of affairs. The blame had to be given to the VC's minions on the UNTC.

The rest of the meeting was lost on Jenny. She sat bolt upright as though she had been slapped around the face with a wet fish. It was obvious what had been going on; the desperate attempt to push up the grades, the students singled out for attack, each one of them hopeless. Jenny had thought it was to do with drugs, but suppose it wasn't that at all? Someone was desperately attempting to get the statistics balanced. More deaths led to an improvement in her classification ratio. She had said it herself, but she was joking at the time. This was no joking matter now. That was what had been happening. There had been a very carefully planned execution of the weakest students, using different methods to avoid detection, so cunning at first that the majority of the deaths looked like accidents. And then she thought of Kevin's warning. Was she being set up as a murderess all along? Somebody was out to get her one way or another.

Why were some deaths more obvious than others? If she could work that out, she could identify the culprit. Who was in the vicinity of the archaeological event, the trip to the Bahamas, and the swimming pool? Who knew about cars? Jenny compiled a register of seven key suspects who had been in the Bahamas when the unfortunate girl had drowned. She had marked out a number of tick boxes by the side to see if she could identify who was best placed. Top of her list was the VC. This was followed by Professors Hardwicke, Carter and Hastings. Next came Medusa, then Lowry and finally herself. By the side of her name she had ticked herself present at every crime scene. No wonder Caldicott was concerned. She was in the pivotal position all the time. But suppose that Maya's death was an accident. Accidents do happen. What about Reg White's assassination? That could have easily been a drugs dispute and nothing to do with the university. And it was the only death where everyone on the list appeared to have an alibi. Except that her book had been found in the car, she had been informed. Had Jenny forgotten anyone? For the deaths in Somerset, Jenny had to add three names to the list: Dr Dryden and Professor Jones, and… no, it couldn't be. In the Bahamas? She had to put it down – DS Caldicott.

As a process of elimination, she texted Tom to ask him if any of the staff had been absent when she was in the Bahamas, just in case it was possible that someone took a flight over there to cause mischief… Now to go through it all.

The VC: He was obsessed with raising the target of 2:1s and firsts. Was the man mad enough to kill his own students? What had he said at the last assembly? "We love you, we love you all, you must come back to us, but first you must spread the word, like the disciples!" No, it didn't make sense for him to be the killer. As much as he wanted quality students, his first priority was students of any kind to increase the cash flow. The deaths had hindered student recruitment, and rightly so. The campus was no longer the safe haven it was supposed to be.

Hardwicke: That man was ruthless all right, a bastard of the first water, but was he twisted enough to kill the students? She thought on balance no. He would want to screw them to death if they were beautiful, but not execute them in cold blood. With much regret Jenny had to cross off his name.

Carter: There is nothing like a detective story for finding the most unlikely character is the murderer, but this was a step too far for anyone's imagination. No, the sweet old man simply couldn't move as fast as he would have had to, to commit all the crimes. Besides which, he was genuinely fuming that someone had ruined his archaeological fieldwork.

Hastings: He had tried to warn her off. Was it because he wanted to stop her finding out it was him? No, she remembered now, that she had been told that Hastings had an alibi for at least two of the deaths.

Medusa: Now there was a real possibility; ruthless, totally self-protectionist, not as talented as she would like to think, but a killer? Prostitute – yes, she would happily sleep with the VC if it meant keeping her job, but killing students, and from another department? Perhaps they had all turned her down, sexually. She was a woman who desired revenge for any trivial rebuttal. If one merely pointed out a spelling error in her handouts they were in danger of having their tea over-sugared, or indeed having salt put in "by accident". Jenny had seen that happen once to Dr Dryden when he went too far with a joke at Medusa's expense. But murder? Jenny really didn't think that it was likely.

Who next? Lowry? Jenny couldn't analyse why his name might be there, she would come back to him.

What about the reserves? – Dryden had no motive to her mind. Gwen? She would need an accomplice. Caldicott?

Jenny held her breath whilst working through the possible timings of Caldicott's interventions. He could easily have tampered with Dwaine's car, but he could not have pushed Maya off the car park, nor was he anywhere near Nassau the night her student was killed there, but he could have been responsible for Reginald White's execution. She started to see why DC Stone thought that Caldicott was working with her. And what of her situation?

In the cold light of day she was the natural choice. She had means and motive. She could have asked McClellan to fix Dwaine's car at a fee, or have persuaded Caldicott to tamper with the brakes. Perhaps she had murdered her ex-lover? Now she could see why Caldicott was so concerned. She, he said, had the key somewhere in her mind. *Perhaps it really is me* Jenny thought. She began to feel unwell. Had her fall down the theatre school's stairs unleashed a vicious side that she was unconscious of – a sort of Jekyll and Hyde character? How could she have killed anyone? Why would she want to do that? She didn't care about her job that much, did she? Perhaps she did. She felt ill, sick, dizzy. The fact that she had a cast-iron alibi for McClellan's death was neither here nor there by that stage, as she was so struck by an overwhelming sense of guilt. She was about to phone up Stone and make her confession, when a voice from the board called her back.

'Dr Jordan, can you please pay attention? You have been asked by Professor Jones why there are not enough details in the minutes of the research meeting that you chaired on 19 April.'

So Gwen had been up to her tricks again had she? *Heavens defend me from that Welsh fairy*, she thought; although fairy was not quite the right description, troll was more appropriate. She was a snivelling sort of a woman: Untalented, insecure and ugly. Not physically ugly as such, but the ugliness inside her soul oozed out of her body as pus seeps through an unhealed wound. And that woman was always picking away at the departmental scabs. Everything in the last two months that Jenny had tried to do to improve the place, be it on behalf of the students or the staff, there was always one voice of dissention, always Gwen. "Gwynne the snitch", one of the staff called her, and by God they were right. This was a woman who needed to retire quickly, or be retired permanently. Jenny would happily have back the very worst of her deceased students, if Gwen was lying in her coffin with maggots eating her contorted brains.

'I am so sorry Professor Jones,' and here Jenny had emphasised the "ss" in "professor" as though imitating a snake, for that was what the woman was – a snake. 'I'm afraid that we had no adminissstrative sstaff that day, and I am simply rubbissh at typing up lots of detailsss whilsst chairing a meeting. But perhapsss you would like to minute-take next time we have sssuch a problem?'

312

'Fifteen – love, Jenny,' someone sniggered.

'Yes well, I think that we have enough details here to be going on with,' Hardwicke rushed over to the next agenda item.

But the damage had been done. For the first time Jenny had understood the true depth of this woman's personality. She would stop at nothing to discredit another member of staff – stop at nothing. Stop at nothing?

Not even murder? Gwen?

It was at this point that she received a text from Tom informing her that Gwen had phoned in sick on the Wednesday and didn't reappear until late on the Friday, the week that Jenny was in the Bahamas. My God, it was possible too!

Could Gwen have carried out the murders singlehandedly? No, there were technical problems with that idea. How Jenny wished that Gwendolyn was the murderer but she didn't think that she had the guts to carry out the acts herself. She was squeamish if she saw a dead worm. She could imagine Gwen pushing someone off the car park or into a swimming pool, but sabotaging a car? No, this was a woman who could not physically do the act herself; she would require the help of others. But which others?

What if there was more than one set of crimes? How would the groupings fall then?

Jenny re-wrote a list:

Group 1: "The letter writer/graffiti" artist
Group 2: The "student accidents", with or without Henry Fielding and, of course, Tony.

Group 3: The outright assassinations: Kafka, White, McClellan.

Suppose the letter writer/graffiti artist was separated from the deaths. What about the "accident" group? They couldn't all be accidents. How were they linked? Were they linked to the "assassinations"? The White assassination could probably be removed from the list; everyone had an alibi for that – except, of course, Caldicott and perhaps Medusa. Medusa had not flown back to the UK with the others, Hastings had informed her.

Amelia had told her that everything comes in threes – three persons; that was it! Three different murderers with three different motives. Nothing to do with degree classifications after all; drugs' related certainly… if only she could work out who…

At that point Jenny looked down at the pile of marking that Tom had given her. And now whilst struggling to survive to the end of a tedious meeting she finally saw the whole picture. Why the deaths had occurred, who was responsible and who had the nerve to carry them out. It was a most unpleasant realisation… and on top of it all, there was one poisonous old woman writing filthy letters to attractive women.

'And so ladies and gentlemen that brings us on to the last item on the agenda, the vice-chancellor's birthday. I am afraid that we have all been summoned to kiss his ring on his special day.'

'What, what, what?' Gwen looked horrified.

'For God's sake Gwendolyn, I am not instructing you to offer him rimming services, merely pay homage to the man as one would to the Pope. Do you or do you not want a job next year? That is all I have to say. Any other business? Dr Jordan, have you something to hold us all up?'

'I am sorry Chair. During this meeting I have been unable to concentrate fully, as I have been preoccupied with the increasing number of student deaths. I apologise, Chair, for my lack of attention. However, I have now worked it all out.'

With that, she stood up and collected her belongings, gave one last glare to Gwendolyn and walked out of the door. Silence enveloped the room.

CHAPTER 33
THURSDAY, 12 MAY:
Afternoon

Jenny rushed to her office and phoned Caldicott. She knew that she should contact Stone but she would not be able to explain it clearly to him. She needed to talk it through with someone intelligent. Caldicott's phone was switched off. She attempted to leave a message with Stella. Her phone was switched off too. 'Bugger,' she said to no one in particular.

Her next action was to try to contact the person that she should have phoned at first, DC Stone. He was not at his desk.

'Did the caller wish to leave a message?'

'Oh, sorry, no thanks, wait yes, can you say that Dr Jordan from the university has some news and would appreciate it if DC Stone could contact me as soon as he receives this message?'

'Yes, of course madam, good day.'

Jenny started to write an email to Kevin explaining her thoughts whilst they were fresh in her mind, but she was interrupted by a knock on her door. It was Gwendolyn.

'Ah Gwen, come in.' Gwen stepped tentatively into the room, and sat on the wooden chair. 'Nice of you to come to see me, I wanted to have a chat with you. Gwen, why do you hate me so much?'

Gwen sat still, the colour draining from her face. 'Dr Jordan, I don't know what you are talking about.'

'Why did you want to incriminate me as a murderer?'

'I haven't a clue what you are talking about Dr Jordan. You probably killed all the students, yourself.'

'Gwen, that is an outrageous accusation. You phoned up the police when I was in the Bahamas, and told them I had pushed Maya off the car park, didn't you? This is all because you were not made head of department isn't it? Is this why you tried to kill me by making me fall down the stairs?'

'Don't be ridiculous. I didn't mean for you to tumble down the stairs; that was an accident.'

'Ah, well that isn't strictly the truth is it?'

'What do you mean?'

'I believe that you tried to make me fall down the stairs to get me out of the way permanently. Are you the one who swapped over my iron tablets?' Gwen was looking more and more scared by this point, particularly as Jenny was brandishing her paper-knife.

'You knew that I was taking them because we had discussed it during the term break. Why did you want to hurt me? Was it because you wanted to be head of department or was it so that you could go to the Bahamas?'

Gwen stood up. 'It was my holiday, mine by right! I had worked so hard for it! You are a jumped-up little lecturer who has only worked here five years... And you're always having sex. Everyone knows that you have been having it off with that policeman. I suppose he's been round to your house on many occasions hasn't he?'

317

'Really Gwen, that's a slanderous accusation! I have not been "having it off" with Mr Caldicott – he is far too professional to get physically involved with a suspect. But for your information, I very much intend to have lots of sex with him, once all this nonsense is cleared up!'

'You are nothing but a slut.'

'And you are nothing but a shrivelled up old bitch, who doesn't know how to use computer technology for lecturing, who doesn't know anything about English, and on top of that is vindictive towards attractive and talented students.'

She pulled out the coursework paper written by Ashley Roberts.

'Gwen. Look at this. Is this your writing?'

'Yes, of course it is. *Beowulf*; this is my module.'

'Thank you for confirming that. Now tell me why you did not have that paper second-marked by Percy?'

'He obviously forgot to do so.'

'Gwen, you will remember that you sent Percy to me to answer in regard to a complaint that you made about his marking. He told me that he second-marked everything submitted to him.'

'Of course he would say that.'

'Very well Gwen, let us try something different, shall we?'

Jenny retrieved Bernice's letter from *Ulysses*. Look at this. This is a copy of a note sent to Bernice the day of her accident. Would you like to make any comment on that?'

Gwen looked at it and screeched. 'I didn't do it! I didn't fix the brakes on Dwaine's car. I wouldn't know how.'

'For the first time this afternoon Gwen, I believe you. Now talk. I can tell by the handwriting that this is from you. It has taken me a few weeks to realise it, but now I see that you are the author of this unfortunate letter. Did you also write on Medusa's wall?'

Gwen was defiant. 'No, what are you on about? Of course I didn't!' Then, on noticing that Jenny was waving her paper-knife again, her resolve failed her. 'Well, all right, yes I did. I was fed up of her atrocious behaviour seducing all our students.'

Jenny put her paper-knife down. 'Again, I agree with you. Do you think she does it purely for her own satisfaction or to get the theatre studies statistics to look better than ours? Either way Gwen, you must stop *your* behaviour. No more nasty letters, no more vindictive tittle- tattling. I will have to tell DC Stone what you have told me; they will decide if they want to follow it up. Come what may, I am going to recommend that you receive an early retirement settlement at the end of this term. I will ensure that the university pays you until Christmas. That is when you informed Simeon that you were going to leave. Hand me all your keys now, please. I will ensure that Tom lets you into your office when you need to go in there. '

'No, you can't, you can't; I have nothing in my life but my job!'

'You should have thought about that before you injured me and, more to the point, before you attempted to prevent a bright student from being awarded a first class degree. See yourself out.'

Gwen left the office in a hurry. As the last part of

Jenny's message had been delivered *a forté*, the whole of the English building enjoyed the exchange. There was a sound of applause from the office outside. Tom, Shelley and Percy all clapped at seeing Gwen leaving so quickly.

'That's enough!' Dr Jordan roared.

'Tea now?' Tom asked, grinning from ear to ear.

'Yes please, Tom. Any chance of a biscuit?'

'One down, two to go…' Jenny said to herself. She tried to phone Stone again, but with no more luck than before. So she returned to her email to Kevin and wrote a verbatim account of the scene that had just taken place in her office. She knew that he would enjoy reading that.

It was some twenty minutes later when Jenny received another knock on her door.

'Professor Hardwicke to see you,' Tom announced.

'Ah, Professor, the ideal person. I have just told Gwen that I want her to pack up her books for good at the end of this term, but we will pay her until Christmas. Can it be arranged?'

'What has precipitated this forceful decision, Dr Jordan?'

'Poison pen letters… and graffiti, amongst other stuff.'

'Ah, so it was the old witch after all; I did wonder.'

'Well, if you wondered, why the hell didn't you do something about it earlier?'

Hardwicke spoke quietly for the first time in his life. 'I've had other things on my mind.'

Jenny saw Hardwicke looking somewhat forlorn. It was a look that she hadn't seen on him before.

'Simeon, if I may; take a seat in your old office. What can I do for you?'

'What do you know?' was the reply.

'Not as much as I would like to. Tell me are you, or were you, in a relationship with Bernice Pye? I saw you drop a copy of *Zoo* magazine in Heathrow Airport. I read the caption… eventually.'

'Well, do you blame me? She was beautiful and perfect, all natural her own. I'm sure that people thought she had implants. No, as soon as I got my hands on them, I knew they were real. She liked to… I liked to… well, I won't say, but it involved her breasts…'

'Yes, I get the picture. Are you the one funding her studies?'

'Only in the last six months… why do you ask?'

'Did you fill in a "declaration of interest" form?'

'Oh no, I forgot to do that. I would have done if she had sat the exams of course, but… well… she is still in hospital I believe.'

'Simeon, if you don't mind me saying so, you are getting old. Are you going to stay with this one, or are you moving onto another one without scars?'

For the first time since Jenny had met Simeon Hardwicke, she detected a streak of humanity in him.

'Jenny, I don't know how you guessed, but I feel awful. She was coming to see me on that day. If we hadn't arranged to meet up, none of this would have happened… I… '

'Have you been to see her in hospital?'

'Once… she was in a coma… I haven't been back since. I can't face it.'

'She's not in a coma any more, and I expect that she could do with some company. Don't be so selfish, go and see her. Do it tonight.'

'Jenny, when did you learn to be so forceful? I rather like the new you. Perhaps you would like to…'

'Simeon, fuck off! Visit Bernice and ask her if she wants to sit her exams in August. And whilst you are there, ask her if she would prefer to finish her degree programme by studying in the theatre studies department next year. And sign a conflict of interest form.'

'Yes, Jenny.'

Just as a little act of revenge she added, 'Tell you what, Simeon, marry the girl, you two are an ideal couple.'

'Steady on Jenny, that's a horrible idea.'

'Oh for God's sake Simeon, grow up! Just one more thing: Can you tell me what was in this?' Jenny retrieved the brown "naked ladies" envelope from its hiding place in *War and Peace* and handed it over to him.

'Oh God yes, that was the stupid present that Malcolm gave me – you know I said he had given me flowers? It was actually flower bulbs. They were in here. I put this on my desk, but the bulbs disappeared. I think Henry Fielding took them but he died before I could ask him.'

'Were you in a relationship with Henry?'

'No I bloody wasn't! But I think he wanted to be…'

'Simeon, I think Henry did take the bulbs. I suspect he thought that he could get a kick out of them. What were they?'

'Malcolm thought he was being funny; he asked me if I would like some naked ladies. Well, you know me, Jenny… I said "Of course!" I tell you I was bloody disappointed when this envelope turned up. I asked him what was with the joke. He said that these were naked ladies. He said it was the common name for a plant… can't remember what… well, immaterial now.'

'No it's not. Henry smoked them or ate them or something. The bulbs must have been poisonous. I'll have to find out what they were. Thanks, Simeon, that's cleared up a huge mystery.'

'Pleasure! Don't work too late. By the way, I haven't seen that Coleridge lookalike for a while. Isn't he the one supposed to be investigating this? What's happened to him?'

'I'll tell you another day, Simeon.'

And with that Hardwicke left Jenny's office.

Straight away Jenny attempted to phone Stone once again. This time the university phone system was down.

'Typical,' she said to herself. She reached for her mobile, but she saw that she had no signal. 'Oh bollocks, not now!'

There was nothing to be done in the interim, so she searched the Internet for flowers with the name "naked ladies"; it took her mere seconds to find them out. She read:

> *"Colchicum Autumnale" or "Autumn Crocus": The spring crocus is a non-toxic flower. The unrelated autumn crocus flowers in September. It contains unstable alkaloids, which are poisonous if ingested. Death may result.*

There was no may about it. One person, if not two people had died as a result of eating the plant.

She had been so engrossed in her research that she had

only just realised that it was now after five and Tom had gone home, leaving her isolated at her end of the English building. This was not good news. She was pretty certain that she would to receive another visitor shortly. Where were the police? Where was Kevin? She suddenly realised the danger that she had put herself in. She still hadn't finished her email… she typed frantically. She reached the last sentence, and got as far as writing "sorry", when she was interrupted for the third and final time.

CHAPTER 34
THURSDAY, 12 MAY:
Afternoon

Caldicott had taken his mother to an afternoon production at the Brewhouse Theatre in Taunton. It was only after the performance had finished that he received Jenny's call and an email which ended abruptly.

In the email, it told him how she knew she shouldn't contact him at the moment, and hoped that she wouldn't get him in trouble. She had tried to contact Stone, she wrote, but that he was useless. *Tell me something I didn't know* thought Caldicott. Then she described the conversation with Gwen (that made him laugh) and explained the cause of Fielding's death.

She then meticulously set out her deductions for the student murders. She had written, "I am telling you the solution but you have to find the evidence." Caldicott's view on her intelligence was confirmed. He had always recognised her first class brain, but had not appreciated its logical confidence until receiving this. She added that she had progressed no further on the student rape but was certain that it was incidental to the recent deaths. Up to this point, the email was a pleasure to read. And then his heart sank as he read the final paragraph.

"Kevin, I know that you will be cross with me because I did something daft. You know how I just come out with things that I am thinking? Well, I told everyone at the meeting that I had worked out who was responsible for the crimes, without naming any of them. I can't think how I managed to do something so stupid, as now I am a target, aren't I? The phone lines are down, and my mobile has no signal. I am anticipating the worst. I just wanted to tell you, in case I don't get another chance, that I love you and that I'm sorry…"

This was where the email had ended.

*

A third knock sounded on Jenny's door. She pressed the "send" button.

'Come in Malcolm,' she said.

Malcolm Lowry came across the room and sat down in the chair opposite to where Jenny sat. Until now Jenny had rarely looked at Malcolm. He had minded his business and she had minded hers. But this was different…

Jenny studied the man carefully. The heat of summer had finally allowed staff to remove their winter layers, and jackets were temporarily abandoned on the backs of chairs. Malcolm had rolled up his sleeves. Telltale blue pathways could be seen meandering towards his fingers. *Drug addiction, not alcohol after all*, Jenny thought.

'Was it satisfying removing our weaker students?' she asked him. 'I think a number of us would have liked them to leave, but preferably alive.'

'They were abominations to the name of

undergraduate; stupid and talentless with no chance to improve.'

'What went wrong, Malcolm?'

'What do you mean?'

'Why did an intelligent man like you decide to kill?'

'Ever since the new vice chancellor arrived, our business, my business, has diminished. Not only has he cut our admissions in half by his farcical policy of admitting "only the best" but he has clamped down on my trade.'

'Your trade? Do you mean drug dealing? You are behind all the drug dealing on campus?'

'Does that surprise you?'

'Yes, it bloody does, I thought that you were a serious researcher.'

'Are the two mutually exclusive? Opiates can stimulate the mind. My ideas flow after administration.'

'Pity that it doesn't seem to work for our students… But I don't get this at all. Why on earth would you want to kill your customers? You've just complained that your market was diminishing; is this some type of revenge?'

'I wanted to pay back Simeon.'

'You were in love with Simeon?'

'No, of course not, but I hoped that he would support my promotion application. I gave him some bulbs; he kept going on about what a keen gardener he was at the time, I thought he would like them. Then that stupid Henry Fielding stole them. Fielding was always in our offices, helping himself to things that he had no right to take. I suspect that he mistook them for hallucinogens. You know the rest. Well, that gave me a chance to get revenge on Simeon. I was hoping that Simeon would be arrested in connection with Fielding's death and then he would know what it felt like to suffer and see all his plans turned to dust. But he wasn't… he wasn't… I even tipped off the police at the time. Useless bunch of pricks. And then your ex-lover dies in a similar way. So the university finally gets the attention it needed from the CID. Well, I thought, let's give them something to focus on.'

'Did you kill Tony?'

'Of course not, but I thought his death was wonderfully poetic. He was a crashing bore, Jenny; you should know that better than anyone. He was forever droning on about that bloody case of *Barnett v Kensington and Chelsea Hospital*, I found it greatly ironic that he died the same way as the claimant.'

'But that case was about arsenic poisoning.'

'That's irrelevant. I tampered with Hardwicke's car. I wanted him dead. Only it wasn't Hardwicke's car at all. It was Saunders'. I didn't mean to kill *him*, nor hurt Bernice. And Hardwicke was left untouched again! I decided to get at Hardwicke another way, a slower way, by finding a mechanism to incriminate Simeon beyond doubt. I devised a plan using some of our weaker students. They were my clients in the past, so I knew them well, but they all owed me money. I knew that they would not be buying any further supplies from me, they were expendable.'

If she hadn't appreciated it before, this speech convinced Jenny that she was dealing with a madman. Whether through anger, despair or drugs, this was a person whose moral compass had completely misaligned; all compassion in Lowry had evaporated. She knew that she was destined to be his next victim… If she could just keep him talking she might stand a chance…

'I understand the mistake with Dwaine. That must have been awful. What happened next?'

'That dreadful Maya girl: She came to see me about her appeal, so I told her to meet Hardwicke in the car park on the Friday night. "Give him a blow job," I said. "It's worked in the past, hasn't it?" So whilst she was waiting for Hardwicke, I was waiting for her. I had given her some of my mix earlier in the night. It was easy to push her off.'

'Why were you using my books?'

'I found out that Dwaine had one of your books in his car. I thought that it would be rather funny to use one of Dr Jordan's books as an inspiration for the method of execution. I wasn't trying to incriminate you initially. I didn't seriously believe that the police would be so stupid as to think that a murderer would leave his property by a body.'

'How did you know who to choose in the Bahamas?'

'The victim chose herself. She was, of course, one of my clients, I knew her habits, knew that she couldn't swim. Hardwicke had been flirting with the girl previously, so she was a perfect choice. In her case it was a matter of method. I knew that drowning would be a possibility. When an argument flared up and she fell into the pool, apparently unwitnessed, it was time to act.'

'But why did you use *my* books, rather than Hardwicke's?'

'I wanted to make the list of suspects longer, it was nothing personal.

'And that dreadful Reginald White?'

'Now there, unfortunately, I cannot take any credit, as much as I would like to. White was a person who could make an enemy out of anyone who came into contact with him.'

'And my book; how come that was in White's pocket?'

'He probably stole that himself.'

'Who helped you with Kafka? You couldn't have done that on your own.'

'McClellan. McClellan was onto me from the start. He held me responsible for Henry Fielding's death. How was I supposed to know that Fielding would eat the bulbs that I gave to Hardwicke? But McClellan guessed.'

'That's not surprising. If anyone would spot an oddity it would be McClellan, he was the most intelligent of the third years – and on target for a first.'

'Rubbish! He couldn't even write his own name, never mind discuss symbolism in *Jane Eyre*; in fact, I doubt that he even knew who wrote the book, yet alone read it.'

'So how come he did so well in his second year exam?'

'Isn't it obvious? I gave him a copy of the paper to look at, after he accused me of killing Fielding. He had ample time to devise good answers, and then memorise them. That was his talent; he was exceptionally good at memorising things, particularly when he knew that he wasn't supposed to.'

'But then, why did you give him the paper, why not just remove him?'

'I didn't plan to kill anyone at that stage. I didn't intend Fielding to die, and I wasn't going to be held responsible for his death. McClellan saw me walking across the car park on the morning of Dwaine's death. He challenged me with his accurate guesstimate that I had sabotaged the car. He wanted money. I started to pay him, but he became more and more greedy after that. He, of course, had to go in the end, but not until he had helped me to lay Kafka to rest.'

'But why kill Kafka?'

'Why not? The man bore the name of a literary genius, yet he had the brains of the beetle that his master had created. No, he had to go. Well, Dr Jordan, we have had possibly the longest chat of our acquaintance this afternoon, but now it's time to end it.' Lowry pulled out a pistol from his jacket pocket.

*

On reading Jenny's email, a sense of absolute panic hit Caldicott. He had never known such intensity before, not even at the death of his first wife. He tried to reach Stone, but was no more successful than Jenny had been. He left an extremely assiduous message for his DC, and headed for his car. He had been told that he was forbidden from entering university property, or risk losing his job permanently. *Fuck that!* he thought. He sped off to Sedgemoor.

*

Stone's mobile signal was finally restored, and his phone received several messages. He thought he had better do something about them.

*

Jenny knew that Lowry was going to kill her, yet she almost had sympathy for the man. This was what years of frustration and embitterment of a person's lack of promotion could lead to; that, mixed in with drug addiction. God, this was a horrible mess.

Lowry pulled out a familiar book and placed it on the desk directly in front of Jenny. 'This is one of my all-time favourite novels, if not my actual favourite. I was so pleased that you had it in your collection, Jenny; I think it only fitting to allocate this to someone who truly appreciates literature: Ernest Hemingway's *Death in the Afternoon*.'

He raised the gun and aimed it at Jenny. 'Goodbye, Dr Jordan.'

*

How long Jenny had laid out on her desk she could not tell, but the searing pain in her shoulder led her to believe that she had been shot, but somehow she was still alive. Of all the sensations she could have experienced her brain registered only that of surprise. Why had Malcolm not finished her off completely?

The pain stopped her moving any part of her body. *If I stay here I will be all right* she thought. *He may be watching me now waiting to shoot me again. Perhaps he doesn't know that he hasn't killed me.* She attempted to move but passed out again; she had lost more blood than she had realised. When she came round for the second time, she knew she needed to summon help or die. Perhaps she shouldn't. Perhaps she should just let nature take its course. After all, that was the easy way out, and wasn't that what she had wanted for years?

And then she realised that, although she may be expendable, it was her duty to stop Malcolm striking again. It mattered little whether he was still around and watching her or whether he had left, she knew that she should attempt to summon help.

With her energy quickly sapping she made a monumental attempt to lift up her head and move her whole torso forwards. The excruciating pain of the movement made her pass out once more. This time there was no swift recovery.

*

By the time that Caldicott had reached the university, his worst fears were realised. A composite group of blue flashing lights illuminated the English building. Caldicott pushed through the crowds until he met Stone coming out of the building.

'What the fuck has happened? Where is Dr Jordan?'

Stone indicated over his shoulder at an ambulance. 'In there,' he said. 'Not a pretty sight –touch and go.' Then as an afterthought he said, 'You are not supposed to be here!'

'Fuck off!' was the reply.

CHAPTER 35
SATURDAY, 14 MAY:
Afternoon

Jenny was in a critical condition for two days. She drifted in and out of consciousness for hours on end, but throughout her moments of lucidity felt so miserable that she wished that she had never woken up. When she finally came to, she found herself on her back with a bright light shining in her eyes. For a moment she thought that she was on her Never-Never Land journey but her acute senses adapted to a background sound of arguing some twenty or so feet away.

'No, Mr Caldicott, it is completely out of the question. Even if she was conscious there is absolutely no way that she can receive visitors at the moment. She is improving but is still weak.'

'No.'

Jenny startled herself as much as she did the unseen visitors. The first person to respond was Caldicott. Ignoring all the healthcare worker's instructions he ran over to her side, but far from offering any words of love or comfort, he said somewhat angrily, 'I could kill you myself after all the trouble you have given me. What do you mean by "no"?'

'I haven't a clue…' was all that Jenny could say, before bursting into tears.

'See!' the sound of the banshee wailed down the hospital corridor. 'I told you to leave her alone. Staff! Staff!'

'Oh, shut up you old bag!' Caldicott called, much to Jenny's surprise. That stopped her crying straight away.

'Kevin! What is the matter with you? You are not normally like this, you are normally… normally…' She started to drift back off again.

'Oh no you don't! You are not going to pass out on me ever again! How dare you risk your life to try to help me! I know what you were doing! I couldn't care less about my job, do you hear me? I couldn't care less, not if it means losing you.'

'I'm sorry; you know what I'm like… I just come straight out with things, I…'

'Jenny,… I,…'

'I'm sorry Mr Caldicott, but I am going to have to ask you to leave.' The banshee had brought reinforcements. *Well, no one was going to talk to Kevin like that*, thought Jenny.

'If he leaves, I leave…!' Jenny exclaimed, and promptly collapsed again, ruining her speech.

It was over an hour later that Jenny came to again. She opened her eyes, and found herself alone. But in this she was mistaken. Caldicott had merely moved out of view. She saw DC Stone arrive. She hoped that he had not seen her looking at him, she did not want to speak with him – he had caused enough trouble already. She would pretend to be asleep.

335

'I understood that she had come to,' Stone said to nobody there.

'Yes, briefly.' Caldicott's voice brought a smile to her face. 'She isn't going to help us much today; it will take a while for the effects of the general anaesthetic to wear off… I've had a devil of a job fighting to stay here. That old battleaxe out there is determined to see me out.'

'Keep going Kevin, if you can't stick it out here, no one can. I think it's common knowledge that you have a vested interest in this one. Do you need a break?'

'Okay, I'll get a cup of coffee and come back.'

This was the first time that Jenny had heard the two policemen conversing; they appeared to be working together. Stone was not preventing Kevin from assisting after all. How long had she been there? She had many questions to ask, but she wouldn't utter a sound until Kevin was back.

*

It was some while later that Jenny fully recovered consciousness. She was brought to by a nurse scalding Caldicott for sitting on the bed.

'You can't do that, it's unhygienic!'

'That bloody woman!' Caldicott was heard to say.

'Kevin.' Jenny reached out her hand towards Caldicott, who grabbed it immediately.

'Darling.'

'What's happened to Lowry?'

'Don't worry about him. I'm only sorry we couldn't get to him before he got to you. Oh Jenny, why did you put yourself at risk?'

'I didn't mean to… it just happened…'

'Was he responsible for all of the deaths?'

'Hasn't he told you?'

'No and he won't be able to now.'

'What?'

'He isn't alive.'

'What?'

'He shot himself.'

'Really? He shot himself? Oh… *Death in the Afternoon.*'

'What?'

'The book, his favourite, I thought he brought for me, but he chose it for himself. Owwoh… Where did he hit? Everything seems to hurt.'

'You stupid woman, he didn't shoot you, you stabbed yourself with your bloody paper-knife! I told you to get rid of it!'

'Oh… ohhh… Owwoh… I see Ohhhhh… that's funny.' Jenny started to laugh.

'No it fucking isn't. You were very lucky that it just missed a major artery. Even so, you lost a lot of blood. They had to knock you out to repair you. But thank God they managed to save you.'

Jenny was really laughing now, and crying at the same time. 'No Kevin, it *is* funny. Of all the ludicrous things that I did on that day… still, it helped me get a confession out of Gwendolyn.'

Jenny sat up with a big smile on her face, remembering that she had written a verbatim account of her conversation with Gwen, in an email to Caldicott.

'Ah yes, Dr Jordan… about that email…'

But Jenny had moved on to another subject.

'So you know about the awful Professor Jones being the poison pen writer, and that Henry Fielding's death was accidental...'

'Yes, that was clear enough from your emails... but what about the other students?'

Lowry confessed to me that he was responsible for all the student deaths, except Reginald White's. In fact, he seemed most put out that it wasn't him that had killed White!'

'Okay, we will let the Bahamian police know.'

'Kevin, he also said that he didn't kill Tony. That's a problem, isn't it?'

'Yes, in a way it is, but we're pretty sure now that the toxin was introduced in the hospital; which means that you, at least, are in the clear as you did not visit him during his illness. And don't even think of investigating that death, that's my job, as you told me in your email... Jenny, your email... Jenny... I...'

Caldicott attempted to put his arms around Jenny. He was stopped in his tracks.

'Mr Caldicott, you must leave my patient alone now, it's time for her medication.' It was that ferocious nurse again.

'Christ, we never get a minute, do we?' Caldicott said.

CHAPTER 36
THE FOLLOWING WEEK

Wednesday was to be the day of Jenny's discharge from hospital. It was the same day that Caldicott was summoned on three days of intensive training. Jenny would not have been allowed to go home on her own, but Amelia had agreed to stay with her. "This will be fun," said Amelia, "I've got a huge pile of marking to do. We can watch each other failing our students."

The pair spent the next two days drinking tea, eating chocolate biscuits and, in Amelia's case, smoking cigarettes, whilst ploughing through numerous exam scripts. Amelia was in despair with her bundle, 'God, they are even worse than last year!' she said. But Jenny was delighted with hers.

'I think it must be the after-effects of the morphine, but some of these are really good. They have even managed to get the right scenes when discussing *An Inspector Calls*.'

'Does he?'

'Pardon?'

'Is Kevin coming around?'

'Not until Saturday.'

'Right, well I will make myself scarce by then. I don't want to be in the way.'

'Well, we do have a lot to talk about, but talking will be about all, I expect. How's Grant?'

'Oh, he's back in Canada at the moment.'

'Ahhh, that explains it.'

'Explains what?'

'Why you are looking after an old lady when you could have been out with the hunk.'

'Jenny, don't tease me, you know it's not like that.'

'Not yet. I predict it will be, but don't fall for someone who wants to live in Canada. You won't like it.'

'How do you know?'

'You told me you hated the place.'

'Good point.'

*

'Well,' said Jenny, 'they must have done some work, I've counted that we have 72 per cent of firsts and 2:1s here, for this paper. What happened to them?'

'They were probably afraid that they would be executed, if they didn't do well.'

'Yes… perhaps we'll use the same method next year… it seems to have done the trick.'

'I will suggest that we try it in the law school, in future. It looks like all we are going to achieve is the sum of 35 per cent of good degrees, if these scripts are anything to go by. Are you sure that it is all right for me to go now, Jen?'

'I'll survive, and don't forget that I will be getting support from Kevin, tomorrow.'

'That's a new name for it.'

Jenny threw a cushion at Amelia. 'Ouch!' they both said together.

With her marking completed, and the results exceeding her expectations, Jenny was able to sleep well on the Friday night. She was very much looking forward to seeing Kevin in the morning.

*

Caldicott had told Jenny that he would come over about eleven. He had lied. He knocked on Jenny's door at half past nine. It woke her up. She staggered down the stairs in her dressing gown and answered the door.

'Kevin. I was asleep,' was all that Jenny could say before Caldicott grabbed her in a vice-like grip and attempted to kiss her. 'Nooo!'

'Sorry Jen, I forgot about your shoulder.' He let her go.

Jenny gave Caldicott a filthy look. 'Rest assured that I haven't! It takes me ages to get dressed.'

'Then don't bother,' came the reply. 'Ouch!'

It was Caldicott's turn to be on the receiving end of a cushion. He laughed.

'Come on, and kiss me Kate,' he said.

'Oh dear, am I that bad?' Jenny asked.

'Yes, but I quite like it,' he replied.

Jenny kissed him. 'Sorry Kevin, I need my first cup of tea of the day, I get quite violent without it.'

'Hurry up then,' he said.

'Coffee?'

'Well, all right.'

The kettle had just boiled when the post arrived. It was a purple envelope sporting overly fancy writing. She automatically opened it up. Caldicott watched her as she was reading it and saw her turn grey. He thought that she was about to pass out on him again, so he instinctively went up to her to catch her. Then he realised that she wasn't about to faint, she was just incredibly angry.

'Of all the fucking cheek! Read this!' she commanded.

Caldicott took the letter out of Jenny's hand, whilst Jenny went back to making their drinks. The note read:

"Dr Jordan,

We so enjoyed performing Aristophanes' *Lysistrata* with your assistance last year, that we seek your assistance in the performance of the Euripides' *Bacchae*.

As you will know, as part of the plot an orgy takes place. We understand that you are an expert on Greek orgies, so we thought you could help to direct it. There are some nice men for you this year if you want to take part in the play yourself.

Yours

Medusa"

Caldicott burst out laughing. 'Are you an expert on Greek orgies?'

'No, I am fucking well not! And even if I was I would be completely out of practice!'

This was too much for Caldicott.

'Right, we will have to do something about that,' he said grabbing hold of her and kissing her. He started to rip off her dressing gown.

Jenny wasn't the slightest bit upset by this somewhat

342

violent action, although she did protest, 'Mind my shoulder!'

'Sorry Jenny... Jenny,... I...' Caldicott's phone rang. 'Fucking phones!' he exclaimed.

It was Jenny's turn to laugh, although, secretly, she was praying that he wasn't being called out to a work emergency.

'Oh, hello Mother,' he said in a not very respectful voice. He put her on speaker phone.

'Have I called at an inconvenient time?' she asked.

'Yes, you have!' he replied. 'Is it urgent?'

'No, don't worry, I was only phoning to see how Jenny is.'

Jenny beckoned for Caldicott to hand over the phone, whilst pointing to his coffee.

'Turn it off speaker phone, honey, I hate that... Hello Stella. Yes, I'm fine... as well as I can be under the circumstances. ... I've got some painkillers, they seem to be doing the trick... no, no, Amelia looked after me for the past three days, and Kevin is taking me out to lunch later... Yes, I think so. Kevin, are we free about mid-afternoon tomorrow? Your mum wants to take us out to tea.'

Caldicott just glowered at the phone.

'He says that's fine.'

'No it bloody isn't,' Caldicott said under his breath.

'Don't worry Stella, we'll be there.' She gave the phone back to Caldicott.

'Bloody families,' Caldicott said, 'always phoning just at the wrong moment.' He turned off the phone and threw it on the sofa in disgust. 'Why is it that every time that I am about to tell you that I love you I get interrupted?'

Jenny burst out laughing, 'Well, you have now.' And taking his hand she added, 'Come with me.'

She led him upstairs to her bedroom. They stayed there for the rest of the day...

EPILOGUE
TUESDAY, 21 JUNE 2016

On the day of the English department's examination board, Caldicott waited for Jenny on the grass where they had first met. Her shoulder was more or less healed, and since her release from hospital, there had been no more episodes of fainting. Nevertheless, her friends were not allowing her to do anything for herself – much to her annoyance. Both Dryden and Percy decided to escort Jenny to meet Caldicott.

'You see,' she said, 'I can't go anywhere alone these days.'

It struck Caldicott that they were all looking extremely pleased with themselves.

'Well?' he asked.

'Seventy per cent good degrees,' Jenny smiled. 'We all have a job for another year.'

'Huh, yes, but don't hold out any hopes for the year after that. The VC said he was satisfied with that percentage, but only as the department has such outstanding mitigating circumstances. Bloody cheek!' said Percy.

'Come on Percy, let's leave the lovebirds alone,' said Dryden. 'By the way,' he addressed Caldicott, 'how do you know so much about literature? Jenny said that you studied forensic science at uni.'

'My mother is responsible for my training. She teaches English in a secondary school and forced me to take it for one of my A levels.'

'That explains it. I think that makes you better qualified than some of us.'

'Yes, notably the dean,' Percy added. Dryden and Percy walked off laughing. Their place was filled by Amelia and Grant.

'Hi Amelia, did it go okay?' Jenny asked.

'It could have been worse, but we are going to get it in the neck as we only have 35 per cent of good degrees. Ted is thinking of stepping down as acting dean, but everyone has begged him to stay on. Grant and I are off to the pub, do you want to join us?'

'No thanks, we can't. We have to visit Kevin's mother – it's her birthday.'

'Okay, another time. By the way, Kevin, Grant and I are curious… I know it's a sensitive subject but has there been any progress with the investigation into Professor Carstairs?'

'No, not yet, Amelia. So a word of warning: Be careful which cup you drink from in the law school.'

'Ha! Very funny,' said Amelia. 'Well, see you soon!'

Amelia and Grant walked off down the hill. Caldicott turned to Jenny. 'Is it just me or do they remind you of Echo and Narcissus?'

'Oh no, don't say that. I've thought exactly the same before now. I do hope not for Amelia's sake.'

'Oh, I'm sure she will recover, she's young and very beautiful.'

'Are you trying to make me jealous?'

'Yes. Am I succeeding?'

'Yes.'

'Good, come on. I think that we should go back to yours before we go to see Mum.'

'Why? It's out of our way.'

'It's not really. Besides, you only have another three months left before you start directing the orgy scene in the *Bacchae*, and I think that you need some more practice.'

'Kevin,' she laughed, and stood on tiptoe to kiss him.

It was at that point that Cedric the cockerel decided to announce his presence once more.

'Didn't they have animal sacrifices in Ancient Greece?' Caldicott asked.

'It can be arranged,' she said.